The Kingdom Come Series

Book Three

The Kingdom Come Series

Book Three

by

Brandy Ange

Printed in the United States of America

First Printing, 2022

ISBN 978-1-947992-06-1 (paperback)

Marturia Publications

www.brandyange.me

For Distribution Inquiries:
Ingramspark
Global Headquarters
Ingram Content Group
One Ingram Blvd.
La Vergne, TN 37086

For all those
Fighting a battle
The rest of the world
Doesn't see.

Acknowledgements

First, I would like to thank you, for reading the series up to this point and continuing. Without the continued support of my readers, I would not be able to continue doing what I love. There are so many people who helped to bring this book to fruition. I would like to thank those who help me keep the typos to a minimum (though every book has them), Debbie Broyles and Marcia Eatmon are the most encouraging editors an author could hope for! I would also like to thank those who keep me motivated to keep at it, my best friends Christina Cison and Jo Beth Elliott, as well as Teri Woolard, Liz Walker, and Cyndi Downing. I am fortunate to have probably the most supportive family on the face of the planet, so I have to thank my mom for being a sounding board for all of my venting and frustrations, my sister for being my brainstorming buddy, and my dad for always supporting my dreams. I would also like to thank those in my writing community who continue to inspire me, and at times commiserate; S.J. Pratt, Tina Capricorn, A.M. McPherson, and K.L Kolarich y'all are seriously superheroes! I would like to thank my bookish crew for their enthusiasm and support, which keeps me energized and excited to hear their feedback, Ashley, Jennifer, Skylar and Anya. I also want to say a very special thank you to Katie Broyles, my first patron. It means the world to me and is such an honor to have your support! I would be remiss to not mention the man who has added color and intrigue to this series with his beautiful cover designs and character art, Phil Thomas is a genius with an ink pen, and I am so thankful to have him to help me build this world.

Last but not least, from the very depths of my heart, I want to thank each and every one of you who have ever left, or will ever leave, a review on Amazon/Goodreads and or share my books on your social media platforms. You don't know how much that means to me. It not only helps me to know what I've done well, and/or where I can improve my craft, but it also helps other readers to find my books, and that is HUGE! So, THANK YOU

Praise and glory and wisdom

and thanks and honor and power

and strength be to our God

for ever and ever. Amen!

Revelation 12:7

Books by Brandy Ange:

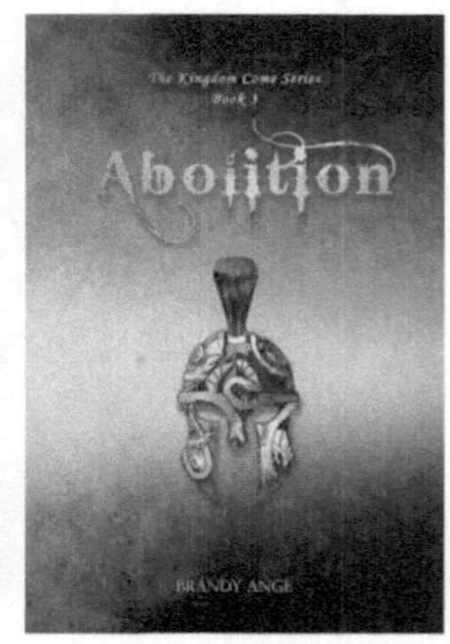

Choose

Or Be Chosen

The Wake

"Out of suffering have emerged the strongest souls;
the most massive characters are seared with scars."

-Kahlil Gibran, The Broken Wings

Achaia sat at the base of a waterfall on an enormous boulder. She crossed her legs beneath her, and held her eyes closed, her eyelashes resting gently on her cheeks. She took deep, slow, measured breaths, listening to the cascading water, letting it fill her mind with white noise. A gentle breeze rustled the lush green vegetation carrying on it the salt from the sea and the scent of damp earth. It surrounded her, brushing her ear like a whisper. *Achaia.*

Achaia's eyes startled open, though she knew there was

no one near her calling her name. The first few times this had happened, Achaia had asked Jude if it had been him or if he'd seen anyone near their camp site, but she'd long since stopped looking. She had hoped meditation would help, but it only seemed to make it more common. The more relaxed her mind, the more she heard the voice- when she slept, when she meditated, as she zoned out into daydreams.

After three months of trying everything that occurred to her, she'd finally come to accept that whenever the voice wanted to inform her who they were or what they wanted, they would. Either that, or she was being driven mad by her guilt, which she thought was possible, given the extent of it, but improbable. She decided this was another one of those spiritual things she just didn't yet understand. She'd tried talking back to it a few times, thinking it might be God, but it didn't *feel* like God. She'd questioned if it could be demons, but she didn't think so.

Achaia stood up on the rock, taking off her white tank top, and shimmying out of her cut off jean shorts which had become her basic go to daily wear. Beneath them, she wore an olive-green swimsuit. She dove from the rock into the swimming hole at the base of the waterfall, relishing the cool water on her sun warmed skin, the rush of it through her hair. She had bathed here every day since Jude had brought her to the island. It felt sacred, like a spiritual cleansing as well as a physical one. She figured she couldn't get enough spiritual cleansing to wash away the stain of Amelia's blood, or her father's.

Achaia had spent the first few weeks on the island almost catatonic. She barely ate, hardly slept, and rarely spoke. But that

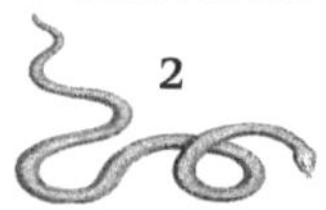

time had been crucial for her mind. She didn't have energy for anything other than processing. And process she did. Gradually she returned to life, but she bore the scars inside, and out. Her fingers ran across her bare stomach, feeling the raised skin of the wound Luc had dealt her, the one that had taken Amelia's life, and bought her friends' freedom. Achaia often wondered if Amelia had known what she was doing. If she had been willing to sacrifice herself, or if Achaia had forced her hand. Amelia's gift had been her curse. Luc had told Achaia that she had made good use of her resources- that thought made her sick. She shook the thought from her head and plunged back beneath the water.

When she surfaced, she saw a figure on the bank that hadn't been standing there before. Achaia turned to face the man, recovering quickly from her shock. Luc stood, his feet in the water, smiling at her. Achaia treaded water, trying to steady her breathing. "What are you doing here?" she asked.

"I would have thought that was obvious," Luc smirked giving her a once over.

Achaia swam back to the opposite side of the waterfall where her clothes sat on the rock, and climbed out of the pool, putting her shorts and tank top back on.

"No need to get dressed on my account," Luc laughed.

"How are you out of Hell?" Achaia asked.

"I have my ways of making temporary visits to the mortal world, though they can't last long." He shrugged.

"Is this the first time you've watched me?" Achaia asked, feeling nauseous.

"No," Luc said simply.

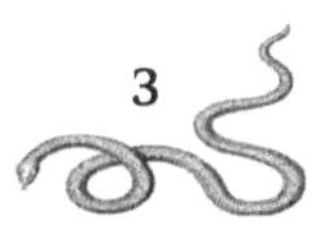

"You're disgusting," Achaia seethed.

"I haven't been ready to talk," Luc said, sounding serious.

"That's a first."

"*Touché,*" Luc shrugged. "Will you come over here and have a proper conversation with me?"

"Not likely," Achaia scoffed.

Luc nodded as if he'd expected as much. "I see I've left my mark on you." She felt like his voice was crawling over her skin, the way he said it as he gestured to her stomach with his eyes. "You've left one on me as well."

Achaia tried to focus on the place where her feet stood on the stone, the warmth it held from the sun- she breathed slowly and deeply but said nothing.

"I still want you," Luc said, his eyes lingering over her with a weight Achaia could feel in her stomach.

"Sucks to be you. I'm not an option." Achaia cocked her leg and crossed her arms in a stance that told Luc he could shove it.

"I am giving you this one last chance to come with me willingly." Luc's eyes were intense. Somewhere between pleading and threatening, they bore into hers.

"Or what?" Achaia spat back.

Luc disappeared for a fraction of a second and appeared on the rock just in front of her. Achaia startled, though only slightly, taking a step back.

"I will shake the foundations of the Earth to rattle you free of it," Luc said as if it were a romantic sentiment. He reached for her, taking her arms gently in his frigid hands. Achaia stiffened

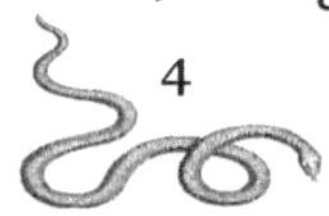

at the touch. "Come with me," he begged.

Achaia stared into the depth of his eyes, feeling his charismatic pull. But she knew who he really was, and that trick no longer worked on her. "Has it been you?" she asked.

Luc rubbed his hands up and down her arms. She fought to appear unfazed. "Has what been me?" Luc asked.

"Calling to me, have you been calling for me?" Achaia asked, wondering if perhaps the voice she'd been hearing had been Luc all along.

Luc leaned closer to her. He was uncomfortably close to her face. "What are you talking about?"

"Nothing," Achaia said turning away. "It obviously wasn't you."

Luc grabbed at her arm and closed the gap between them, standing against her back. He was using all of his powers of manipulation, every ounce of charm and gentleness, and though his touch should have repulsed her, the thought that it felt nice kept banging on the doors to her brain. "Come with me," Luc whispered in her ear. "I can give you eternity."

Achaia breathed out, staring straight ahead, focusing on the trees, the sun-drenched Earth. "Only in Hell," she said coolly.

"We can make the most of it, rule it." Luc's hands wrapped around her waist, grabbing at her stomach, across the wound he'd given her. The wound that had killed Amelia.

"No!" Achaia turned around, and jumped away from him, out of arms' reach.

"You want me. I know you do."

"Only Lucifer could believe his own lies," Achaia said

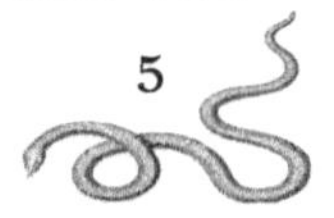

sadly, pitying him, not for the first time. He desperately wanted to be desired, but he never would be, at least not by her.

"You owe me," his voice turned cold.

"How so?" Achaia asked.

"You robbed me of your father. I wouldn't have been alone. But now he's…" Luc's voice cracked.

"So," Achaia said, curiosity getting the better of her, "he-he isn't with you?"

Luc looked up at her, his eyes filled with sadness and something else, something darker, "No. He's just- gone."

Achaia felt the words like a blow to her lungs. She wasn't sure what happened to Nephilim when they died, but her father had also already sold the angelic portion of his soul to Lucifer. She thought he would die like a human, and go to either Heaven, or more probably Hell. Achaia knew this was a ploy to guilt trip her into believing that she deserved to be in Hell with Luc, but she couldn't buy in. She'd been reading the human scriptures, and they made God look fiercely jealous, but full of love and mercy. She prayed that her father had somehow made it to Heaven and that's why Luc thought he was gone.

"Luc, listen to me," Achaia took a step facing him. "I don't know what the truth is. But I know enough to know that I will never choose you."

Luc's form was starting to fade, and as he reached out for her, his hands passed right through. He looked livid that he could no longer touch her. "I meant it, you know."

Achaia shook her head, not following his train of thought.

"I will shake the Earth to free you from it." Luc closed the

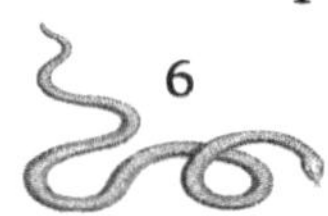

small space between them, leaning down to stare her in the eye. "A time is coming Love, when my bonds will be cut, and I will have free reign on the Earth. I will come first, for you. Together we will burn the Earth to ashes. And out of them we will begin a new Eden."

Achaia shook her head, trying to comprehend, but before she could respond, he disappeared.

Achaia cringed, unable to believe that she'd allowed him to be so close to her. His gift for manipulation was disturbing. Even when you knew it was happening, it was hard to resist, and she was out of practice. She still felt her mind battling thoughts of his lingering touch and questioning whether or not she had liked it. What it would be like to give into it. She cringed with a full body spasm feeling like spiders were crawling all over her. "Guh!!!" She groaned, trying to shake free of the disturbing thoughts. "Gross, gross, gross!" She jumped and leapt away from the place where they had stood. She looked at her beautiful, once serene waterfall, her oasis. Her face scrunched angrily as she thought about how Luc had said today wasn't the first time he'd watched her. "Perve."

Olivier was walking as slow as he reasonably could, but Yellaina was struggling to keep up. "Olly! Wait!"

Olivier sighed. "I'm sorry."

"I know you probably feel like you're crawling, but I feel

like I'm running a marathon." Yellaina was breathing heavily trying to catch her breath.

Achaia was in better shape than Yellaina, and she never complained during any of their walks to the comic book store. He missed his best friend. This wasn't usually a trip he would have taken with his girlfriend. But Yellaina said he didn't need to go alone. Olivier stopped where they stood on the sidewalk. His new purchases swung in the bag in his hand. He wasn't really ready to go back to the safe house just yet, so he wasn't even sure why he was in such a hurry. It was more like he just felt desperate for some kind of forward momentum, eager to put as much distance between them and the events of May, when he'd watched his sister, Amelia, die.

Moscow was almost tolerable in the summer. Olivier still wasn't a fan of Moscow, too many horrible memories- but on this beautiful August day he tried to make himself stop and be grateful that he was alive, when Amelia and Shael were not. He was there with his beautiful girlfriend, on the verge of proposing, while his idol, Noland's girlfriend had run off with Lucifer's son- He was lucky, right?

As if knowing what he was thinking Yellaina smiled at him sadly. "What would you and Achaia have done next?"

"Is there anywhere in Russia we could get a decent grilled cheese sandwich and soup?" Olivier's phone rang and he answered it, still looking at Yellaina's sad smile. "Sup?"

"Is that really how you answer the phone?" Dina's voice came from the other end. Olivier had partnered with Dina to go undercover in the council to try to uncover evidence that their

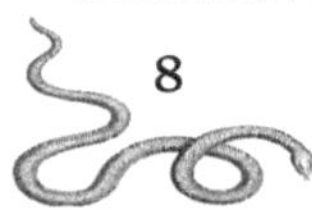

leader Joash was corrupt. She was pretty cool, for an ancient Greek anyway.

"I'm trying new things," Olivier joked, though his voice fell flat.

"Keep trying," Dina said, and he could tell she was smiling. "Is Yellaina with you?"

"Yup." Olivier held out the phone so that Yellaina could hear as well, without putting the phone on speaker.

"I hope you know I'm not trying to rush you, but are you guys ready to come back to work?" Dina asked, and Olivier could tell she was eager to get back to it. She had been giving them time to mourn for Amelia, and truth be told Olivier kind of wished she hadn't. He preferred to keep busy, to feel like he was doing something about it. Emile told him he was still in the anger stage of grief, and nowhere near ready to be trusted in the field, but Olivier was over sitting around.

A glance at Yellaina was enough for Olivier to tell she agreed with his brother. Olivier should say no and hang up the phone. Yellaina smiled diplomatically, even though they weren't on video chat, and said, "There's just one thing I want to do first. Give us a few more weeks?"

Dina sighed. This was obviously not the answer she wanted. "I'm assuming I don't need to remind you that time is nonexistent…"

"I thought it was relative?" Olivier said cocking his head in mock befuddlement.

Dina ignored him and went on, "… and that the fate of the world literally hangs in the balance."

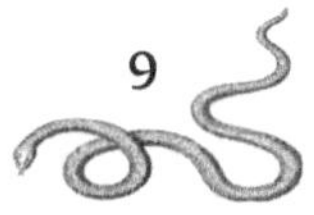

"Hangs on what?" Olivier said, still unwilling to be serious. There had been too many conversations over the last few weeks. Enough low tones, and downward glances…

"What do you mean hangs on what?" Dina asked annoyed.

"You said 'literally', so what's it hanging on? Surely not rope…"

"Call me when you're ready to come back to work." Dina hung up the phone.

Yellaina smiled and shook her head at him, amused. "Sometimes you remind me of what's-his-name?" She thought for a moment, wearing her cute thinking face. "Tony Stark! He is the snarky one, right?"

Olivier smiled and pulled her to his side, wrapping an arm around her. "That is the greatest compliment you've ever given me."

"Really?"

"Yes."

"But isn't Tony Stark known for being immature, and a bit of an irresponsible playboy who is super reckless—"

"Okay, it *was* the greatest compliment you'd ever given me. I guess I should have asked in what way I remind you of him. May I remind you the man is also a rich genius?"

"Well you're obviously neither of those things." Yellaina laughed playfully.

They were coming up on a bridge, and Olivier pulled over to the side, to look out at the city, with all of its colors and shapes. Moscow was beautiful.

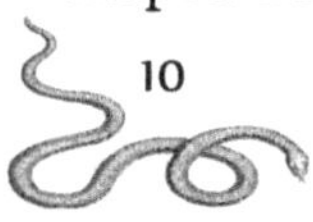

"What was that one thing you wanted to do before we go back to work?" The sun was at that point just before setting where it turns the world to gold. Yellaina's deep brown eyes caught the light and turned to honey.

She glowed as she answered, "Well you lived. You came back to me. So, if I remember correctly, you owe me a wedding."

Travel wasn't as easy without the blessing of the Nephilim council, especially not between countries during a world war. After going through and clearing out Achaia and Shael's apartment, Noland had hopped on board a cargo ship. It had taken him from New York to the French side of the English Channel. There he had taken the train to get back to Moscow. The world was changed. No one trusted anyone. Everyone was living their lives on bated breath, waiting for the next bomb to drop, or to be invaded.

Noland went straight to Bale's office to give his report. He shoved the door open without knocking since it was already cracked and let down the old Army duffle of Shael's that he had taken.

"And?" Bale asked without preamble.

"The apartment has been wiped. No trace of them remains, save for what I myself carry."

Bale nodded. "Good," he looked over his desk and with a

sigh of relief repeated the sentiment, "good."

"Have you been? Is she-"

"Amelia is getting settled. She is beyond well." Bale smiled.

Noland knew it must be a struggle for Bale to contain his enthusiasm in front of Emile, but in Noland's presence there was no need. Noland was happy that Amelia was happy, and that she still existed at all, let alone in Heaven. It was the best he could have hoped for, under the circumstances. As far as he knew, his parents had just ceased to exist when they perished. The working theory was that what became of the original generation when they died was still a mystery, but perhaps those born on Earth were being shown more grace, not bearing the full punishment for the sins of their fathers. Amelia had given them that hope, at least, as the youngest Nephilim to be slain. Noland wondered about all the missing guardians, and if any of them would be found in heaven. They hadn't gotten around to making an actual list, at least that he was aware of. He didn't want anyone to die, but more confirmation would at least give some peace of mind, with the end feeling so close.

"Will you stay?" Noland asked, curiously. If he were in Bale's shoes, and he had the power to go to Achaia that moment, nothing could prevent him.

"The time has not yet come. There is still work to be done, here." Bale's smile faded. "Not that I would aid Lucifer, but I am ready to have this over."

Noland felt his agreement but wasn't so ardent as to verbalize his concurrence.

"What did you keep?" Bale asked, eyeing the Army duffle.

Noland reflexively pulled the bag half behind him. "Just a few things I thought Achaia might want when she comes back."

"You think she will come back?" Bale asked, looking genuinely curious.

Noland didn't take offense, but he didn't answer. The truth was he hoped, but he was by no means certain. If he said as much aloud, he might convince himself that she wasn't. "I'm going to let Emile know I'm back," Noland said nodding toward the hall behind him.

Bale's lips thinned in understanding as he nodded.

Noland turned and lugged the duffle bag with him to Emile's room which was closer to Bale's office than his own. He knocked on the closed door. There was no answer. Noland opened the door anyway and found that the room was vacant. In fact, it looked decidedly un-lived in. Noland sighed, knowing exactly where to check next. He walked down to the next door, and knocked again, still receiving no answer. He opened Amelia's door to find Emile was lying on her bed with headphones on, staring out the window. Seeing the movement out of the corner of his eye, he sat up and looked at Noland.

Noland waved, and Emile removed his headphones. "Melody Gardot—"

"She has a soothing voice." Noland granted, sitting at the foot of Amelia's bed.

"She's going to be ruined for me after this." Emile frowned. He was wrapped in his sister's comforter, leaning against her plethora of pillows in varying shades of grey and purple.

Noland took in the room. The staleness in the air, the half

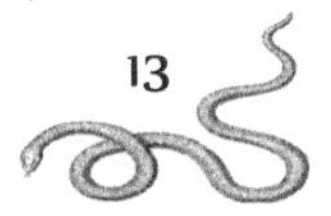

empty cups of tea littering the nightstand, the untouched plates of pastries on the chest of drawers and yet, still the faint lingering scent of Amelia underlying it all, the gentle hint of lavender-

It looked like Emile hadn't left her room in weeks. Noland regretted being away as long as he had.

Emile took a deep breath. "How was it?"

Noland shrugged. Truth be told going through his estranged girlfriend's and her dead-father's things had reminded him a little too much of losing his parents. And, if Noland was honest with himself, he had started to look at Shael as his soon to be father, at least wishfully thinking.

Noland had taken his time, spending much of it musing over the conversations he and Shael had had the last couple of weeks they had spent together. It really had felt like having a dad again. And Achaia- Noland tried not to think about her too much, though that wasn't easy. All signs this time pointed to that she left willingly, especially the note that had been left in her own handwriting explaining that she had run away with Jude. Noland kicked the bag away gently.

"What's all that?" Emile asked. "Stuff you thought Achaia might still want?"

Noland shrugged with his chin. "Or stuff I did."

Emile cocked an eyebrow.

"When your girl leaves with another man, I think you're entitled to go through all the crap she left behind for you to clean up." Noland tried to sound joking. Truth was, he wasn't mad about it. He tried to compartmentalize and approach the task not as her abandoned boyfriend, but as her guardian. In God's

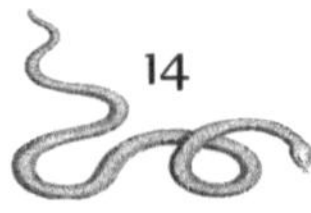

eyes, that was still his calling, even though he was otherwise doing a pretty crap job of that at the moment, since he didn't know where in the God-made universe she even was. "Look, I'm more worried about you." Noland leaned back on the footboard of the bed, really looking at Emile. He'd lost weight, and there were dark circles under his eyes, and a hollowness to his cheeks.

"Half of me is gone," Emile's voice choked off. "The str- stronger half."

Noland shook his head. "You are whole on your own." Noland leveled Emile with a firm, but loving look. He scooted up the edge of the bed to sit next to Emile.

"I feel like I am half floating, half falling in this endless void, and I can't find footing to steady myself." Emile's eyes were bloodshot as he looked up at Noland. "I've felt grief subside enough in others to *know* it isn't permanent, but right now it *feels* like it's threatening to consume me whole. And I have this insatiable appetite for solitude."

Noland took hold of Emile's hand and squeezed it tightly in his own. He closed his eyes, and concentrated, remembering when he had lost his parents and had felt so alone. He had moved to New York and met Yellaina, but when Emile and Amelia had moved in and Emile could feel his loss, and understand his pain, that was when Noland had finally felt like he wasn't alone. When no other Nephilim had understood or experienced his pain, Emile did. Noland focused on that feeling- of being understood, of no longer being alone.

"What is that?" Emile asked "Comfort?"

Noland opened his eyes to look at him. "I wasn't alone

anymore, then; you aren't alone anymore, now." Noland looked Emile determinedly in the eye, willing him to hear him loud and clear. "You've helped us all carry God knows how many of our burdens. It's time you let *us* help carry *yours*."

Emile swallowed hard and nodded. He took in a deep steadying breath and nodded some more. Noland knew Emile was having a hard time being on the other side of comforting, but he didn't have to walk his grief alone. He needed to let them in. Noland was determined to see Emile open back up before he left again. He needed to know that Emile was going to be okay.

"So, does that mean you're ready to come back and rejoin humanity? And us?" Olivier appeared in the open doorway, "because we're not really included in '*humanity*.'" Olivier made air quotes around the word. Yellaina smiled behind him. Olivier's eyes looked concerned, but hopeful.

Emile smiled weakly. "I suppose so." He shrugged, sighing. Noland patted him on the shoulder, proud of his effort. "It's going to take me more time than I deserve to take, so I had better just start trying."

"Good," Olivier said, throwing an arm around Yellaina. He stepped tentatively into the room with her. "Because we're getting married."

Noland looked back and forth between Olivier and Yellaina, and Emile. Slowly, Noland watched Olly and Yellaina's happiness flood into Emile. His eyes lit up with a little surprise, and a hint even of joy.

Achaia made her way back to the beach, where Jude was teaching a yoga class to tourists. She kept her distance and clung to the tree line until he finished and jogged over to her.

"Hey, wanna go surfing today?" he asked. His dreads had been lightened by the sun, and his eyes matched the turquoise blue of the water behind him.

"Actually, we need to talk," Achaia said, quietly, even though the tourists were all too far away to eavesdrop on their conversation. "I saw your dad today."

"What?" Jude's smile dropped. "Are you okay?" He grasped her shoulder but let his hand slide down her arm to grab her hand. He squeezed it as he looked worriedly into her eyes. Even though she had tanned, living on the beach in Thailand all summer, and she joked that she was finally showing her Israeli-half, she still looked pale next to Jude's mocha tone.

Achaia smiled weakly. "I'm fine. He just creeped me out is all. He didn't try to hurt me. He wanted me to come back to him."

Jude barked a humorless laugh and rolled his eyes in disbelief. "Still, he knows where we are."

"I think he's always known. I don't think we can actually hide." Achaia was still talking in a hushed tone, as the yogis filed off the beach past them. "I should have known this was a pipe dream."

"Let's go somewhere else to talk about this." Jude tugged Achaia by the hand he still held and led her toward the cliff-like rocks that surrounded the little bay. Checking for onlookers, they half climbed, half flew to sit on the top. On the horizon, the sun was setting casting the sky in glorious shades of orange and pink.

"I don't really know what to do," Achaia said, staring out at the setting sun, rather than at Jude. She licked the sea spray off her lips and listened to the waves crashing far below. She wondered how long it would take before the water won, and the seemingly solid rocks eroded. "We can't hide. I can't go home." Achaia swallowed as she considered 'home'. "I don't even have a home anymore to go back to. I'm sure the landlord has thrown out all our stuff." Achaia thought of all she wished she had been able to grab and pack before she left, especially the tear-stained picture of her mother that her father had clutched a million times in his hands. Achaia felt the tears well up in her eyes.

If she was honest, these last few months with Jude had felt like an extended retreat, and at times a vacation. But it had never felt permanent, and everything she'd left behind, no longer felt entirely real. There was a definite line in her mind, the life before her father had died, and the one after.

Jude slipped his arm around her and kissed her temple. Achaia's breath caught. "You don't have to figure out everything today." He rubbed up and down her arm comfortingly. He smelled like coconut and sea salt. "What do you need right now?" he asked smiling encouragingly, his lips mere inches away from hers.

Achaia leaned back and cleared her throat. "I don't think meditation is helping. I think what I need is action. I need to be doing something." Achaia hadn't told Jude, but while he slept, and she took the midnight to morning watch, she trained. She worked out her muscles until they ached. She dove off the cliffs to practice her aerial maneuvering. But she wanted more. She needed purpose.

"I have some ideas on that front." Jude's voice was low, and only half joking.

Achaia's eyebrows raised in surprise.

"Joking!" He raised his hands in mock surrender. Jude stood to his feet and offered her a hand to help her to hers. As she stood, she realized just how close they were standing. Jude put a hand on her waist, holding her there. "Maybe, I was only half joking." Jude's tone had changed, becoming low and serious. The pink of the sunset was reflected in his sea blue eyes.

Achaia's heart raced. She wanted to back away, and she thought of Noland.

Jude propped her chin up with his fingers and lowered his face to hers. Achaia gasped and turned her face away, as Jude kissed the corner of her mouth.

Achaia stepped back. "Jude."

"No, that was my bad. That was terrible timing." Jude's face flushed. "Not what you need right now, obviously."

Achaia stared at her feet, feeling nauseous with awkwardness.

"You want to feel like you're doing something," Jude said, pushing forward, uncomfortable with the silence. "Let's train. We should be prepared if my dad comes back. We can set up more parameters. What would make you feel more comfortable?" He was eager to help, or to compensate.

Noland, Achaia thought sadly. In that moment more

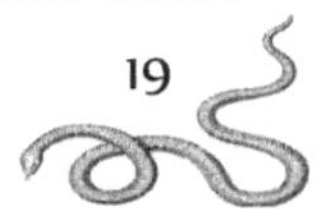

than ever, she missed him with an aching in her chest. But she reminded herself, he probably didn't want to see her ever again. The thought of her, probably made him sick. One of their closest friends was dead. And it was all Achaia's fault.

2

"Keep a little fire burning;
however small, however hidden."

-Cormac McCarthy, The Road

Yellaina stood in a dress shop with Noland. She looked at herself in the mirror, shrouded in lace wearing a delicately elegant satin dress with lace overlay, 'obnoxiously feminine' Achaia would have called it. What would Amelia have thought? When she had imagined shopping for her wedding dress, she'd always imagined Amelia and Achaia with her. Instead, it was Noland who sat in a velvet chair in the corner, watching Yellaina try on dress after dress. None of them matched what she had always pictured. Or maybe they just didn't make her feel the way she'd always anticipated, happy. That was a lot of pressure to put on a dress, when your two best friends were gone.

Yellaina had invited Veronica to come, but dresses weren't really her 'area of expertise'. And Yellaina suspected this was not the distraction she needed at the moment, when she was still grieving her father. Everyone was grieving. Was it selfish of Yellaina to want to get married right now? Was she trying to force everyone to be happy for her? No. She really just wanted the next chapter of her life to start. You can't wait for grief to end. It never does. Slowly it just becomes a part of the landscape of your heart. So, while the territory was shifting anyway, why not add a little joy to the mix?

"What do you think?" Noland asked, behind her.

Yellaina startled from her reverie, to look again in the mirror. "I don't know. What do you think?"

Noland stood and came to stand behind her. He put his hands on her shoulders and met her eyes over her head in the mirror. He was more than a head taller than her. "*You* are stunning. The dress is just an accessory. Olivier is going to be thrilled no matter what you're wearing." Yellaina could see the sadness in his eyes. She knew he was thinking of Achaia, who could come home in a potato sack and it would be the most welcome sight either of them had ever seen. Yellaina didn't want to presume to miss Achaia as much as Noland did, but it had to be awfully close.

"But, is it too much? Over the top?" Yellaina spun around to look him in the eye directly.

"Yellaina, since when do you do anything half-way when

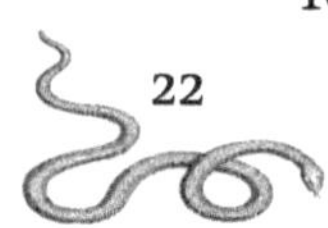

it comes to clothes or makeup?" Noland cocked an eyebrow. "But if you're not sure, try on a hundred more! I have nowhere else to be. I'm retired, remember." Noland winked and sat back down in his chair.

Yellaina followed him and pooled the dress around her as she sat on the floor at his feet. "This isn't anything close to what I hoped for. And I feel incredibly selfish for being sad about it." She felt the warmth of the tears welling up in her eyes. "I want Amelia here. I need Achaia. I don't want to ask Veronica to be my maid of honor if it is going to make her feel obligated."

"You could always ask Inessa," Noland joked, trying to ward off the hysterics in the tenseness of her voice.

Yellaina scoffed at the idea of the ancient, shrewd safe house healer in a rosy pink dress and a corsage. The tears overflowing as she half laughed, half sobbed, Yellaina laid her head in Noland's lap and cried as he smoothed his hand over her hair.

"I'll do it," he said gently. "But I'm not wearing a dress."

Yellaina barked an unladylike laugh as she continued to cry into Noland's lap. After another minute, she collected herself and looked up at him. "Would you really?"

Noland grabbed Yellaina's face in his hands gently and leaned forward. "Yellaina, I would do anything for you."

Yellaina smiled weakly and hiccupped. "You've been more like family to me than my own father. I would be honored if you would stand by my side and give me away."

"*Ya lyublyu vas*, Yellaina." Noland smiled, wiping her tears away with his thumb.

"I love you, too." Yellaina stood to her feet, and kissed Noland on both cheeks.

"Next dress?" Noland laughed.

Yellaina smiled and headed back into the dressing room.

Achaia and Jude boated over to the private little island they had called home. Jude had built a bamboo hut on it before he'd been captured by Luc. It was a modest dwelling, filled with scavenged furniture pieces. They cooked over the fire outside, and slept in shifts, though the bed was big enough for both of them. Achaia helped Jude start the fire, and thought again of Noland, as she often did.

As she walked the beach collecting firewood a young monkey ran toward her excitedly and climbed her legs up onto her shoulder. "Hello, Winston," Achaia said affectionately, petting him, and feeding him a piece of her banana.

Winston patted her head in thanks and ate.

"Will you be joining us Winston?" Jude asked as he saw Achaia approach with her bundle of firewood, and Winston in tow.

"Since when does he miss dinner?" Achaia laughed, eager to pretend the events from earlier hadn't happened. In truth, she was ready to head into the shack to be alone with her thoughts. The silences during dinner were awkward, and Achaia was grateful for Winston's antics to provide distraction. As they finished eating, Achaia claimed fatigue and went toward the shack. Jude only nodded and took up his post for the first watch. Achaia would relieve him in the early morning hours.

As Achaia settled into the bed they shared, she could smell coconut and sea salt coming from Jude's side. It was a bright, cheerful, comforting scent. However, it no longer helped her feel at ease. She really wished he hadn't tried to kiss her. She kicked herself for being surprised and for not being more guarded with him. Had she led him to think that she felt more than friendship for him? Was she a horrible person for wanting to pretend it hadn't happened, rather than talking to him about it? She was emotionally exhausted and spent, and this was really the last thing she needed to add to everything else she had going on at the moment. Was it time for her to leave? Was she getting into a habit of running away when things got too hard or uncomfortable? Where would she go? Achaia moaned, and rolled onto her other side. It was a hot and humid night, and the sheets were already growing damp with her sweat. Because of the heat, and the fact that Jude never came into the hut while she was sleeping, Achaia usually slept in the bare minimum, her bra and underwear.

Achaia tossed and turned until she finally gave in to exhaustion. Her dreams were once again haunted by the voice calling her name.

Naphtali stood on the clouded floor before the gates, amazed that he wasn't sinking through with the weight he carried. For months he had searched to the ends of creation for Shael and had found no sign of his soul. The gates swung open to admit Naphtali without a sound. The streets of Heaven were busy. Angels marched here and there on missions too important to take notice of Naphtali. He found himself at Lailah's door, and steadied himself with a breath before knocking. There was no answer, but he heard a clatter from within.

Trying the door, Naphtali pushed it open. "Lailah?" he called into the entry way.

"Naph?" Lailah's voice was weak.

Naphtali entered the drawing room and found her curled in on herself on a curved daybed of gold, covered in ivory cushions. Her face was sunken and wet with tears. She looked absolutely devastated.

"Where have you been?" she asked, sitting up a little straighter as he came to sit next to her.

"Lailah." Naphtali spoke her name softly and pulled her into a hug that he held.

Lailah sobbed. Naphtali smoothed down her hair and leaned his face against the top of her head.

"I have searched everywhere for any trace of him," Naphtali said, feeling the knot in his chest tighten.

Lailah pulled away and looked up into his eyes, devastated. "He is gone, Naphtali. I felt him cut from me. I no longer feel myself bound to him. He is gone." Fresh tears cascaded down her cheeks.

Naphtali pulled her into a tighter embrace, that was now just as much to comfort himself as it was to comfort her.

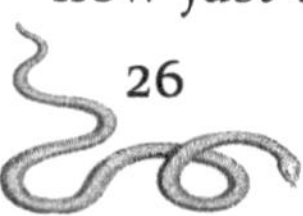

Confirmation that Shael was truly gone was one of the reasons Naphtali had put off coming to see Lailah for so long. He wanted to hold on to hope for as long as possible.

"I didn't want this." She sobbed. "I was angry with him. I was hurt, betrayed. But I never wished this." Her whole body convulsed as she wept.

"Shh," Naphtali cooed, gripping her tighter. "I know Lailah, I know."

"A part of me hoped he would come home, if he died. And," Lailah gasped a sob, as she pulled away from Naphtali, her face full of anguish and shame. "Part of me was relieved that I was no longer bound… until," her words were unintelligible in her cries, "what that meant…"

Naphtali felt a wave rise up inside of him, all of the grief and anguish he had been pushing down as he clung to hope in his searching. It rose up with the force of accumulated interest and overtook him.

Yellaina was grateful that Nephilim weren't typically sentimental, as she stood outside the doors of the seldom used ballroom of the Russian Safe House. Noland stood beside her instead of her father.

"If you should feel happy today, Yellaina, it would be okay." He smiled at her and took her hand, wrapping it up into his arm. "You look radiant."

Yellaina smiled up at him. He looked handsome in a

suit. She'd never really seen him dressed this high. His hair was combed back into a neat manbun, and though some scruff covered his jaw, it was neatly trimmed.

"Are you ready?" Noland smiled down at her. Her comforting older brother. She drew on his presence to steady her and took a deep breath.

"Yes."

Noland pushed the doors open and led her into the room. Olivier stood before her, smiling wider than she'd ever seen him smile. Emile stood next to him. Noland walked her slowly across the room, where the safe house staff sat, with Veronica. A very small crowd, but Yellaina only had eyes for Olivier. His eyes were shining with what couldn't possibly be tears. As she got closer, one escaped down his cheek, and he chuckled as he wiped it with his sleeve. Yellaina beamed at him.

Noland handed her off to him and took up his place behind her.

"Olivier DuBois and Yellaina Rosanov, are you ready to commit yourself unto each other, and your service unto the Lord?" Bale asked. He wore a deep blue suit, which Yellaina absently thought would have looked very well with Amelia's eyes. She smiled back tears and nodded.

"Oh, heck yes," Olivier said, smiling back at her.

Yellaina laughed and heard Noland chuckle behind her. Emile wore a half convincing smile behind Olivier.

Olivier grabbed her hands in his and squeezed them.

"Would you like to exchange vows?" Bale asked. He had never been asked to perform a Nephilim wedding before, and

Yellaina had asked for something between a Nephilim wedding and a human one.

"We would," Olivier said, taking a knee. "Yellaina Mignonette Rosanov, I swear unto you my loyalty as your mate, as your husband, and as your friend. I will stand at your right, and at your six," Olivier smiled his nerdy grin, and Yellaina laughed, "to have your back, and to hold your heart. I swear to fight for you, and not against you. I will seek every day to love you as the Lord loves his bride, selflessly, protectively, and generously. I promise to forgive the few moments where you're not perfect. And to put none but the Lord before you. For now, forever, and for always. Until the end of days, and after." Olivier stood to his feet, smiling with wet cheeks.

Yellaina smiled through her tears of joy, and took a knee herself, looking up into Olivier's shimmering eyes. "Olivier Jethro DuBois, I swear unto you my loyalty as your mate, your wife, and your friend. I will stand at your right and take up arms in defense of you. I will cherish your heart, and the generosity in which you give it. I will comfort you in times of despair." Yellaina's voice caught, and Olivier swallowed hard as a few new tears escaped down his cheeks. "I will encourage you in times of doubt. I will support you in your pursuit of God and follow with you in His ways. I will put you before myself in all things and do my best to love you selflessly and generously, withholding nothing from you. I give you all that I am as a companion, and partner. For now, forever, and for always. Until the end of days, and after."

Yellaina stood, and Olivier pulled her into a firm embrace and kissed the top of her head. He was shaking with silent sobs.

Yellaina squeezed him back. Then he took a deep breath before stepping away and looking at Bale to continue.

"You said you would like to follow the mortal tradition of exchanging rings?"

"Yes," Olivier said turning to Emile. Emile dug in his inner jacket pocket and pulled out two rings. "I hope you like it," Olivier said to her quietly as he placed a delicate gold ring on her finger. It had an engraving of a rose on it, with a diamond flanked by rubies on either side. It was breathtaking.

Yellaina smiled in answer. She took the band that she had picked out from Emile. "I hope it fits," she giggled, sliding the band onto his finger. Luckily, it did. Olivier took her hand and held it.

"Then, with the power vested in me by, well," Bale shrugged, "the creator of the universe, I hereby bind you to your vows, to each other, and unto the Lord; to serve, and to love. You may kiss your mate."

Olivier smiled mischievously and pulled Yellaina into him and kissed her more passionately than he ever had before. She smiled against his lips and giggled as he spun her around in a dip. It was a long moment before he set her back on her feet.

Noland clapped politely, and Emile laughed, feeling their overflowing happiness. Veronica whooped, and clapped, standing from her seat. A moment of melancholy passed as Yellaina wished Amelia and Achaia were there. But she smiled through it and leaned her head against Olivier's shoulder, squeezing his hand, in case he was feeling the same.

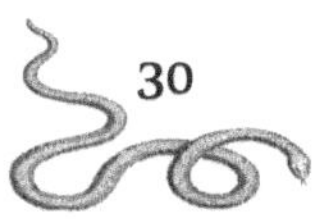

Dina entered her office to find Joash sitting at her desk. He spun around in her chair, where he'd been facing out of the window looking over the city. It was a sunny, hot day in Rome. Dina was just returning from stepping out to grab lunch. She'd relished her time watching humans live, no matter how stressed they were. They had no clue of the actual magnitude of what was happening. Their resilience in still showing up to work to make a pizza, or craft an espresso… She loved humans. Many fallen Nephilim, especially Joash, did not.

"You're back." Joash smiled. It was a genuine smile.

Dina wondered if her gift was actually for espionage. She was amazed that Joash hadn't discovered that she was working against him. He looked at her with so much trust, like she was his conspirator. How could he not see?

"What's up?" Dina asked coolly, taking a sip of her espresso.

Joash rolled his eyes. "These interrogations are tiresome. What do they really expect to find? They need to stop. We have work to do and can't waste any more time on some girl's vendetta. This is not the time for us to be distracted and divided." Joash stood, offering Dina her seat back. His words were pretty, and they would have sounded logical and wise, if Dina didn't believe him to truly be working his own angle. This wasn't the first of his rants she'd listened to since Yellaina had petitioned the council to look within for enemies. Dina knew he was deeply bothered for the council to be so influenced by a teenage girl, over him. It was a topic of immense bitterness.

She took her seat, and set down her cup, leaning forward onto her desk thoughtfully, and looking up at him. "If you could have it your way, what should we be doing right now?"

"If we weren't so focused on ourselves, we could be tracking down those weapons, to better serve humanity," Joash answered sagely.

"Would you destroy them?" Dina asked, curiously.

Joash cocked his head at her as if he were disappointed by her question. "You never throw out what is valuable just because it is dangerous. You just handle it very intentionally."

Dina nodded placatingly.

"How are you handling all of this my dear? Your interrogation is this afternoon, is it not?" Joash asked, with a meaningful look. Dina nodded. "I just want you to know that whatever happens, I'll take care of you." Joash patted her hand on her desk, before turning to leave.

Dina's lunch turned in her stomach. Whether that was a threat or a promise, Dina didn't doubt that he would.

Achaia stared into blue eyes in her sleep. "Amelia," she moaned. "I'm so sorry."

The specter of Amelia didn't speak. She was a blur of incomplete images. Blue eyes, black hair, a red lipped grimace.

"Amelia?" Achaia cried. She felt more than perceived that

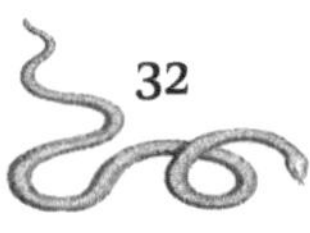

Amelia was growing distant and further away. "Please come back! PLEASE!" Achaia sat upright, awakened by her own scream.

"Achaia?" Jude stood at the window next to the bed. "Are you alright?"

Achaia struggled to catch her breath. Realizing too late she was in a sports bra, she grabbed at the sheet to cover her chest. "Nightmare," she said, still breathing heavily. She swung her legs off the edge of the bed and stared at her feet for a moment trying to re-ground herself in reality. She took a few more steadying breaths. "Is it time for my shift?" she asked.

"Achaia, it's okay. If you want to try to get some more sleep, I'm fine," Jude said compassionately.

Achaia felt bad for not feeling so generous to him the night before. "It's fine. I won't be able to sleep after that anyway." Achaia stood, and took note that Jude did not look away as she grabbed for her shirt and pulled on her shorts. She knew that her bathing suit probably showed more than her underwear, and Jude was probably just used to seeing half naked girls walking around. But it felt different when it was undergarments instead of a swimming suit, and she really wished he had looked away. Noland would have. She shook the thought from her head. It was an unfair comparison.

Achaia walked out of the shack and took up a seat on a log by the bonfire they kept at night, to serve as light, and if needed as a weapon. Jude sat next to her. "Do you want to talk about it? Would it help, to get it out of your head?"

Achaia stared into the fire for a long moment. "I just thought they'd stop by now." She bit her lips together and released them slowly, thinking. Would she have the nightmares for the rest of her life? Nightmares from her escape from Hell. Nightmares of her time imprisoned, of the duel, of their escape from Luc's clutches once again. Nightmares of her guilt. Was this what sleep looked like now? Would she ever experience true rest again?

"I've heard that it helps to talk about your traumas. I guess the more you talk about it and say things out loud, the more you process it, and it eventually starts to feel more like a story that happened to someone else." Jude looked like he was itching to scoot closer, or to touch her, but he kept his distance. Achaia was grateful. She wasn't the touchy feely type. And right now, she really just wanted space.

"I screwed up," Achaia said flatly. "I have to deal with the consequences. This is my lot." She smiled at him halfheartedly. "It's not your problem. Go get some sleep."

Jude stood, looking perturbed. "Burdens are lighter when you let people help carry them, Achaia. Just consider it."

Achaia knew what he said was true. But she also felt like she didn't deserve the relief. Not yet.

As Jude went into the shack, and Achaia found herself alone with the fire, she drew closer to it, even though the evening was warm. She missed Noland. She missed Emile, his ability to know when she wanted comfort or to be left alone. It wasn't any fairer to compare Jude to Emile than it was to compare him to Noland. She missed Olivier, who would have been able to make her laugh or distract her with comic book recommendations. She missed Amelia who would have told her to get over herself for thinking she was so important to have made this whole mess with no help from anyone else. That she wasn't impressive enough to have brought this all about on her own. She missed Yellaina who would have tried to make her feel new and revived with facials and manicures, to glimpse a fresh start through a makeover.

For the first time she allowed herself to wonder if she was wrong, if maybe they missed her too. If maybe she was wrong to do their thinking for them. She wasn't Emile. She sucked at picking up on people's feelings. Maybe they weren't angry; maybe they didn't hate or blame her. Maybe it was just easier for her to assume they did because she was clinging to an excuse to withdraw. That taking the blame and flogging herself for perceived wrongs was easier than facing the truth, that she hadn't had *any* control of what had happened, that she had merely been powerless to stop it. Was that possible? Would she rather feel guilty than powerless?

This thought shook her to her core. For months she had drowned herself in blame and self-loathing. Could it be that that had been her version of the easy way out? Was this keeping her from where she really needed to be, in the fight? Was this what Luc wanted? Was her sitting on the sidelines actually helping his cause? Achaia stood. She had been reading the human scriptures, trying to learn who God was, who Iesou was. There was a third, even more elusive member of their trinity as well, the Holy Spirit. She had so many questions… Where did she fit into it all? She had said she chose a side, but her actions looked more like retreat. She couldn't stay. It was definitely time to leave.

Noland sat in Emile's room after the wedding. They had shrugged off their suit jackets and loosened their collars. Noland, running hotter than most people, had unbuttoned the top few buttons, and rolled up his shirt sleeves. Summer in Russia didn't get as hot as America, which Noland liked. But still the 70s that it reached in August, felt more like 90s to him.

"What's on your mind? You're emotionally all over the place," Emile asked, curiously. There was no judgement in his voice. Noland guessed they were all a little emotionally scatterbrained these days.

"Would it be stupid to go after her?" Noland asked, sitting at the foot of Emile's bed. "I've given her space before, and it turned out to be all misunderstanding. I can't even pretend to assume I know how she feels, but selfishly I just want her home."

"Where's home?" Emile asked sarcastically, eyeing the duffle bag that was still in the corner of his room.

"With me," Noland said bluntly. More than ever, he knew he had chosen Achaia before he'd known that God had picked her for him. Who knew, maybe God had chosen her for him, *because* he loved her. He loved her because he *chose* to love her. And he wanted to comfort and reassure her. He wanted to walk the path of healing with her. To let her vent, or rage, or cry or whatever she needed…

Emile nodded. "I've been worried that she thinks we blame her." Emile looked down, clenching his jaw for a second.

Noland watched the muscles twitch and flex. "As skilled a fighter as she is, and as good at beating the crap out of some demons, it's nothing compared to what she does to herself when she thinks she's screwed up. If she has taken on the blame for something like this, then she is killing herself slowly, inside. I am intimately aware of how she grieves. She grieves harder than most. But she won't show it. That Jude guy probably has no clue how to comfort her." There was an edge of bitterness to Emile's voice that surprised Noland.

"Are you jealous?" Noland cocked an eyebrow in question.

"You're not the only one who gets to be." Emile was darker these days than he had been. He no longer kept his shadows in check, and he didn't try to fix the shadows in others. He accepted them as a part of the bigger picture of what makes them human, or at least a flattering imitation of it. "Losing my sister was hard enough. Losing both of them was nothing short of cruel."

Noland nodded in agreement. He knew better than to believe that Achaia meant for it to be cruel. But Achaia wasn't the most emotionally in tune with herself, let alone others. Noland was hardly one to judge that. If he could find her, if he could convince her to come home, they could work on that together. "I'm going to ask Naphtali to help me find her. Three months is long enough. I want to know how she's doing."

"Agreed," Emile nodded. "On a lighter note, can we also agree that it is super weird that Olivier is *married*."

Noland opened his eyes wide and nodded. "And, first; before either of us."

"Humans would say he's too young." Emile smirked.

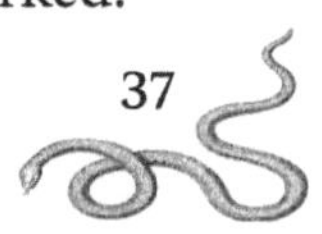

Noland took a sobering breath and nodded looking down. "We know better. This is only the beginning. More mates will be marrying. The end is near, and we need to pool our resources and share our gifts. It does make me feel better knowing that Yellaina won't be as defenseless, with Olivier's gift for speed."

Emile shivered. "Ugh, I don't want to think about my brother consummating his marriage. Change the subject."

Noland laughed. "What about consummating your own?" Noland winked.

Emile blushed. "Ronnie is still grieving her father, and I am still grieving Amelia. Now is hardly the time to propose."

"Speaking of, I need to talk to Veronica about something," Noland said, standing back up.

"Wait. Speaking of consummating?" Emile sat up straighter.

"No, marriage," Noland laughed. "Don't worry I'm not going to seduce your girl. I apparently couldn't if I wanted to…"

"You're not as hopeless as you think," Emile said consolingly.

"Really? As I recall Achaia ran away with another guy."

Emile winced as if he felt the jab Noland had landed on himself. "But not for that reason." Emile looked at Noland seriously. "I can tell you for a fact that she feels more for you than perhaps either of you really know. Breaking my rules again…" Emile rolled his eyes.

"Sure doesn't look like it," Noland said, not sarcastically.

"I think it takes both of you a hot minute to put your finger on what emotion you're experiencing. Then you both want

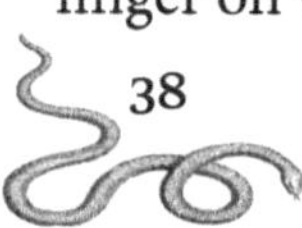

38

to sit back for a few weeks and analyze why…" Emile laughed, poking fun at them.

Noland smirked, and nodded. "Sounds about right," he granted.

Naphtali brought a pot of tea into the drawing room where Lailah was looking a little more at ease. "There's another matter I'd like to discuss with you, if you're feeling up to it." He sat the tea down on a small round side table and took a seat in a chair across from her.

Lailah nodded, "Of course."

"One of them is here," Naphtali said pouring the tea into cups. It smelled like flowers and honey.

"I can't believe I was so overcome, I forgot she was slain." Lailah flushed guiltily.

Naphtali raised a hand as if to stop her self-reproach. "Her parents are both fallen, her friends are still Earth-bound, and her mate is Bale, who comes when he can, but has obligations still on earth. She is very much alone here and could use guidance through the adjustment. She is also now conveniently placed within your reach for a blessing." Naphtali looked Lailah in the eye, intently. "Take her in. Train her to come into her heavenly being. Teach her the gifts of angels who aren't fallen."

Lailah looked down at her lap, her green eyes unsure.

"It could be as healing for you as it will be for her," Naphtali offered.

39

"Am I really the best to teach her?" Lailah asked.

Naphtali reached over, placing his hand on top of hers. "I can think of no one better."

Lailah smiled bashfully. "Very well, bring her forth. I will take her in. She can stay with me until Bale returns."

Amelia stood at a golden door. Everything was so gold here. Gold and white. *Yellaina is going to love it*, she thought to herself, as Naphtali opened the door. A breathtakingly beautiful woman stood inside, welcoming them in.

"Amelia, you are most welcome," she said, and her voice sounded like roses smelled. Amelia shook her head. That made no sense…

"Thank you for agreeing to take me on. I promise I am a diligent student. I won't waste your time."

"My dear, there is no time here," she smiled compassionately. "It will be an adjustment. But you'll get used to the heavenly realms."

Amelia took a deep, unnecessary breath. Breath in Heaven wasn't necessary for life, as much as it was a tool to create it, and a way to express it.

"I am called Lailah," she said as they entered a drawing room. "I am possessed of the gift of blessings, and I would like to bestow one on you."

Amelia looked up at her surprised. "To what do I owe this honor?" Blessings were not given willy-nilly.

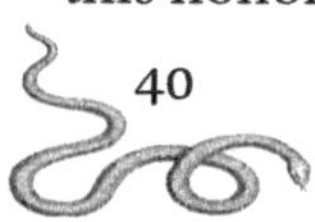

Lailah blushed. "Long have I desired to make the acquaintance of you and your friends. Your arrival has been heralded since the vapors hovered over the waters. You and your friends will be the ending of days."

Amelia felt the blood drain from her face.

"My word, that sounds far more ominous than it is. You are those that will herald the Kingdom come down. It is an honor, child." Lailah gestured for Amelia to take a seat, which Amelia took.

Naphtali smiled at her encouragingly. "Bale was right. Achaia has a very important part to play. But so do the rest of you. Lailah would like to bestow on you a blessing to aid you."

"I would like to give you a blessing, but I will not force it upon you. I would also like to teach you how to move into your Heavenly form, who you've always been intended to be. I see you cling to your human form still. I can help you with that."

"My Heavenly form, is it that different? You look-normal?" Amelia struggled trying to find words. She had always relied on her brothers and Yellaina to do all the talking, on Noland to make all the decisions. Now, she was on her own. She had to interact with strangers, and *that* was definitely not her gift.

"What do you know about your gift?" Lailah asked, taking a seat across from her. Naphtali joined them, which made Amelia feel slightly more comfortable.

"That it has been more of a curse. I take on the pain of those I care about, apparently even to the point of death. I didn't realize *that* was a thing."

"What if I told you that you have only begun to scratch the surface. You can take away the pain of anyone you wish, and once you've fully mastered your gift, you can bestow that pain you've harbored on anyone you so wish, Lord willing."

"What?" Amelia was stunned.

"You can harness the pain of your allies and release it upon your enemies," Lailah said, smiling. "I can teach you how."

Amelia's eyes opened wide in surprise. "Is that your blessing?"

"No," Lailah demurred, looking to Naphtali. "I rather had something else in mind for that."

3

Set in Motion

"Nothing is so painful to the human mind
as a great and sudden change."

-Mary Shelley, Frankenstein

Luc sat in the projection room staring at the images flitting across the fractured ice wall, where months ago he had tried to show Achaia his truth. His mind was scattered and unfocused, so the images were frayed and sporadic. Glimpse after glance, Luc watched Shael's life play out before him. The two of them lounging on a cloud talking about when Shael had known Lailah was his mate but didn't know if she'd known yet. He was nervously fidgeting with his robes, a sword glimmering at his side.

He watched memories of the two of them spying on the

Seraphim as they trained, Luc joking that Shael could take any of them blindfolded, and that he should go down and show them a thing or two.

…. Shael's face after the fall, choosing to settle on confusion before betrayal, giving Luc the benefit of his doubt. Luc choked at the memory of Shael's loyalty.

…. Shael pleading with him, screaming at him, leaving him.

A wail tore through Luc's chest as he lashed out at the projector, slinging it across the room, shattering it against the ice. When he looked back up at the wall, Shael's face flickered then disappeared with the last vapors of the smoke of Luc's memories.

Luc stretched his neck from side to side and shook out his shoulders. He looked at the pieces of the projector on the floor, cursing memory and all of the pain it offered.

He wanted to forget.

But he didn't.

He never could.

Bale had been kind to Veronica when she had turned up at the safe house in Moscow after murdering her own father. They had installed a new kitchen upstairs nearer the dining room, and Bale had helped her convert the old kitchen in the basement of the safe house into a forge. Noland had lit the fires with heavenly flames before he had left to clean out Achaia and her Father's apartment.

Veronica spent most of her days here, working. It was a good distraction, and she liked feeling useful- creating, as opposed to being destructive. Guilt and anger played a constant tug of war with her. At times as she raised her hammer and brought it down on steel, she was raging against her father for manipulating her into agreeing to 'help' him. Other swings were taken out on herself for her patricide. What kind of person kills their own father, just because he'd asked? He had made it *feel* like the lesser evil at the time, but she felt quite differently about it now. In the moment, she hadn't had time to think. The image of his pleading eyes on the beach still burned the backs of her eyelids, whether waking or sleeping. And the bloodied, windblown sea foam still beleaguered her dreams.

A hesitant knock on the door brought Veronica out of her reverie. "Hey." Noland stood, leaning against the door frame in a posture calculated to look relaxed; however, she hardly believed that he *felt* relaxed.

Veronica smiled at the sight of him, though, and placed the steel that she was working on back in the fire. She pulled off her heavy gloves and wiped her hands on her leather apron. She swiped her forehead clear of sweat and moved to take a sip of water. "Hey."

"I have a request." Noland walked into the room and offered her a cold damp rag. She took it gratefully and held it to the back of her neck.

"What is that?"

"Your craftsmanship with weapons is unparalleled. How are you with jewelry?"

Veronica smiled. "Depends, what kind are we talking?"

"Rings." Noland looked so hopeful Veronica smiled.

"What kind of rings?"

"The pledging kind." Noland smirked. "I have some thoughts."

Veronica hopped up to sit on the counter. "I'm listening. I've never made rings, but I could figure it out, I'm sure."

"Great!" Noland looked so happy Veronica would have agreed to anything to keep him smiling. He'd been so devastated to lose Achaia again right after getting her back. And then to lose Amelia and Shael on top of it all…

Veronica totally understood Achaia's inclination to run. She was the last person to be able to judge, having run away herself. She was glad though, that Yellaina and Emile's parents had found her. *Sometimes the moments we most crave solitude is when we least need it,* she mused. "For what it's worth, I think she'll come back, eventually," Veronica offered, not really knowing if the sentiment was actually helpful at all.

Noland smiled in gratitude. "I hope so. I just want her to talk to me. I just want to know how she is handling all of this. And more than that I want her to really understand that none of us blame her for it."

Veronica shifted her weight uncomfortably. She was sure there was no way *her* family felt the same. In that, Achaia was definitely the more fortunate. Veronica was grateful for Emile and his friends, who were slowly becoming her friends, too. But they didn't feel like, nor could they ever replace, her family. Veronica was positive her mother and brothers did blame her.

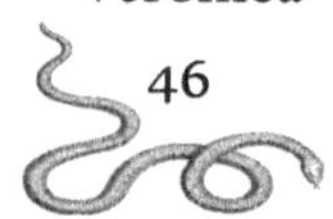

And she couldn't blame them for it.

"There's one other thing I'd like to commission from you as well." Noland's smile widened, bringing Veronica's full attention back to him. Oh, the way her mind wandered these days…

"Oh yeah? What's that?" She asked, matching his grin.

Bale sat in his office pouring over old scrolls. The climate of the world was changing. Nations were in lock down. Trade was strained, leisure and business travel completely suspended. If Bale was right, the end was at hand, and things would be coming to a head very soon. He had confidence the Lord would prevail. Even Luc knew this. But Bale had just as much confidence that Luc would take down as many as he could with him.

Humanity was desperate and panicked. They had grown aggressive and cruel toward one another in their fear. They no longer thought, as much as felt their way through their days, and the absence of logic in their lives was felt in the hostility in the air and their internet. Bale missed the days where news was slower to spread and more localized. People only worried about what affected them in their own lives. The escalation of knowledge of good and evil since the fall had reached a climax in the knowing of absolutely everything that was happening everywhere, and to have it all accessible at their fingertips. Never mind that the 'knowledge' of this age was foolishness and heresy. Knowledge and truth were not the same. Humanity now focused too much on knowing a lot of 'nothing-true'. The pursuit of truth and quality of information had been sacrificed for knowing all.

Bale struggled to focus on the scroll before him. There were five more like it cluttering his desk in various degrees of unraveling. Bale shut his eyes and massaged his temples. He knew better than to think that references to a beast were symbolic as many humans believed. They did not understand the extent and diversity of spiritual beings or warfare. The question Bale had, was where was Luc keeping the beast, and where would it be unleashed. *The east? In the west?*

Bale had questions only the Lord could answer. Bale also wanted for direction and instruction on where the Lord wanted him to focus his strength and resources. Olivier and Yellaina were going under the guise of a honeymoon to rally troops and collect numbers via the outliers. In the meantime, Bale welcomed an excuse to visit Amelia.

Bale felt a presence before he looked up and saw Naphtali appear in his doorway.

"Greetings," Naphtali said smiling. "I bring news of Amelia."

Bale smiled, "How does she fair?"

"Well. Lailah has welcomed her into her home to be blessed and to train her to utilize her full heavenly potential." Naphtali moved into the room and took a seat across the desk from Bale.

"That is good," Bale nodded. "Now, what of Lailah," Bale heard the worry in his own voice, and reprimanded himself for having not reached out to her sooner.

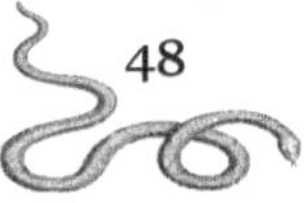

Naphtali frowned at his lap. "Devastated."

Bale let out a breath he hadn't realized he was holding. It was no small thing to be the forgotten mate of a renown traitor. He should have remembered her suffering sooner. Who would offer her condolence? "Is she, has she…" Bale was at a loss.

"She is working through it. There are many things for her to consider and process. It will be no easy grief."

"If that burden is hers, then I wonder at-"

"The Lord's?" Naphtali nodded. "I have wondered that myself. All of Heaven was rocked by the wave of despair when Shael descended. I can't imagine the suffering… The Lord did favor him."

Bale nodded. He had been so swept away in research, in trying to solve problems and move forward, that he himself had not truly stopped to process what the death of another round of Nephilim meant. However, they did have some more answers. Though no one had seen sign of Nathaniel, or his beloved, of Shael or Martinus, Amelia was safe in Heaven. Perhaps the younger generations had more grace than the fallen generation. But what had befallen them? Had they ceased to exist? Or were they banished out of reach in some other realm known only to the Lord?

"It may do well for you to visit Amelia. I think she could use your help with her blessing."

Bale snapped back to the present conversation. "I was just planning on leaving. Might you be willing to stand guard here in my stead?"

"Indubitably." Naphtali smiled. "I was hoping to check in

on Noland and the others."

"You'll find Noland, Emile and Veronica here, but Olivier and Yellaina have left on honeymoon."

"They have wed?" Naphtali's eyebrows raised in surprise.

"They have," Bale nodded solemnly.

"So it begins," Naphtali said, taking it to mean much the same that Bale had. The Lord was binding his forces together, to strengthen them and prepare them for battle.

Noland was walking back to Emile's room, thinking he would go through the contents of the army duffle, and set up a bedroom for Achaia. As he rounded the corner onto the right hall, he saw Naphtali walking toward him at the other end. "There you are!" Naphtali said.

"You're here!" Noland said at the same time.

"How do I find you?" Naphtali asked.

"Well enough," Noland shrugged. "Where have you been?"

"To the ends of the earth, and farther," Naphtali's smile faded; he looked dejected at best, "twice."

Noland let out a breath and with it a shred of hope he hadn't realized he was holding onto. "So-"

"He is gone. I have confirmed it with his mate. She felt herself freed."

Noland hadn't even realized that was a thing. He found comfort in it though, since he still felt very bound to Achaia, she was alive. He hadn't felt her in any serious danger. A time or two he had felt a tug, but nothing in the realm of what he had felt when her life had been in danger. For that, at least, he could be grateful.

"You wouldn't happen to have caught a glimpse of Achaia in your travels?" Noland asked hopefully.

"I have, though I kept my distance. I have checked on her periodically," Naphtali admitted.

"Where is she?" Noland asked bluntly.

"She is on an island in the south of Thailand."

"With Jude?" Noland looked down to his feet, dreading the confirmation.

"Yes," Naphtali said, "though I never witnessed anything between them to cause you concern."

Noland breathed a sigh of relief but wasn't completely comforted. "Thank you."

"You're going after her," Naphtali said, more than asked.

"Momentarily. Will you come with me?" Noland asked, thinking it would be nice to have someone along who knew where they were going.

"I am keeping watch here while Bale is away." Naphtali declined.

Noland nodded. "Can you provide me with coordinates?"

"I can." Naphtali nodded.

"Thank you. I am going to go prepare. I will leave at nightfall," Noland informed him, before going into Emile's room. "Naphtali is here," Noland said, announcing Naphtali behind him.

Emile stood from his bed. "Have you seen her?"

"I am well, thank you for asking." Naphtali said sarcastically. "Yes, she is very well."

Emile sighed in relief, like an addict getting a shot of his favorite drug. "Thank you."

"I'm leaving at nightfall to find Achaia," Noland announced. "I assume you will stay with Veronica."

Emile nodded. "It's growing quiet around here. Everyone is leaving."

"On the contrary," Noland said smiling. "We are but fetching more to come."

"This place will be swarming with Nephilim before you know it," Naphtali said. In truth, the servants were all in a frenzy to ready rooms, and prepare for the influx.

Emile nodded. "Then I guess I should enjoy the quiet while it lasts."

"The calm before the storm," Naphtali added.

Noland looked between the two of them before grabbing the duffle bag and heading out of the room.

He made his way back to his room, which he intended to give to Achaia, taking her less glamorous old room for himself. It felt like ages had passed since they had first shown up on Bale's doorstep, who had been so wary of Achaia's presence. Achaia had never complained about being shown to a dungeon compared to the lavish guest rooms, but Noland wanted her to feel welcome when she returned, and he hardly cared about comfort for himself.

He dumped the duffle bag out gently in the middle of the

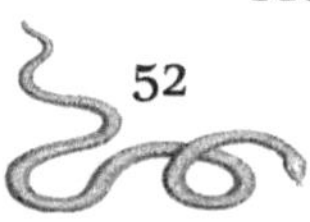

floor. He had grabbed several comic books, not sure which ones were her favorites, and added the picture of her mother to the nightstand. He had found a picture of Shael holding Achaia at a zoo, looking out at some elephants. She was pointing excitedly, and Shael was beaming at her. Noland thought this looked special and added it next to the one of her mother. There was a beaten-up copy of the same picture, that Noland tucked into his pocket. It was light enough to be something he could take to her. In case she decided not to return with him, she could have something. There were also some of her warmer clothes, a throw blanket, and some of her father's weapons that were ancient and weren't really great for use. Noland knew some of them were famous blades. He set them on top of the dresser to figure out how to display later. He had also grabbed a couple of Shael's flannel shirts and the bottle of cologne from his chest of drawers. Noland new how smells were links to memory and wasn't sure if Achaia would like to smell it from time to time.

The sun was setting outside, lighting the sky on fire. Noland threw on some lighter clothes, putting the picture of Achaia's mom back in his pocket from his other pants. He packed a small bag with some essentials, changes of clothes, toothbrush and so on, making sure to pack light. With all commercial flights canceled, the skies were fairly clear to travel. He only hoped for cloud cover to provide spots to land and rest occasionally.

He sat on the bed, feeling hopeless when it came to actually finding her. Naphtali could only give him approximate coordinates. He picked up one of her shirts and smelled it. Then he had a thought and picked up his phone.

Yellaina answered after the third ring. "Noland, is everything alright?"

"Yes," Noland said, not a fan of the worry in her voice.

"Then why are you bothering me on my honeymoon?" she was only half-joking. Noland chuckled.

"The Nephilim who helped you find Veronica. What is his name, and where can I reach him?"

"Adisa? Why do you need to get in touch with him?" Yellaina asked surprised.

"I want him to help me track Achaia," Noland explained.

"You're going after her?" Yellaina asked excitedly.

"What?!" Noland could hear Olivier in the background.

"Noland is going after Achaia." Yellaina's voice was quieter, like she was holding the phone away as she spoke to her husband.

"About time! Thank God!" Olivier exclaimed.

"So how do I reach him?" Noland asked, a note of impatience entering his voice.

"He lives at the Cameroon safe house," Yellaina said, sounding more patient than Noland.

"Great, thank you. Have fun!" Noland said in haste.

"Oh, we are!" Olivier said enthusiastically in the background.

"TMI dude," Noland said before hanging up the phone. He walked briskly through the halls to Bale's office and grabbed the Safe House Directory, dialing the number to the Cameroon office.

"*Bonjour,*" a man answered.

"Okay." Achaia stretched a little more, warming up her muscles.

"And let's make it interesting." Jude smiled. "If you win, what will your stakes be?" he asked.

Achaia pondered for a moment, and studied his face, wondering if she was pushing her luck. "If I win, we leave here. We stop hiding, and we rejoin the fight." With Jude's long arms and powerful legs, she knew her winning was a long shot. If it were a flying race her odds were better. She was lighter, smaller, and more aerodynamic. But Jude had the advantage in the water.

Jude looked shocked. "You want to leave?" His voice held a note of hurt.

"I want us to leave. Aren't you going stir crazy sitting here while the world is going to Hell?" The waves lapped against them, making Achaia have to constantly shift to maintain her balance in the water. It was crystal blue, and clear, a perfect match to Jude's eyes. It was cool where it splashed against her still dry stomach.

"Achaia," Jude reached out for her hands. "We are safe here. Look around," he gestured around them with one hand. "We are in paradise."

Achaia frowned and shook her head. "We aren't though, are we? Not really. Thailand won't be left out of this war. And your dad already knows where we are and how to reach us." Jude dropped her hands and frowned. "Look, this has been wonderful. But it was never meant to be forever. I needed a break. And now, I need to go back. Come with me."

"If you win, I will." Jude's voice had lost any lightheartedness to it. "But if I win," he looked at her intently.

"What?" Achaia asked curiously.

"If I win, you stay with me. So, either way we'll be together. And I mean *really together*, Achaia." Jude grabbed her hands and pulled her closer to him. "I want to be with you."

"You are with me," Achaia said putting a hand up on his chest, to keep some distance between them.

"Achaia," his voice grew low and rough, and he leaned his head down closer. "You know what I mean. We've been playing house long enough. You must have thought about it, too."

"Jude, I have a mate," Achaia said, pushing on his chest, for more space.

"So do I, somewhere… But we have a choice, Achaia. And I choose you."

Achaia stared determinedly down at the water. "Jude-"

"Okay, how about this instead: If I win, you let me kiss you, really kiss you. Then you can tell me whether or not you feel anything for me. Okay? Achaia, look at me." Jude's voice was pleading.

Achaia looked up. His eyes were piercingly blue through thick dark lashes. He was a beautiful contrast. If there was no Noland in the world, or if she'd never met him, she wouldn't hesitate to give Jude a chance. But there was a Noland, and she loved him. She caught her breath at the realization.

Jude took this as encouragement, "Okay, first one back wins. Ready?"

Achaia tried to get her head back in the race.

"Go!"

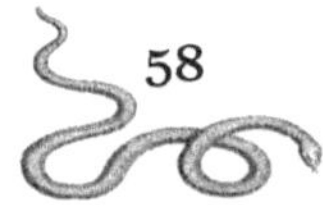

Jude dove, already ahead of her just because of his height. Achaia pushed hard. Every stroke she felt like she was pushing the last three months of grief, heartache, self-loathing, and bitterness behind her. Every stroke took her one closer to home. She pushed, and her arms were already sore before they reached the boulder. Jude had made it there first, but he'd waited for her. "Are you alright?" He asked.

Achaia's arms were sore, but not enough to prevent her from being able to make it back. She was in the best shape of her life. "Yeah," Achaia said, kicking off from the rock and stealing a head start on the lap back.

"Achaia!" Jude cried out. "You can take a rest!"

Achaia didn't listen. She pushed harder, desperate to win. She heard Jude dive back in, behind her. He was gaining on her. Achaia's breaths grew ragged and unsteady. She pushed harder, holding her breaths longer in an attempt to steady them. Jude had caught up to her. The shore was close now, so close. Achaia fought desperately, prayed for her strokes to be longer, for them to push her further, but Jude passed her by, reaching the shore first.

Achaia climbed out of the water, out of breath and devastated.

"Achaia, it was just a race," Jude said putting a hand on her shoulder. "Your stakes weren't nearly as high as mine. Or do you really not want to kiss me that bad?" He sounded hurt.

Achaia struggled to catch her breath. "I don't want to hurt you," she stammered. "Don't make me hurt you."

"Never being allowed a chance to try would hurt more

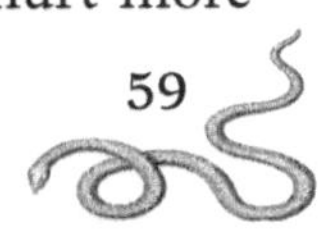

than anything. I'd always wonder what if?" Jude argued. "One kiss, that's all I ask. Just one."

Achaia pulled on a pair of jean shorts over her bathing suit. "I'm telling you, now; it won't change anything."

"It will." Jude assured her. "If not your mind, then it will give me peace in mine."

"One kiss, and you'll be satisfied to remain just friends?" Achaia asked, doubtfully.

Jude flinched slightly but nodded.

"Okay," Achaia stepped forward.

"Oh, I'm not cashing it in now. Besides, you haven't even brushed your teeth yet, have you?" He joked.

Achaia rolled her eyes. "But what if I am leaving?"

"Today?" Jude asked.

"Probably not today," Achaia granted.

"Then kiss me before you go. But give me time. I want to plan it out." Jude took off toward the shack.

"Plan out a kiss?" Achaia asked, following him.

"Plan out our first date."

Achaia stopped. "I didn't agree to a date…" Achaia yelled. Jude continued down the beach. "Jude, I didn't agree to a date!" Achaia stomped in the sand.

Jude stopped and turned. "Achaia, you've been living alone with me for three months. What on earth could you find so intimidating about one evening of my company?"

Achaia rolled her eyes.

"Unless you're worried, I might win you over after all, and that makes you nervous." Jude smiled.

"Please don't do that," Achaia pleaded.

"Do what?" Jude feigned ignorance.

"Get your hopes up. Please don't. I don't want to hurt you," Achaia said, hating the whining tone that her voice had taken on.

"Don't worry about me, Achaia. I'm made of tougher stuff than you give me credit for." Jude turned and walked into the shack to get ready for work.

Marshalling Hope

"Yet hope again elastic springs,
Unconquered though she fell;
Still buoyant are her golden wings,
Still strong to bear us well."

-Charlotte Brontë, Life

Yellaina woke up wrapped in soft white sheets, and Olivier's arms. She rolled over to see if he was awake yet and found him blinking awake in the morning sun. He stretched and sat up against the pillows. Yellaina wrapped the sheets tighter against her chest and laid her head against his stomach.

"Good morning," he smiled down at her.

"*Dobroye utro.*" Yellaina smiled, playing an invisible keyboard on Olivier's abs.

"I understood that!" Olivier laughed. "You know," Olivier

ran his fingers through her hair, smoothing out the morning muss, "when I used to imagine what it would be like to wake up next to you every day- It was always such a far off idea, like I was going to be a completely different person- I'd always thought I'd be happy about it. But I don't think I really ever understood happiness, until now."

"Olly," Yellaina sat up and leaned up to kiss him. "You imagined waking up next to me? Of all the things…" She leaned in and kissed his shoulder.

"Oh, I imagined other things as well," Olivier's voice lowered. "But that wasn't until after I loved you. When I just *knew*, I tried to imagine what life would be like with you as my wife. If marriage is supposed to represent what God feels for humanity, then I just don't understand how he doesn't just burst."

Yellaina laughed. "Do you want to go down and see what Latvians eat for breakfast?"

Olivier eyed her and wrapped his arm around her back. "Priorities wife, priorities." He leaned down and kissed her.

When they finally did make it down for breakfast, a lot of the food was gone, but they managed to grab some eggs and toast before setting out for the safe house in Liepaja. Dina had sent them a list of outlier safe houses, that rarely received attention from the Council, and they were starting in Latvia.

"So, what exactly do you plan to say when we find them?" Olivier asked her as they got off the streetcar near the address Dina had texted her.

"I don't really know. I guess we should start with seeing

how they are doing and asking if they have any needs we can help with. Then just getting a feel for how they feel about the Council. If they aren't overly favorable, we can invite them to the summit in Moscow." Yellaina looked up at Olivier to see if he looked like he thought this was a good plan. He took her hand and squeezed it encouragingly. "God, I hope they come," Yellaina said looking up at the door.

Olivier knocked.

A woman answered the door with a curious stare.

"*Sveiki*," Yellaina smiled.

"*Ka tev iet*?" Olivier added, smiling widely. He was like a kid at Christmas with his new ability to share Yellaina's gift.

"*Kas tu esi*?" The woman asked, not unkindly.

Yellaina explained that she was a Nephilim from Russia, and her mate, a Nephilim of France, and asked if they could come in. The woman looked surprised but pleased, and let them in.

She led them to a small parlor, and Yellaina wondered how they could fit any additional Nephilim in their safe house. It didn't look like they received half the allowance that Bale got in Moscow, but Liepaja was a smaller city than Moscow or New York, and Yellaina hadn't spent significant amounts of time in any smaller safe houses, save for Veronica's, to know if this was normal.

Yellaina started the conversation off light, by asking who all resided in the safe house on a regular basis. The woman's name was Dace, and her mate's name was Ivars. They had two children who were grown and gone, so it was just the two of them. Their son was a guardian, but they hadn't heard from him in a century

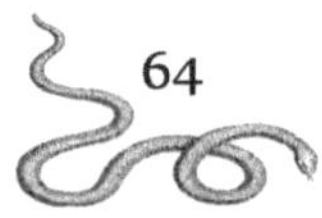

or more. Their daughter was a healer in Kuwait. They heard from her more often, once a decade or so. Yellaina thought that was pretty standard for Nephilim. She asked if they worried about not hearing from their son, and if he had kept in touch more before his extended silence.

The woman said they had used to hear from him every ten or fifteen years, and they didn't know where he was last stationed, and never heard anything from the council, so assumed all must be well in spite of his silence. If something had happened to him, the Council would have let them know, wouldn't they?

Yellaina and Olivier exchanged a look. Yellaina asked if the woman really believed that. A sadness formed in her eyes, like a storm cloud might darken the horizon, slowly, until it moved gradually forward. She shook her head. He had lost track of time before, but a century was too long not to suspect something was amiss.

Olivier nodded his agreement. He chimed in then, explaining how he, himself had worked for the Council, and Guardians had been going missing, and that the Council wasn't doing anything to look for them. The woman looked stunned. She asked many questions which Olivier tried to answer before Yellaina asked her own. "Would you be willing to attend a meeting to learn more?"

The woman nodded. "*Protams.*"

Yellaina and Olivier spent the rest of the day with Dace, and met her husband, Ivars at dinner. They left the safe house feeling pretty confident that their visit had been an encouragement to the couple. "That's two," Olivier said smiling as they started walking back to their hotel. "Did you have a goal number in mind that we are working toward?"

Yellaina hadn't thought to set a goal, just as many as possible. But she liked the idea of being able to have something by which to measure success and to inspire motivation to keep moving forward. "All of them?" She joked, as she thought.

"Ever the optimist," Olivier laughed.

"Save for Joash. Everyone but Joash." Yellaina laughed.

"That's my girl," Olivier high fived her, and Yellaina laughed harder.

"I think God knew what He was doing when He picked you for me." Yellaina smiled.

"I've had similar suspicions," Olivier said throwing an arm around her shoulders, and pulling her in to kiss the top of her head.

Noland perched on a cloud to catch his breath after flying for over an hour straight. He took a water bottle out of his bag and took a huge gulp. He swore he could feel each cool drop descend in his throat, through his chest, to the butterflies wreaking havoc in his stomach. He hadn't really thought too hard before leaving about what it would be like to actually see Achaia again. What if she wasn't happy to see him? What if she wanted to stay hidden? What if she wanted to be with Jude? Just because Naphtali hadn't seen anything to cause concern, didn't mean it wasn't there.

Noland put his water bottle away and sat on the cloud looking out at the horizon, the cool moisture soaking the back of his clothes. It was refreshing after hours of flying. The sun was setting, and the view was painted in shades of pink and orange. Noland sighed. There was beauty in endings. Shael had taught him that. But Noland prayed that he and Achaia weren't over, and that this was just a part of their beginning. The sun itself wasn't visible above the clouds, but its light still painted everything around. Noland reminded himself that though he couldn't see the whole picture, things were still in motion that were leading them all toward victory. The end might be brutal, but it would be beautiful. He got up to his feet and adjusted his bag between his wings, before taking back off into the sky.

Emile ventured down to the forge in the basement, where Veronica spent ninety percent of her time. They had both been mourning so hard, that they hadn't really had much of a relationship. They both tended toward isolation, but Emile knew he needed to set aside his own preference and comfort to support Veronica whose grief had the added layer of guilt that Emile didn't carry.

"Knock. Knock," Emile said, standing in the open doorway.

"Oh, hey," Veronica said turning around. "What time is it?"

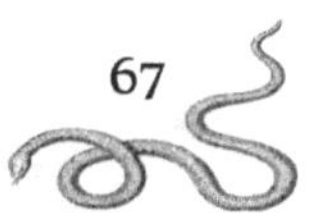

"Almost six. I wondered if you wanted to grab some dinner. Get out of the house for a bit."

Veronica looked down, and Emile could feel her hesitation. Conflict rose within her, excitement at a change of scenery and exploring the city, and exhaustion.

"Ronnie, I think we both need to get out," Emile encouraged.

Veronica smiled and nodded. "You're probably right. Let me get washed up and change my clothes."

"Okay, great." Emile smiled, happy to get out of the same old rut of a routine that they had fallen into.

Veronica looked beautiful, sitting across from Emile at a small table for two, in a simple sun dress and a cardigan that she borrowed from Yellaina's room, because Russian nights were a little too cool for Chilean sundresses. Emile soaked in the view of her and smiled. "I think this is our first actual date."

Ronnie looked up, and thought for a moment, then smiled, "I think you're right. That seems crazy. I feel like I've known you for so long."

"Right?" Emile looked down at his menu with great difficulty. He wanted to just keep his eyes on Veronica.

"I'm sorry if I've been distant lately. I know I have locked myself in the forge." She looked up at him guiltily, wincing an apologetic smile.

Emile's smile fell. "It's okay. I understand."

"I know you do." Veronica's smile lightened, "but that is no excuse for me taking advantage. I think I've just been trying

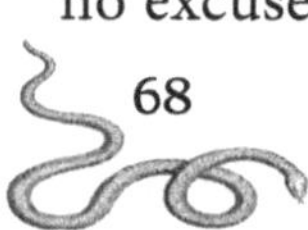

to process and come to terms with—"

"Everything?" Emile asked.

Veronica shrugged her lips and nodded. "There's so much of it that I haven't told you." She frowned.

"Well, whenever you're ready to talk about it, I'm ready to listen." Emile leaned back from the table as their waiter came to take their orders. They made light conversation until the waiter returned with their food, which looked delicious. Emile hadn't been eating as much as he usually did over the last several weeks, and he had lost weight. His stomach growled as if telling him to remedy the situation.

Veronica stared down at her plate.

"What? Does it not look good? We can order you something else," Emile said, looking across the table at Veronica's *Bortsh*.

"It's just so different here. I think I'm just home sick. The food is fine." Veronica picked up her fork.

"Yeah, I don't know that we will be able to find a Chilean place around here." Emile smiled an apology. "But we can cook it at home sometime."

Veronica smiled up at him. "If we can find the ingredients we need, that sounds fun. I could make you *pastel de choclo* with *humitas*!" Veronica's smile faltered as she frowned again.

"Why do you feel so guilty?" Emile set down his fork despite his hunger and leaned forward giving Veronica his full attention.

Veronica sighed and leaned back in her chair, staring down at her hands, folded in her lap. Emile knew she was fiddling her thumbs, a nervous habit of hers that he had noticed several times. When she looked up at him it was through brows contorted by anxiety. "I don't deserve to have fun or be happy."

Emile felt the statement like a blow to the chest and knew Veronica had just taken a swing at herself. He stayed silent, wanting her to go on.

Her voice lowered to a tortured whisper. "I took my father's life. I took it." She breathed out heavily. "And yet, I am angry with him. I am so angry with him. I killed *him*, and yet I feel that *I* was the one betrayed." She sighed as if speaking the words had released a weight. Indeed, Emile felt a tiny bit lighter.

"I think letting it all out will help." Emile swallowed, bracing himself for whatever she was holding onto. "Tell me everything."

"I don't know that I can. That feels like a betrayal to him. I don't want to be like him. Not anymore." Veronica's eyes shimmered with mounting tears.

"Nothing you could tell me would hurt him now." Emile reached his hand palm up on the table, and Veronica took it. "Anything you say here, stays here."

Veronica squeezed his hand and nodded. "There's so much that has been weighing on me." She took a deep breath and thought a moment, as if trying to figure out how to phrase what she wanted to say in English. She was so fluent Emile sometimes forgot it wasn't her first language any more than it was his. But it was their common one. "I don't think I knew at the time just what all he was, what all he'd done. It scares me to say it out loud and to hear it… like that will make my suspicions

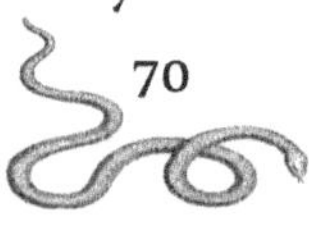

70

true. I am scared that you will agree with me." Emile could feel her heartbeat hammering through where his fingers rested on her wrist.

Emile scooted his chair closer to the table and leaned in over it as far as he could. "Is there another way for you to move forward?"

Veronica thought for a moment. "No, I don't think so."

Emile nodded solemnly. "Well, whatever comes to light, we will work through it together. You don't have to do this alone."

"Emile, I am fairly sure that my father murdered those charges. I think he was the killer all along. I'm afraid that he took the job as a detective to cover his own tracks. He wanted this war, the end, so badly-" Veronica stifled a sob.

Emile felt the heaviness take up residency in his chest, the dull ache that sucked the breath out of his lungs. He took a deep steadying breath, hoping that the pressure in his chest was reducing the pressure in hers.

"He killed those children, and he made us look at them, study them." Veronica shook her head in disgust. "I know each of their names, their faces, all of his victims… and my brothers-" Tears flowed down her cheeks. Emile thought of how her brothers were emotionally stunted and lacked healthy coping skills because of their young exposure to the violence and gore. "He sold weapons to Lucifer, and who knows how many Nephilim are also dead because of them. He had *me* make weapons he knew could kill our own kind. He had me kill him. He made me a *murderer*." Her voice cracked on the last word. "But he didn't make me. I did it." She looked down at her lap, and Emile could feel the shame mixed in with her grief and anger.

Emile spared a glance around the restaurant to make sure they were still talking quietly enough, and to make sure no one was looking at them. The surrounding diners were all absorbed in their own conversations, though.

"I loved him, and he was a monster. I hate him and he was my father. What does that make me?" Veronica looked into Emile's eyes, begging for an answer.

"Ronnie, the fact that this hurts so badly is proof that you desire righteousness, and that you are good. You do not find pride or accomplishment in what has happened or in your father's behavior. You disagree with him and what he manipulated you into doing… You're a good person."

"But I drove my sword through his chest." Veronica released Emile's hand. "When all is said and done, he didn't *really* make me do it. *I* swung the blade."

"We will never know what would have happened if you didn't. Maybe he would have repented. But maybe he would have killed countless others. We can't know. What we do know is that your father's fate was partly his own doing. You never would have done what you did on your own accord."

Veronica nodded. Emile could feel her fighting not to allow his words to comfort her.

"Veronica, nothing we do in the present or the future will be able to change the past. You won't be repeating the transgression. Don't let it hold you back from all the good you can do with your future. That would just be another casualty. We

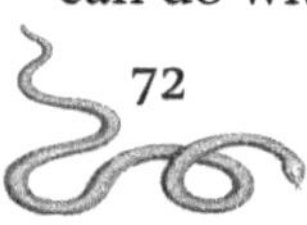

don't need any more ongoing casualties right now." Emile knew his words might be harsh. But if what Veronica needed was a challenge or a conviction, then he would give her anything she *needed*, at whatever cost.

Achaia sat on a rock by the waterfall, staring at a tree across the pool, just listening to the thunder of water on rocks. She wanted to go home, desperately. She acknowledged that home wasn't a specific place; it was a person. She knew it in her bones, and every ounce of her being ached to be near Noland. Was this what knowing felt like? If so, she felt cruel for leaving Noland and thinking he was better off being away from her. Is this what he felt the entire time she'd been gone? Why had she been so stupid to agree to race Jude? Now, she was just going to hurt him as well, and all three of them would be miserable, and it was her fault.

"You torture yourself more than I ever did. I guess I should just leave you to it."

Achaia sighed. "What are you doing back here?" She turned to see Luc standing on the rock behind her, slightly see through, and not entirely present.

"Oh, you know. Just waiting for the day you wake up and realize we are cut from the same cloth. Noland doesn't deserve you, and you'd be settling with Jude. You and I-"

"Would kill each other." Achaia rolled her eyes and stood, turning to face him. "Why won't you just give up?"

"I'll never give up on you." Luc stepped forward. It would have been a sweet or romantic sentiment coming from *anyone* else. Luc made it *sound* appealing, but it *felt* foreboding.

"Even if I want you to?" Achaia asked with the biting edge to her voice that Luc, unfortunately, loved so much.

"Sorry, I stopped listening after 'you.'" Luc winked at her.

Achaia sighed and rolled her eyes. "I told you. I've made my choice."

"And I told you what I would do if you didn't change your mind." Luc's voice grew cold. "How many will die because you refuse me?"

"How many would die if I didn't?" Achaia nearly shouted. "You can't manipulate me anymore. I *see you*, Luc. I see who and what you are. I've shed your blood and saw you bleed. I've seen hurt in your eyes, and watched you envy. You're not unbreakable. You're weak."

Luc went as if to grab her arm but passed through her.

"You can't reach me anymore," Achaia said taking a step nearer to him. Her voice dripped with venom.

"Maybe not in this form." Luc went as if to brush his knuckles across her cheek. Achaia felt the chill like a breeze. "But I have others." He disappeared.

Amelia lay across a beautiful daybed in Lailah's golden drawing room. Her lashes brushed her cheeks as she tried to lay still and relaxed.

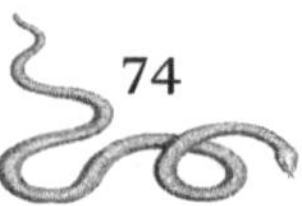

"That's good. Now reach out with your mind. Picture his soul, his personality. Where do his deepest thoughts rest?" Lailah's voice was lulling.

Across the room, Bale reclined in a chair. His eyes were also closed.

"Slip between his thoughts and seek out his consciousness."

Amelia shook her head, trying to concentrate. She loved Bale, but this would have been easier to learn with Emile. Bale's mind was so much more complex than hers. Instead of a room, or even a house, Bale's mind was like a city. She was searching everywhere for the right door to find him. She gasped, as he appeared before her in her mind. *Bale?* She asked in her mind. *Is that you? Did I do it?*

Bale's smile lit up his face, as he reached for her cheek. *Yes Amelia, you did.*

"You're both smiling. Did you do it?" Lailah asked excitedly.

Amelia smiled widely at Bale before opening her eyes.

"She did," Bale laughed, sitting up. "Well done, Amelia!"

"I spoke to you, in your mind?" Amelia sat up, amazed. "What does this mean?"

"Your blessing is the ability to speak to people in their dreams. With enough practice, you should be able to reach the dreams of your brothers and your friends on Earth. As long as their mind is relaxed, you should be able to slip into their subconscious thoughts."

Naphtali smiled widely at her. "Where do we stand on your abilities with your gift?"

"Well that is more difficult to practice, seeing as how I haven't experienced any pain in heaven, and I don't really want to inflict it on anyone here."

"Yes, that will be more difficult to hone. We may have to focus on the theory, and then hope that when the opportunity arises that it comes naturally to you." Lailah winced.

"She's stubborn, like you," Luc said, sounding annoyed. He paced back and forth along the side of the icy alter where Shael's body lay, perfectly preserved in the utter cold. "But despite everything, you loved me. I know you did. And so does she. That just scares her."

Luc stopped and looked down at Shael. "You chose me in the end; you pledged yourself to me. And we are going to be together forever now." Luc sat on the edge of the altar staring down into Shael's face, more familiar to him than his own. "When all of this is over, I will find a way to bring you back. I'll prove to Achaia that I am more powerful. Resurrecting you will be an incredible gift, and she will understand her desire for me. The three of us will outlast them all." Luc looked down at Shael's unmoving face. "You'll see brother, you'll see. She and I will start a new race, in a new Eden."

5

The Weight of Resolve

"She had not known the weight
Until she felt the freedom."

-Nathaniel Hawthorne, The Scarlet Letter

Dace and Ivars were planning to head north into Estonia, while Olivier and Yellaina headed south into Lithuania.

"We don't have much time. I think we need to multiply our forces," Olivier was saying, as they checked into their hotel room. "What do you think about calling your mom?" Olivier scanned Yellaina, trying to interpret her body language.

Yellaina dropped her bag on the floor and turned to face him. "I don't know where she stands. I don't actually know her very well at all." Yellaina didn't seem upset about this fact. It was fairly normal for Nephilim to not be close to their parents.

Olivier knew he was lucky to have what relationship he did with his. "Might be worth calling and checking in to feel her out?"

Yellaina nodded. "You're right. If she can get the ball rolling in China, if that's even where she still is…"

"My parents have gone back to France and said they've been reaching out to the more rural safe houses. They said they also have close friends in Egypt and have talked to Adisa's parents in Cameroon," Olivier said as he unzipped his duffle bag on the bed.

Yellaina smiled at him and unzipped her bag to pull out her toothbrush and shampoo. "We really aren't in this alone, are we?"

Olivier crossed the room and took her hands in his. They were so small. Her usually pristine nails were chipped. "No, this movement will spread. We just have to make sure they all know we mean peace, not civil war. If violence breaks out, it won't be started by us."

Yellaina's smile fell as she nodded. "I've never felt this much pressure. It's like the world is coming to a boiling point and the pot is getting ready to overflow. We're all going to get burned. I just want to minimize the damage. At the same time, I am just so full of dread, waiting for it to happen."

Olivier nodded and sat on the edge of the bed and pulled Yellaina onto his lap. She smelled like rose petals and ylang-ylang. She leaned her shoulder against his chest.

"When I think about it too long or too deep, I feel like I

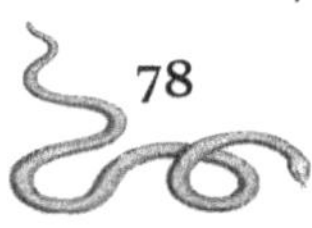

can't even breathe. It's so much." Yellaina's breathing was shallow, and Olivier could see the signs of her anxiety in the way she barely took each breath and in the way she had stopped the things she usually did to take care of herself. Olivier ran his hand over Yellaina's back, playing with the strands of her curled hair. "Is this what Noland has always felt like? Responsible for more lives than just his own. I never questioned him, I always just trusted that he would know and do what was best. Did he feel that pressure?"

"Noland?" Olivier huffed skeptically before stopping to actually think about it. "I don't know. He carried himself like it was the most natural thing in the world for him. But maybe part of us having so much trust in him, is because he never showed if he was scared or stressed. He just always kept moving forward. That's what we have to do. Don't critique every move we make. Just keep those moves going in the right direction one step at a time." Olivier kissed Yellaina's shoulder.

"You're right. One step at a time. Let's just focus on the next step." Yellaina kissed Olivier's cheek before standing and heading off to the bathroom.

Olivier nodded, more to himself than to his wife. "So, meeting with the Mosėdis safe house keeper. That's the focus- shouldn't be hard. We've got this."

"I'm also curious about the museum of rare stones." Yellaina looked at Olivier with a pensive scrunch of her brow.

"Some sight-seeing?" Olivier cocked his head to the side in question.

"Some recon…"

"For a friend?" Olivier cocked an eyebrow.

"Veronica's experiments got me thinking. What if there are other stones with properties we haven't tapped into? What if some have healing properties? If she can use gems for weapons, then why wouldn't we be able to use them for healing or protection?"

"That's a thought," Olivier granted, though it confused him.

"God's breath swept over all of creation. We don't yet know what all that means."

"Okay?" Olivier nodded consentingly. "I'll follow your lead here. What is it exactly you're hoping to find?"

Yellaina frowned, "I'm not sure. But I think it's worth considering."

Emile looked up at the sound of someone knocking on his door. "Come in."

The door creaked as it opened. Bale slipped inside and closed the door behind him. Emile sat up straighter. "I can't make promises," Bale smiled. He looked happier than he had since Amelia's death. "How have you been sleeping?"

Emile cocked an eyebrow in confusion. "What?"

"Has your sleep been restless or deep?" Bale asked, looking eager.

"I guess a little restless." Emile shrugged. "Why?"

"Tonight, I want you to drink some chamomile and take some melatonin." Bale walked further into the room. "Amelia

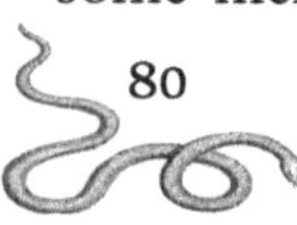

has been blessed. We'd like to try an experiment. We've been practicing."

Emile sat up straighter. "I don't want to hear about you practicing with my sister."

Bale tilted his head in confusion until realization dawned, and he looked annoyed. "Practicing with her blessing, you-" Bale took a deep steadying breath. "Lailah has given her the ability to speak in dreams. Amelia wants to talk to you. It will work best if you enter a deep sleep."

Emile sat up straight. "Would Inessa have a tonic?"

"I don't know about a tonic; I think it's just Nyquil."

"That'll work." Emile smiled, feeling exhilarated, but desperate to fall asleep.

"So far, she hasn't intentionally tried to reach beyond heaven, so I can't promise that it will work. If you can reach a deep sleep, that will make it all the easier for her," Bale explained.

Emile lit up with the possibility of being able to once again, hopefully, see and talk to his sister. Would he be able to feel her emotions? To know for certain that she was safe and happy. The peace that would give him would be immeasurable. "I'll have Inessa put me in a coma if that's what it takes."

Bale laughed. "I thought this would cheer your spirits, but let's just try the Nyquil first."

Veronica was grateful for her gift. Since her conversation with Emile, and airing everything out in the open, she felt a slow shift taking place in her mindset. She held a tiny piece of iron in the fire, watching it heat to a glow. What would it feel like to be that metal. Heated beyond what it could bear, then pounded into a new shape. Yet, in the end, it wasn't left bruised and battered, but more beautiful and more useful than it had ever been before it faced the fire. She wondered if God was doing something similar with her. It was a painful transition. But how was he using these blows? How was he forging her soul? Her mind? Her heart?

Veronica worked for hours in a trance of introspection. She submerged the tiny piece of metal left in her tongs into the fire, and when it rose back out, it was something completely new. She set it next to the others, a matching set. Veronica hadn't gotten to know Achaia like she had hoped. But based on everything Noland had ever told her, Veronica thought, she hoped, the girl would like them.

Emile was right. She couldn't undo what had been done. But there was nothing good in ruminating on the event or stewing in the guilt and the shame. It was easier to do that. Not enjoyable, but easy. It was much harder to push forward, to work toward being able to forgive herself, to forgive her father.

Her father hadn't been all bad, nor had he been entirely good. Veronica wasn't perfect, but she was a saint. She had a duty to this world, a duty to God. Paying penance for her sins wasn't helping anyone in this downward spiral the world was in. Paying penance only worked to make her feel less guilty by receiving punishment and feeling like she was repaying the debt she had taken out when she took her father's life. But penance didn't really help; and no punishment could cancel out her debt. It was an excuse to not move forward.

It was time to do the hard work of moving on, however slowly. Veronica wasn't exactly sure what direction forward was, but she couldn't sit in the puddle she had been. Nothing good ever came from metal staying in the fire. It had to be worked, and then it had to be cooled. It was a hard and repeated process. But Veronica was familiar with it, and she knew now what to expect. It wouldn't be easy, but it would be a work worth doing, and she would be stronger once it was completed.

Luc stood in the empty office waiting impatiently. It smelled like cigar smoke and leather. Warm scents. Luc clenched his jaw in annoyance, maybe even envy? It didn't matter what he felt. It all felt like anger in the end.

The door opened, and Luc stepped into the shadows in the corner of the room until the door closed, and he knew they were alone. He waited for Joash to take a seat at his desk. He watched the arrogance with which the other Nephilim pulled his chair in and looked at his desk as if he had so much control of his life, of his situation. Luc was filled with loathing for the man. "In your element here, Joash?" Luc said with a sneer.

Luc was satisfied to see Joash's surprise. "What are you doing here?" Joash spat.

"I've waited in the wings long enough," Luc stepped forward into the dim lamp light.

"You'll wait a bit longer. The pieces are not yet all in

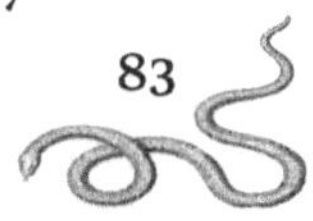

place." Joash was arrogant and thought himself more powerful than he really was. He had never been one of the main players on the board. He just didn't realize he was only a pawn.

"I've been watching you a long time, and I've known you for even longer," Luc drawled as he strode up to the desk opposite Joash. "Too long have you selfishly pursued your own desires. You've warped mandates to your own ends and used power for selfish gain. You have a despicable tainted heart."

"Everything I've done has been for the good of the Nephilim. Unlike you," Joash spat, standing to his feet, face purple with rage. "You chose not to repent. It's your fault we fell in the first place."

"I may have started the war, but you chose to follow me. Your falling was your own doing. You can't blame me. Not anymore. Especially when the truth is so evident." Luc smiled, stepping closer.

"What are you talking about?" Joash said, showing the first hint of hesitation.

"At least I owned that I was not loyal. You're in denial, but I can sense it in you." Luc adjusted Joash's collar, which was disheveled.

"What?" Fear now mixed with the hatred in Joash's voice.

"Your allegiance has waned. There's no conviction in you. You haven't truly chosen the Lord. You haven't chosen a side." Luc's hand moved swiftly to Joash's neck. Joash's eyes widened in surprise, and alarm. "You can't choose yourself Joash. That's not how it works. You must have a master. You have not made yourself a master as I have. You don't truly hold anyone's allegiance."

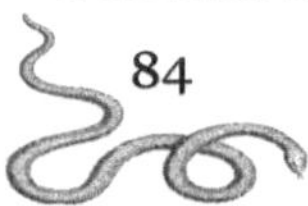

84

"Lucifer-"

"Silence your vile tongue. We had an agreement, brother." Luc squeezed tighter. "I am here to cash in. I have need of your abilities." As if ink were bleeding into them, Joash's eyes turned black. Smoke filled the air between them, and Joash's body shook violently, as Lucifer took it.

Achaia dressed simply, in normal everyday clothes. She didn't want Jude to think she'd put in an effort to impress him. Her stomach was tangled in knots. She had dreaded this night since she had lost the race against Jude. Jude knocked on the doorframe of the little shack they'd called home the last few months. "You ready?" he asked, smiling.

The sun was setting outside, turning the world to sherbet. Achaia sighed, not wanting to be mean, but wanting to be honest. She decided not to say anything. She shook her head, and followed him out onto the beach. He led the way to the tree line, where there was a path lit with candles. Achaia felt the knots in her stomach tighten. The path led to the waterfall; she was very familiar with it.

"This is one of your favorite places, isn't it?" Jude asked smiling. There were more candles covering the rocks surrounding the pool, casting dancing reflections along with water. The effect was magical. On the largest rock, where Achaia usually meditated, there was a picnic set up. Jude helped her up, and she sat on the beach blanket he'd laid out. To her relief he sat across from her, on the opposite corner, giving her plenty of space. He was trying to make her more comfortable.

"My lady," Jude smiled, handing her a coconut with a straw sticking out of a hole chopped in its top.

Achaia took it and attempted a smile.

"Breathe Achaia. It's just me," Jude laughed. He pulled food out of a basket, bread, cheese, and some sliced cold ham. Achaia's stomach growled. Jude laughed. "Go ahead, dig in."

Achaia smiled in earnest then, reaching for a piece of bread.

"So how was your day?" Jude asked.

Achaia thought, knitting her eyebrows. "That's not what I was expecting you to say."

"What? You thought I'd dive right into confessions of my love?" Jude shook his head, "Lighten up Achaia."

Achaia sighed. "I don't think you want to hear about my day."

Jude leveled her with a look of hurt. "Of course, I do."

"No," Achaia amended, "I mean, you're not going to like it."

Jude nodded for her to proceed.

"Your dad came back again. I think he has something planned, and I'm pretty sure he is going to come after me, maybe with force."

Jude scoffed. "Let him try."

"I think he means to hurt a lot of people in the process. I really feel like I need to leave. If he comes here, people are going to get hurt. If I can draw him out-"

"Let's not talk about my dad." Jude cut her off.

Achaia felt the abruptness. Jude didn't usually interrupt her or tell her to stop talking about something that mattered to her.

"I mean, let's talk about something happier," Jude said smiling. He reached his hand over to grab hers, but Achaia reached for a piece of ham at that moment to avoid it.

Achaia avoided his eye and took a sip of her coconut. "Like what Jude? The world is going to hell in a handbasket. What happy things do we have to discuss?"

Jude looked determined. "Look around you. We are in one of the most beautiful locations on the face of the planet. The company is par none, and we have good food…"

Achaia sighed and looked at Jude sadly. "I'm not saying I'm ungrateful, but don't you see it, Jude?" She felt herself growing annoyed. How could they see the world so differently, and Jude care so little?

"See what?" he asked losing a bit of his cheeriness.

"How not-right we are for each other. You prefer to avoid the hard things, and I dwell on them. I am too heavy for you. We make great friends, we balance each other out, but we don't fit that way. I want someone who will take a closer look at those hard things with me, not ignore them." Achaia sat down her coconut.

"I think you're good for me, and I make you lighter. I remind you of the bright side."

"Yes, but you don't sharpen me. And sometimes we have to deal with the darkness. We can't just ignore it or run away."

Achaia's voice was doing a poor job of masking her frustration. "I need a partner who will tackle the darkness with me, not try to distract me from it."

"Is that what Noland would do?" Jude asked, a bitter twinge to his voice, that was out of character for him.

"Yes," Achaia said almost harshly. "I know you don't want to hear it. But he sharpens me. He pushes me and makes me stronger. He doesn't coddle me, or just try to make me feel good all the time. He knows when I need to be pushed." Achaia sighed. "He isn't afraid to upset me. He doesn't walk on eggshells to make it happy all the time. He isn't afraid of the hard stuff."

"You think I am?" Jude asked, hurt.

"I think you like to be happy," Achaia said smiling sadly at him. "And yeah, sometimes that means you avoid things. After everything I've been through, I can't just be light and cheerful all the time. I need to spend some time in the muck, to sort through it, to process it. I can't just-"

"Achaia, I hear you, I do." Jude nodded. "You're the best friend I've ever had, and I want you to be happy. I just want the chance to be the one who does that."

Achaia looked down at her hands. "I think that's the problem Jude. Being happy isn't my prerogative. That isn't even on my list of priorities. It feels selfish with everything happening. I don't want to be happy; I want to be on mission. I want purpose. You're perfectly happy to sit it out on this beach and pretend the world isn't burning, and I can't!" Achaia's voice broke.

Jude took a deep slow breath and let it out even slower. "I can't change your mind, can I?"

"No more than I can apparently change yours." Achaia felt tears burning the backs of her eyes. The pressure of holding them back ached in her throat. She hated that she cried when she was frustrated. She didn't like people thinking she was sad or hurt, when she really just felt out of control and frustrated. She didn't want her tears mistaken for weakness or vulnerability. She wasn't the sort of girl to cry over a boy not doing what she wanted. But she was the sort to get frustrated when someone she cared about didn't show any interest in understanding her point of view or doing what she really truly believed to be right.

Jude reached over, and drew a gentle knuckle along her cheek, wiping away an escapee tear. Achaia turned her face away from the touch.

"You still owe me a kiss before you go," Jude said, offering her a hand to help her to her feet.

Achaia bristled with disbelief that he was really going to collect after she'd thoroughly explained her feelings. "Then you better take it now. I'll be leaving in the morning," Achaia said shortly.

Jude smiled sadly, slipping his hand around the back of her neck, and cupping the base of her skull, wrapping his fingers through the hair at the nape of her neck. He tilted her face up to his, and she felt more tears of frustration escape. She wished she could make him see that he had to choose a side. He wouldn't be able to just stay on this beach and not be affected. He would be caught in the middle of this war, in one way or another. If the world was really ending, Achaia dreaded to think about what would happen to Jude if he refused to choose a side.

Jude brought his mouth down to hers and kissed her hard. Achaia put her hand to his chest, keeping him at a distance. She could feel his heart hammering in his chest, while hers was breaking. Tears poured down her cheeks, seasoning the kiss with salt. A sob escaped her, against his lips. Achaia pulled away, unable to look at him, or to even remain standing in his presence; she turned and ran back down the candle lit path toward the beach.

Noland landed in the small courtyard of the Bankok safe house in the wee hours of the morning. It would have been dark if not for all the city lights casting a fake twilight across the sky. Adisa had beat him there and was waiting on the steps.

"Noland," Adisa stood and walked out into the grass to meet him.

Noland stretched his wings, and his back, sore from days of exhaustive flight. "Adisa, thank you so much for meeting me."

"Come in and rest. They are ready for you." Adisa took Noland's bag from him, and Noland felt five thousand pounds lighter. He withdrew his wings before entering the house. Adisa led him to a small room with a simple wooden framed bed with a thin mattress. On the bed was a tray with some fruit and bread. Noland was famished. "Please, eat." Adisa gestured to the tray and handed him a bottle of water from a small table in the corner.

Noland sat on the bed and dug in. He hadn't realized how ravenous he'd grown. He wasn't actually sure when he had last

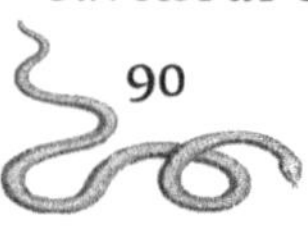

stopped to eat. He had been so focused on getting here.

After Noland had polished off the whole tray of food, Adisa smiled at him. "Feel better?"

Noland nodded.

"You'll be more refreshed after a night of sleep. I was." He stood to leave Noland to it. "You have something of your mate's?" Adisa asked.

Noland nodded, pulling out a dark grey and well-worn Marvel t-shirt Achaia loved. Adisa took it and smelled it. Noland looked at him hopefully.

"This will work very well," Adisa said. "We can leave tomorrow. Unless, you'd rather rest?"

"No," Noland said quickly. "Tomorrow." Noland felt weariness mount its assault on his muscles. He laid back in the bed, and before even reclining entirely, he was asleep.

Noland woke a few hours later to bright sunlight filtering through sheer red curtains. Noland's muscles clenched in protest as he sat up, a Charlie-horse in his calf, and a brutal ache between his shoulder blades from the days of flying and his night of sleeping with his head hung to the side. He stood to relieve the calf cramp and massaged his neck and shoulders, stretching in front of the window.

The smell of something sweet and coconutty drifted on the air, making Noland's stomach growl. He followed his nose to the main room where a tray of *kanom krok* was prepared along with sliced mangos and milk. "Do you have anything stronger?" Noland asked the safe house keeper, Chayan.

"Coffee is brewing. It will be done soon. In the meantime, enjoy the coconut pancakes." Chayan spoke in perfect English, without even a hint of an accent.

"Are you a polyglot?" Noland asked.

Chayan laughed, "Yes."

"My friend Yellaina is, also." Noland took a seat on a cushioned daybed. The room was coated in rugs and cushions in rich reds and purples. It was the warmest safe house he'd ever inhabited. *Yellaina would love this place*, Noland thought.

Adisa came into the room stretching and smiling widely, his large white teeth a stark contrast to his ebony skin. "Morning," he said groggily.

"Morning," Noland nodded, "mango?"

"Yes, please." Adisa joined him at the table. "These smell divine."

"They might be. I've often thought my wife's gift was cooking." Chayan smiled.

Noland nodded in agreement. He'd never heard of that as a spiritual gift, but if this simple breakfast was any indication, Noland was sure she was blessed. It was also possible he was still starving from the days of travel and neglecting meals.

"Chayan, can I ask you something?" Noland started, after swallowing his third pancake.

"Of course," Chayan took up a seat at the table with them. "Ah, here's the coffee."

Chayan's wife entered the room carrying a tray of steaming mugs. She set it down on the little table and unloaded the mugs.

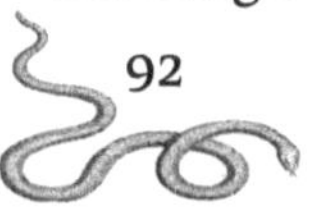

"This is my wife, Som Wang. She doesn't speak English." Chayan thanked her in their own tongue, and Noland nodded his appreciation. Som Wang looked him in the eye with a sad smile, and tenderly touched his cheek in a very motherly gesture. It had become so foreign to him. Noland was caught off guard but couldn't deny there was comfort to be found in the simple show of concern and kindness.

"Som is gifted with hope, encouragement and hospitality. Many come here to be refreshed." Chayan smiled as his wife left the room. He gazed after her adoringly. Noland felt an ache in his chest to share something like they had with Achaia. Though he couldn't see Achaia waiting on people and playing hostess, he smiled at the ridiculous mental image.

"Will you come back with your mate once you find her? Take rest here for a while before embarking back?"

"That would be nice." Noland nodded. He could use a few recovery days, but he wouldn't rest until he had found Achaia and knew her answer.

"Eat, there's more where that came from," Chayan bid them as he stood to go help Som Wang in the kitchen.

Achaia watched the sun come up over the horizon. She hadn't slept at all the night before. Jude hadn't argued about taking the night off. He had gone straight into the shack and remained there the whole night, giving her space, or moping. Achaia didn't care. She breathed in the salt air and took in her last sunrise over the turquoise waters, the cliffs bathed in gold. The breeze was cool, but she wasn't willing to enter the shack or to see Jude to grab a sweatshirt.

She had sat close to the fire and thought of Noland and his warmth. Would he be happy to see her? Angry at her for leaving? She could bear his anger; she deserved it. He would forgive her, and they could move forward. Everything she'd told Jude the night before solidified it in her. Noland was what she needed. Not because she was nothing without him, but she was stronger and better for knowing him. He was a good influence, a patient teacher, a compassionate friend, and a steady companion. That's what she needed, steadiness. Her world had crumbled around her, but he was unshakable. Yet, she wondered if he was, really. She was filled with a desire to be there for him, to be strong enough for him to have someone to rely on, and to share his fears and burdens with. He had Emile, but Achaia wanted to share everything with him- life's joys and pains.

Achaia watched the waves roll in and withdraw. They rallied in perpetual assault of the shore but were inevitably drawn back out by an invisible force. Achaia wondered if that is how God worked. How many times had he drawn back the tide, or calmed the onslaught? How many times had he put in check forces of darkness that she'd scarcely acknowledged? Achaia's thoughts roamed and wondered, her sleep deprived brain unable to keep focus on any one train of thought.

Jude emerged from the shack, looking rumpled and miserable. "Will you go rest? You shouldn't head out with no sleep." He squatted down, sitting in the sand across the fire from

her.

Achaia nodded, knowing he was right and stood without a word. She walked back toward the shack.

"Achaia," Jude called after her.

Achaia turned, bracing herself. For what? She didn't know.

"I *know* you're right. It just *feels* wrong to me, ya know?" Jude winced.

Achaia nodded. If she'd learned anything over the last eight months, it was that *feelings* had value, but she couldn't always trust them over what she *knew*. She'd been led astray too many times. There was no more trying to explain that to Jude, though. They were never going to agree.

Schism

> "The primary cause of unhappiness
> Is never the situation but your thoughts about it."
>
> -Eckhart Tolle, A New Earth

Noland and Adisa landed on a stretch of crystal-clear beach tucked between a half circle of cliffs. Noland spared a glance at Jude, who looked up at them in surprise and stood, next to a fire. Adisa nodded to Noland that Achaia was in the shack a couple yards away. Adisa went to talk to Jude, to give Noland a chance to talk to Achaia. Noland felt his stomach tighten, and he took a deep steadying breath. He knocked on the open doorframe. There was no answer.

Noland ducked his head inside, and saw a bed, big

enough for two, but only holding one. Achaia was curled up on the far side of the bed, but the nearside was turned down as if someone else had just crawled out of it. A wave of nausea washed over Noland. He stepped inside and wondered how he should go about waking her.

Achaia was standing on the beach, but there was a thick mist surrounding her. She couldn't see the cliffs on the horizon, or even the tree line a few yards away. A voice was calling her name. "Where are you?" Achaia called.

"Here," the voice said right behind her. Achaia turned, and was pierced through by bright blue eyes. Brighter than they had ever been in life.

"Amelia?" Achaia fell to her knees.

"Achaia, stand up." Amelia's no-nonsense attitude was just as Achaia remembered.

"I'm so sorry," Achaia felt the warmth of tears flood her cheeks.

"Achaia, I knew what I was doing." Amelia reached out a hand to help Achaia to her feet.

Achaia looked up at her in disbelief. "What?" She stood, with shaking knees.

"I knew what I was doing. We need you for what's coming. I was a liability, with the exception of one thing, my ability to take your afflictions. It worked perfectly. Why are you wasting my sacrifice?"

Achaia's stomach dropped with the weight of conviction. "I guess I felt like I needed to be punished. I deserved exile." Achaia stared at her feet.

"God, that is so stupid, Achaia." Amelia sounded annoyed, and very much herself.

Achaia looked back up, unable to hold back a slight guilty smile. Amelia looked the same but perfect. Any slight blemish or imperfection she may have had in life was smoothed away. She was stunning.

"You can't exile yourself. That's just called running away." Amelia rolled her eyes. "You need to go back with him."

"With who?" Achaia asked.

"Achaia, wake up."

"Achaia," Noland shook her leg gently. Her cheeks were wet with tears. She was crying in her sleep and moaning. "Achaia, wake up."

"Amelia, don't go!" Achaia sat up.

"Achaia?" Noland scooted closer, grabbing Achaia's shoulders.

Achaia's eyes met his, in confusion. "Noland?"

"Achaia," Noland closed the space between them and grabbed her up in a fierce hug.

"Am I still sleeping?" Achaia asked, puzzled.

"You really need to learn to tell when you're awake." Noland chuckled, pulling away to look at her. Her skin had

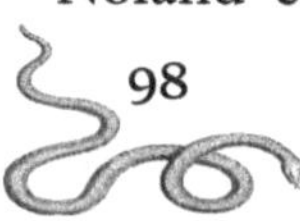

grown gold, and her freckles had darkened in the sun. Her hair was streaked through with sunshine itself. Her eyes shone even brighter in her tanned face. She looked more like Shael than she used to. Noland smiled at the thought. Her Israeli heritage was shining through, and it was beautiful.

"How are you here?" Achaia leaned forward tucking her head into his chest and squeezing him. Noland's eyes drifted back to the other, unmade side of the bed and he stiffened.

Achaia pulled away and followed his gaze. "We sleep in shifts." She said answering his unasked question. Noland breathed a sigh of relief.

"Noland," Achaia swallowed. Noland turned his eyes back to hers. "Noland, I *know*." Achaia grabbed his hands. "I am so sorry. I was going to leave today to go back to Bale's, to find you."

Noland pulled her head to his lips and kissed her forehead. "You have no idea how relieved I am to hear that."

"More than that," Achaia looked up at him, studying his face. "I love you."

Noland lost his breath. In all of his wildest dreams and hopes for seeing Achaia again he had never hoped for this much. He couldn't speak; he couldn't breathe. He couldn't believe he was hearing her right.

"Noland?" Achaia asked, looking concerned. "Are you alright?"

"Say it again," Noland said, cupping her face in his palm.

Achaia smiled. "I love you."

Noland leaned forward and brushed his lips against hers.

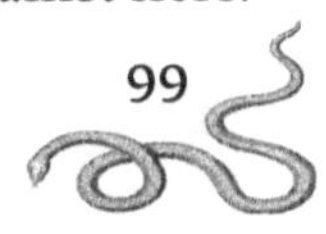

Achaia reached up, grabbing the back of his neck and pulled him nearer. Noland smiled against her mouth. "That was a warmer welcome than I was expecting." Noland laughed, pulling away. "But tell me, how are you? Are you alright? You were having a nightmare?"

Achaia's cheeks were flushed, and she looked down demurely. "I've been having dreams about Amelia, but this one was different. Noland, I think she was actually talking to me. She told me to wake up and that I needed to go with you. Could she really have been talking to me?"

Noland wasn't as surprised as Achaia was. "I mean, angels have appeared in dreams before. I'm not sure how it works. I assumed it was either a specific gift, or maybe something angels in heaven can accomplish. It's possible it was her."

"It definitely sounded like her. I don't think I'd talk to myself that way, even in my subconscious." Achaia smiled. "I think it was her."

"We can ask Bale when we get back to Moscow." Noland smiled, squeezing her hand. "I've missed you."

"I've missed you more than you could ever imagine." Achaia scooted closer to him, laying her head against his chest. "You're really here. God, I took this for granted before." Achaia laughed, wrapping her arms around him and squeezing him tightly. "I just can't touch you enough."

Noland laughed. "As much as I love hearing you say that, this is hardly the time or place," he winked down at her.

Achaia sat up and slapped his shoulder. "That's not what I meant!" Her cheeks turned a brighter shade of pink.

"Do you need help packing? The Bangkok Safe House is waiting for us. We will rest there for a few days, and then head back."

"I don't have much." Achaia stood and started throwing piles of clothes into her beaten and busted bookbag.

They stepped out onto the beach where Jude was sulking. Adisa shrugged.

"So that's it, then?" Jude asked Achaia, ignoring Noland altogether.

Achaia squeezed Noland's hand, and he squeezed back. "Come with us Jude," Achaia pleaded. "You don't have to stay here alone. Come with us. Pick a side."

Jude finally looked at Noland, as if sizing him up. He sighed, and without bitterness mumbled, "I'd rather not."

"If you change your mind, you'd be most welcome," Noland offered.

Jude looked like this wasn't at all the right thing to say to him. "Shouldn't you hate me? I've been shacking up with your girlfriend for three months."

"That's not a good enough reason to hate you." Noland shrugged. "I don't know much about what your life has been like, but I know enough to guess that it hasn't been easy. You don't have to go through it alone."

"Thanks for the charity, but I'm fine." Jude nodded.

"Jude, please," Achaia pleaded, sounding almost desperate. "Don't stay here. Your dad-"

"Wants you more than he ever wanted me. If you leave, I'll be safer here-" Jude stopped, looking like he regretted the words even though he hadn't finished them.

Noland felt Achaia flinch next to him, as if struck. "Maybe you're right." Her eyes were shining with unshed tears. "You're better off without me."

"Achaia, that's not what I meant," Jude said, sounding just as hurt.

"You're sure you won't come with us?" Noland offered again.

"You shouldn't want me anywhere near you," Jude said looking thoroughly confused by Noland's kindness.

"You helped keep Achaia safe. You were a friend to her when she needed one. Why should I be angry with you?" Noland asked.

"Because I fell in love with her," Jude said bluntly. Achaia flinched again next to him. Jude looked as if he hadn't meant to speak the truth aloud.

"I can hardly hold that against you," Noland said sadly. He felt bad for Jude. He didn't know what all he and Achaia had been through together, or how they had spent their time, but Achaia was choosing him, and for Jude, that had to hurt. "I won't hate you for that either, still not a good enough reason." Noland smiled, as if it would lighten the mood the tiniest bit.

"Just go," Jude said sullenly, taking off toward the trees.

"Jude!" Achaia called after him.

"LEAVE!" Jude yelled back over his shoulder without turning around.

"Come on Kaya, he's made his choice." Noland rubbed her arm gently. "Even if you don't like it, it's his and you can't take

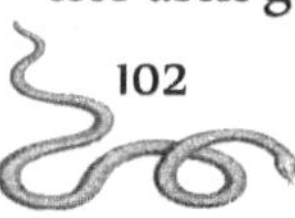

that away from him."

Achaia looked up at him, surprised, but nodded.

"Shall we?" Adisa asked, breaking his silence.

"Yes," Achaia said, still staring into the trees where Jude had disappeared.

"He can always change his mind. He knows where to find us," Noland added quietly. Achaia nodded.

Veronica smiled down at her work. If she had ever been proud of anything, it dulled in comparison to this. This creation wouldn't take any lives but mark the beginning of a new one. It was a symbol of love, not war.

"Hey," Emile stood in the door.

"Look!" Veronica said excitedly, holding up the ring for Emile to inspect.

Emile took it from her hand, and smiled, slipping it onto her ring finger. It was too small for her. "It's not for me, silly." Veronica laughed.

"A man can dream, though." Emile smiled, rubbing his thumb over her fingers.

"But look at it!" She urged, slipping it back off her finger and handing it to him again.

Emile held it up in the light and studied its details. She had engraved the diemerilium band with a serpent twined around the *Alicanto*. The *Alicanto's* wings were spread protectively around the serpent. For such a small surface she had fit in a surprising amount of detail- down to the feathers of the *Alicanto's* wings and the scales of the serpent. The serpent's face was arched up emerald eye to onyx eye with the *Alicanto*.

"Veronica that is beautiful." Emile was breathless in his admiration of her work. "For Noland and Achaia?"

"Mostly for Achaia," Veronica grinned. "I hope she comes home with him. He's been miserable. Do you think she will?"

Emile thought for a second. "I *hope* she will. But I really don't know."

Veronica nodded. Emile's face was drawn, sad. "You miss her too, don't you?"

"I do." Emile swallowed, hard. "I think you'd really like her. She's a firecracker," he smiled. "I think you'd be good for each other. You have more in common than I wish you did."

Veronica cocked an eyebrow in question, not knowing what he meant by his assertion. "What's that supposed to mean?"

"I just mean, your dads… You could probably just relate really well with what the other is going through right now."

Veronica nodded. If her experience could help her to show compassion to someone else facing something similar- well, that didn't make it good or worth it, but at least there was a redemptive aspect to her suffering. "I hope she comes back with him." Veronica smiled, "I want to see her reaction to this!" She held up the ring again, admiring her handiwork.

Emile nudged her shoulder with his own. "If you were designing a ring for yourself, what would it contain?"

"I don't know," Veronica thought for a moment, "but perhaps a flame floating along the waters. At first you might think

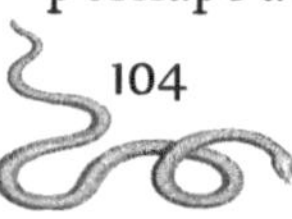

them opposites, that undo each other. But," Veronica looked over to her fire and cooling bucket, "when they work together, they can create fierce beauty, and mark a new beginning. Afterall, when the Spirit hovered over the waters, the first thing they created was light."

Emile leaned down and kissed her temple. He pulled back, smiling, "Guess what."

Veronica looked up with curiosity, "What?"

"I spoke with my sister last night."

"What?" Veronica stepped back in her surprise. "How is this possible?"

"She came to me in my dreams. She's been practicing with Bale, and she is improving."

"Oh Emile, that is wonderful!" Veronica reached for his hand and squeezed it.

"She is okay. She's in heaven, and she's not alone. Naphtali has stayed with her. She is studying with a Nephilim named Lailah. She's good." This was the most at peace Veronica had seen Emile since Amelia's death.

"I am so glad." Veronica only felt a twinge of envy. She wished she had the option of talking to her father again, but maybe it was better that she couldn't. She also envied knowing where Amelia was. Veronica didn't know what had become of her father, and if she was honest with herself, that was part of what made it so difficult to forgive herself or move forward. Had her actions sent him to hell? She doubted he would be welcomed in heaven. Or, had she wiped out his existence all together?

Jude sat by the waterfall where Achaia had usually sought refuge. This would be his place now, though it would forever remind him of *her*.

"Judas ben Lucifer, what are you doing?" a low voice asked behind him.

Jude scowled. "Don't call me that." He whipped his head around to stare into eyes almost identical to his own. "What are you even doing here?"

"Just checking in on my little brother. What are you doing here?" Tobias was about a head taller than Jude and built like a lumber jack. Where Jude was lean and toned like a swimmer, Manasseh Tobias was broad shouldered and had the kind of muscles that made it hard to wear shirts with sleeves. His brown skin was a shade or two darker than Jude's. "I saw what happened. Why didn't you go with them?" Tobias climbed the rock and took a seat next to Jude, making him feel small, as always.

"Why do you care?" Jude asked bitterly.

"Because Jude, if you don't choose, you'll be chosen. Don't you want a choice? Don't you want to decide?"

"You really think either side will choose me? Neither side wants me. If I don't choose, I can just keep out of it and let them all annihilate each other. Serves them right."

"Pity party isn't your color," Tobias said sounding annoyed. "And don't tell me you're arrogant enough to really think that's how this is all going to play out. Do you really think

you're the only exception to the rule?" He huffed a laugh devoid of any genuine amusement.

"How do we really even know that it's even a rule to begin with? Has anyone ever not chosen?" Jude didn't look at Tobias as he spoke but stared into the gaps between the trees. He could see through to more and more trees, but eventually it all just turned black.

"Of course, plenty. And none of them ever like the result of that inaction. God, Jude, how long do you need to mope around before you make a decision? Isn't your gift supposed to be strategy? You can't feel sorry for yourself forever. Sooner or later you have to take up your place in this world. You've got to make a move."

"Nobody wants me!" Jude yelled, standing. "You wouldn't understand. You're the treasured prodigal dad can't have, and the would-be leader of our generation. You chose to stay in the shadows and not join the council. But you are a son of soul mates. Maybe not the council's first choice, but they would have taken you for your mother's sake. I'm just dad's bastard spawn that will never be good enough for him, never be bad enough for him, and an abomination to the council."

"Achaia doesn't seem to be letting that stop her and she has just as many obstacles as you." Tobias stood, towering over Jude, looking at him like he was a petulant child. "Difference is, she took ownership and isn't letting what anyone else thinks, wants, or believes stop her from doing what she believes is right."

"Don't talk to me about Achaia," Jude spat.

"When are you going to grow up and get over yourself?"

Tobias struggled to keep his voice even, but frustration was fighting its way through. "You sit here all *woe-is-you*, while the world is literally on fire. Do you know how many innocent people are dying? How many children are left parentless? How many vulnerable people are being taken advantage of and abused? Meanwhile you sit here on your pebbled beach drinking your coconuts thinking you've got it so hard. Entire countries are being ended, identities lost. They have no choice! Don't squander yours. Jesus, Jude, take your head out of your butt for one damn second and look around you!" Tobias ran a hand over his face, trying to calm himself.

"As appealing as you've made that sound," Jude rolled his eyes, "I'll pass." He slid down the rock into the water. When he surfaced, and looked back up, Tobias was gone. Jude could hear the sound of his brother's wings beating in the distance and wasn't sorry.

Achaia, Noland and Adisa landed in a beautiful little courtyard in the afternoon sun. A woman with hip length silky straight black hair swept out into the light, her hair reflecting the sun like a raven's wings.

"Som Wang, this is Achaia," Noland smiled.

The woman looked exuberantly happy to see her. She took her by the shoulders and stared into her face. Achaia had heard it said that the eyes were the windows to the soul. If that was true, Som Wang's soul was a place of tranquil beauty that

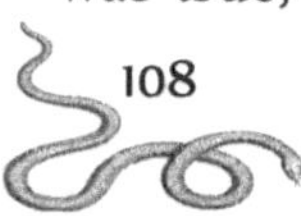

Achaia wished she could possess. The woman was only an inch or two taller than Achaia, but she looked down on her with all the authority of a mother, as she smoothed down Achaia's wind tossed curls, and pulled her gently by the back of the head in for an affectionate embrace. Achaia felt like the prodigal daughter being welcomed home.

Achaia wasn't the touchy feely type, especially not with complete strangers, but the woman had a comforting presence that made the gesture welcome. Achaia wondered if this is what it would have been like to be hugged by her mom. She closed her eyes, and imagined that was who was holding her, and she felt her cheeks wet with tears. As the woman released her, she wore a faint but kind smile on her lips and gestured for them to follow her back inside. Achaia looked over at Noland, astonished by her reaction to the woman. Noland smiled and mouthed, "I know."

Inside, there was food and drinks, and cushions everywhere. Achaia wondered if they were early for a party. She felt a staggering sense of welcome. "Som's gift is for hospitality. I hope you don't mind hanging out here for a few days," Noland said, taking up a fuchsia pouf on the floor next to a round wooden coffee table laden with treats.

"Twist my arm," Achaia laughed, reclining next to him on a sunshine yellow pillow.

Adisa sat across the table from them and was already sucking on a mango wedge which he had squeezed a lime over.

Achaia grabbed up the fruit as well, and dug in, the sweetness filling her mouth, and the bitterness puckering her lips. They drank ginger turmeric tea and ate until Achaia was ready to fall asleep. She didn't want to sleep though. She wanted to hear everything that she'd missed in her time away.

"We have time for all that," Noland said, as he showed her to a room with a wooden framed mattress shrouded in mosquito netting.

The breeze coming through the window danced in the curtains, and made the room feel almost ethereal. She nodded and gave into the exhaustion, curling up on the bed, and letting Noland pull a blanket up over her.

"We are here to rest. Take advantage of that."

Olivier and Yellaina left the museum of rare stones at closing time. Olivier's feet hurt from standing and staring and taking a few steps then doing it all over again. As they reached the street, Olivier studied Yellaina's face. "So, was it everything you'd hoped it'd be and more?"

Yellaina's brow was scrunched, and her eyes were distant. She was deep in thought, somewhere else entirely.

"Yellaina," Olivier said, tapping her shoulder.

Yellaina looked up at him, her face still drawn in remnant concentration. "Huh?"

"The stones, what did you make of them? And note how well I've done at not making any jokes."

The joke went over Yellaina's head, as she finished her summit, coming out of her reverie. "I'm not sure."

Olivier nodded, staring at her blankly.

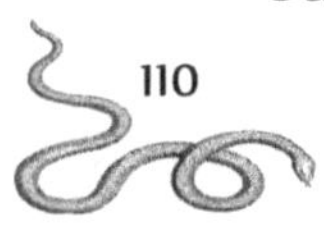

"I feel like-" Yellaina sighed. "I'm missing something."

"Okay, let's walk. We're standing in the middle of the exit." Olivier guided her gently by the back of her arm, down the sidewalk. "What kind of something do you feel like you're missing?"

"Like a step. Like stones in and of themselves don't do anything. But, maybe it's more like herbs. Like they have properties, and then under the right conditions they come out. Like the oils of plants. You don't just eat the leaves and expect the cure. You have to extract the oils. Maybe there's something about Veronica's forging process that released the properties of the stones to give the weapons their abilities? How is it? What part of the process woke them up that much? It's not like Pyrite is our Kryptonite. We don't just grow weak standing next to the rocks…"

Olivier stopped walking and grabbed Yellaina's face and kissed her, hard.

"What was that for?" She smiled looking shocked.

"You just made an extraordinarily relevant Super Man reference, and I've never loved you more." He continued walking down the street, "That's my girl." He fisted the air bringing an ecstatic knee up to his chest.

"You're such a nerd." Yellaina laughed.

"You made the reference, not me." Olivier smiled widely.

"What is that?" Yellaina asked stopping in her tracks and pointing up to the sky.

"What?" Olivier looked up and saw it too. "Not a shooting star…"

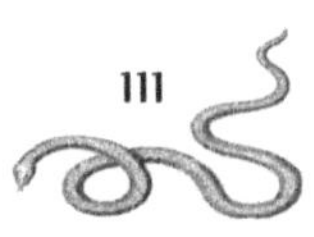

"No…" Yellaina agreed.

The closer it got the larger it grew. Sirens started blaring in the streets. Realization dawned in agonizingly slow motion in Olivier's mind.

"Yellaina!" Olivier tackled Yellaina to the ground and covered as much of her as possible with his body just as the bomb detonated, what must have been miles away. Still, the earth shook around them, and foundations of buildings cracked. Windows shattered, and bricks fell. Yellaina screamed in his ear.

Lithuania had just been attacked. The scary thing was, there were so many options, Olivier didn't even know by whom. "Are you alright?" Olivier asked, still kneeling over her, but taking his body weight on his hands and knees.

Yellaina nodded. "Olly, we're running out of time. We need to recruit faster."

Olivier nodded and helped Yellaina to her feet.

"Do we go help?" Olivier said, looking toward the city that had been hit.

Yellaina looked sad. "I think we have passed that phase of the end. I don't think there's much more in that way that we could offer. I mean we can, until the world ends. But I think our efforts are needed elsewhere, as horrible as that feels to say. And we had better get a move on."

Olivier nodded in agreement. Their meeting that afternoon with the safehouse director had gone well, and they were going to help recruit, too, just like Dace. But they needed their numbers to spread faster, or there would be no Moscow to host a summit in.

Tobias landed on the front porch of the rickety old houseboat he called home. It was pieced together with miracles and looked like one false move would send its splintered rotting boards back into the Tonle Sap. He watched the local children paddle their long thin boats full of soda cans back to their parents floating shacks for the night after the tourist boats stopped running at sunset. He shook his head, wishing that his brother wasn't so oblivious to the poverty in the world, and that there were people out there more helpless to help themselves than he was. But he couldn't make him see that. "Mom?" He called.

"Out here," Hilmaya shouted from around the side of the house, where she balanced on a long bamboo boat that was just wide enough for her to sit in. She balanced with all the grace of a dancer and unpinned the laundry from the line with the deft hands of a warrior. She said she was paying her penance for not leaving his father sooner by helping the impoverished people of Cambodia, but after growing up in the floating village, Tobias knew the truth. This wasn't a punishment at all, not anymore. She loved the people. She helped the children and found joy in sticking it to the corrupt privately owned companies that exploited them. She was a force to be reckoned with. They called her Momma Blue, at her request. Her electric blue and purple hair made her stand out from the other people of the community, if not from her vibrantly painted houseboat. "How'd it go?" she asked.

Her dark eyes gleamed with hope in her ebony face. Her smile blindingly white.

"Not well," Tobias granted.

Hilmaya frowned. "Tell me you didn't argue with him."

Tobias shrugged. "I'm telling you, we will never see eye to eye on anything, if he can't even see what's right in front of his face."

Hilmaya frowned. "Manasseh, you were raised with love, and knowing who you were, the good and the bad." She looked at him with so much compassion, he felt like he was being pushed to his knees. But he remained standing.

"He was raised in a very loving home if I remember correctly." Tobias argued.

"But imagine how he must have felt when he realized the truth of who he was. His whole life was a lie, a coverup. I knew I should have found him, taken him in," she said bitterly, shaking her head with self-reproach.

"Mom—"

Hilmaya held up a hand cutting him off.

"That boy had no idea what he was in for, and whatever your father has put him through since, he has borne remarkably well." She frowned with sorrow for the boy. "He needs family. He can't decide because he feels like no one wants him. We need to show him he is wanted. We don't do that by arguing." She looked at him scornfully.

Tobias was a big guy, an adult of twenty-two, but when his mom looked at him like that, he folded. He knelt his head and nodded. "Yes, I see."

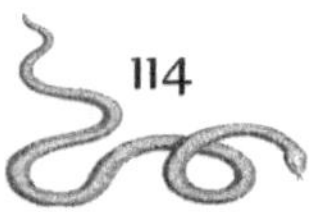

The humidity of the night settled on Tobias' skin making his shirt stick to him annoyingly. He inhaled the fishy smell of the Tonle Sap and looked out at the last bit of sun disappearing over the horizon. Time was running out. Soon, Jude would lose his chance to choose, and Tobias feared what that meant for him.

Hilmaya climbed out of her boat behind him and put a steady strong hand on his shoulder. "You've flown far," she said with a squeeze. "Come have some dinner."

Tobias thought of the families floating all around them and wondered what they were having that night, and if everyone had enough…

7

Shifter

"People worshiped the dragon because he had given authority
To the beast, and they also worshiped the beast and asked,
'Who is like the beast? Who can wage war against it?'"

-Revelation 13:4

Dina sat in her office, picking at an incredibly unappetizing salad that she had picked up on her way in. She was staring between her phone and her computer- willing the first to ring and filtering through news reports on the bombings and the lists of casualties' names. Yellaina and Olivier were in Lithuania, and she hadn't heard from them since the bombing.

Her phone rang, and there was a knock on her door at the same time. She startled upright, staring back and forth between the two until her door opened without her. Joash stuck his head in. A chill ran the length of Dina's spine. She stared at her phone longing to answer it but looked back up at Joash.

"Are you going to answer that?" he asked, gesturing down.

"Whoever it is, can't be more important than you. They can leave a message," she said coolly.

Joash smiled and took a seat opposite her. "I'm assuming that you're up to date on all the most recent bombings?"

"Lithuania, Belarus, Latvia, and Estonia." Dina frowned.

"Surprising targets, are they not?" Joash shrugged.

Knowing what Dina knew, that those countries held the Nephilim most likely to join the Remnant, she didn't think so. But it was better if Joash didn't see that. "They aren't exactly the powerhouse players on the board," Dina granted.

"I wonder why they were targeted?" Joash narrowed his eyes, studying her for an opinion.

"At this stage of the game, maybe just because they could be." Dina shrugged. "Those countries lack the defenses to deflect attacks the way the main players do. The world is mad. Other than that, I'm not sure if man has any strategy left in their arsenal."

"And you think this is men?" Joash leaned back, eyeing her face speculatively.

"Well, I assume, as always, there are demons at play. But I don't think Lucifer pulls all the strings that end in death. We can't give him that much credit. Men are more willful than we've ever given them credit for, and he can't control them any better than we can." Dina smiled encouragingly.

Joash didn't look encouraged though. He frowned

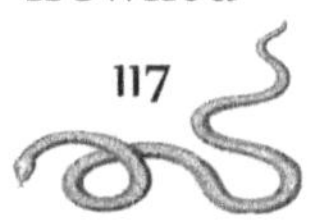

pensively, almost pouting.

"Brother Joash?" Dina asked, watching him closely.

At the mention of his name, Joash's nose twitched up in contempt. The expression was gone in less than an instant. If Dina hadn't been watching so closely, she would have missed it entirely.

"Are you alright?" Dina asked, eyeing him even more carefully.

"Of course, just ridiculous times, aren't they? Can't wait for days to be over." Joash shrugged, standing. "Anyway, I'll let you get back to it." He knocked on her desk, a casual gesture, something he'd never done before. He turned with a little too much of a flourish, and a wicked gleam in his eye, as he left her office. There was a charisma to him he didn't naturally possess, and a contempt for himself that he most certainly didn't usually harbor.

Dina sat back in her chair and thought of the chill that had run down her spine at his entering. Dina didn't know what to think, but something wasn't right with Joash. Maybe she really was overly stressed. She was definitely sleep deprived. Surely Joash was too, knowing that many of the council were watching him more closely. Maybe he was trying to act more charismatic to win people over? But there was no need to waste those energies on her-

Dina shook her head and picked up her phone to check her voicemail.

"Hey Dina, sorry to keep you waiting so long. We're okay!" Dina breathed a sigh of relief at the sound of Olivier's voice. "We are wondering if you have any ideas about how we can move this along a little faster? It really looks like we are running low on time, and travel is getting harder. Yellaina can only fly so far, and people are watching the sky now more than they used to…"

Dina hung up the phone and dialed him back.

Noland woke up the next morning to Chayan shaking him awake. "You have a call."

Noland sat up confused. "On the safe house phone?" He squinted in the early morning sun. "Who even knows I'm here who doesn't have my cell number?" He moaned to himself as he stretched out his still sore back muscles.

Noland followed Chayan to a small office, with an ornately carved wooden desk in its center. He leaned over it and picked up the phone Chayan gestured to before he left, closing the door behind him.

"Hello?" Noland asked.

"Hey," a woman spoke on the other line.

"Hey, you…" Noland said in obvious doubt of whom he was speaking with.

"It's Dina," the woman said quietly.

"Ah, so you're probably not meant to be talking to me. Why are you talking to me, and how did you know where I was?" Noland said waking up a little more and growing suspicious.

"Olivier has been working for me. He told me where to

find you. He and Yellaina need help with their recruiting efforts."

"I'm already on it. Adisa was going to recruit back in Cameroon, and I've already invited the safe house family here in Bangkok."

Dina sighed in relief. "Did you hear about the bombings?" she asked.

"No," Noland stood up straighter, and gripped the phone harder. "Where?"

"Lithuania, and the surrounding countries, but don't worry; I've already talked with Olivier and Yellaina and they are fine."

"Why are you asking for my help?" Noland asked after the relief washed over him.

"Because you have more power and freedom than any of us. And Joash fears you."

"Joash fears me?" Noland scoffed.

"And right now-" Dina stopped short.

"What?" Noland found himself leaning into the phone conspiratorially.

Dina's voice grew quieter. "I'm not sure, but there's something off with Joash. And that makes me nervous the more I think about it. I don't want to wake a sleeping dragon."

"I've always loved that expression. Great mental images," Noland said off handedly.

"It's not an expression." Dina said sounding legitimately worried. "He hasn't used it since the fall- Joash is a shapeshifter."

"Like he can change form, shapeshifter?" Noland asked grabbing the desk for support.

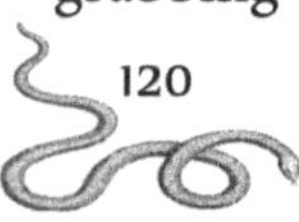

"His angelic form is a seven headed dragon." Dina said woefully.

Noland sat, no longer wondering how on earth Joash had been voted head of the council. Now, it all made perfect sense. Why no one wanted to stand up to him… The original generation was scared of him.

"Dina," Noland started, full of dread, "tell me he has a weakness."

"The man has several, but if the dragon does, I don't know it. That's why I've been trying to take him down before it comes to that."

Achaia walked out to the smell of a very promising breakfast, and to Noland pacing in the lounge room rubbing his temple absentmindedly.

"I don't like the look of this," Achaia said gesturing to his entire person.

"Thanks Kaya," Noland said sarcastically. "It's called stress."

"I know, Nole, I meant I don't like what the stress implies. You look hot stressed. That little vein in your neck pops out and you just look undeniably bad ass." Noland looked at her blankly. "No joking with you when stressed. Check. Got it." Achaia pointed at and checked an invisible box in the air.

Noland shook his head and looked like he was trying to smile encouragingly at her, and apologize at the same time, which contorted his face in an anguished looking expression.

"I've never seen you like this. What has you this stressed? Or do I want to know?" Achaia let Noland take her hands and sit her gently on a pouf. He knelt in front of her.

"I had a strange phone call this morning, from someone in the council. She's on our side and wanted to warn us about something. I checked with Olivier and Yellaina and they've been working with her for a while. They trust her. So, I called Bale to ask a few questions."

"Okay, so I take it, it's bad news?" Achaia studied his handsome face. He cocked a consenting eyebrow and nodded noncommittedly toward the floor. Achaia's stomach dropped. "What is it?"

Noland pursed his lips as if trying to find the right words to say something awful. Looking like he gave up, he finally said "Joash can turn into a dragon."

Achaia stared at him in disbelief. "A dragon?" She asked slowly and carefully as if she must have misheard him. "Like fire breathing scaly monster with wings?"

Noland nodded, "And seven heads."

"SEVEN?" Achaia shouted.

Noland took her hands in his and squeezed. "Apparently."

Achaia's eyes widened in surprise and indignation. "How are we just now finding out about this?"

"It's his angelic form. He hasn't taken that shape since he fell."

"So, does that mean he can't? As long as he is earth bound?" Achaia asked hopefully. "Does the chameleon-effect

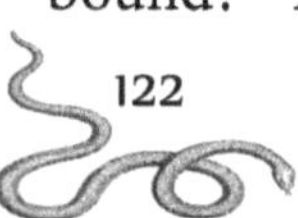

keep him human?"

"I don't know. But if he can use it, it makes sense why he was put in power. Wouldn't you want that ability for your team captain?" Noland asked, as if pointing out the obvious.

"No, I wouldn't," Achaia said placing her hand over his. "Joash is a bully and leads with intimidation. Granted a lot of things may make more sense now, I still wouldn't have voted for him. I value inner strength over brute force or bravado."

Noland smiled at her. "He hates us both."

"That's his problem." Achaia cocked her head to the side, absorbing the facts, "Am I stoked about the fact that he can turn into a beast that could swallow us whole?" Achaia shrugged and studied the air for a second, scrunching her face in mock thought. "No. But," she looked Noland in the eye, "I feel like as long as I'm with you, I am immovable. Whatever comes, I know where I stand. With God, and next to you. I feel like that is the safest place on earth, if not elsewhere as well."

Noland leaned forward and kissed her forehead. "Bale wants us to start heading back to Moscow ASAP, and we need to recruit as many outlier Nephilim as we can along the way."

"I've got Africa covered. I will leave for Cameroon today, and stop everywhere along the way, and send my brothers out west and south." Adisa joined them, sitting at the low table where their breakfast was spread out.

"Thank you," Noland said crossing the room to join him at the table. Achaia followed.

"Of course, we will help. I have contacts all over Asia. I will make some calls," Chayan said, coming out carrying the

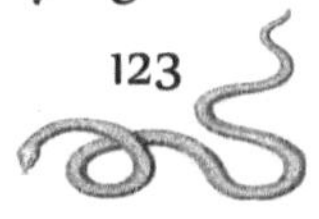

tray of coffee for his wife. Som Wang smiled entering the room behind him.

Achaia helped her with the tray of pastry she was carrying, not sure if she should run away with it to be alone, or to continue the route to the table. It smelled heavenly. "You surely have a gift." Achaia smiled. She knew Som didn't speak English, but she was able to pick up via the context and Achaia's expression that she was being complimented, and she smiled warmly back.

"Som Wang can pack you provisions for your journey back. When will the summit take place?" Chayan asked.

"Tell everyone to make their way to Moscow as soon as they are able. We are going to need to bump up our timeline. Next week at the latest. I'm sorry I can't give an exact date and time."

Chayan and Adisa nodded. Chayan spoke to his wife in a quiet voice, and she replied with purpose, turning and heading back into the kitchen.

"She's going to pack your provisions. Eat. You'll need your strength."

Achaia didn't need telling twice. She ate until she was almost uncomfortably full. It was with a great effort that she refrained from eating the entire tray of donuts. She went back to her room and eyed her old tattered bookbag. Oh, the adventures they had been on together, but it had definitely seen better days, and she wasn't sure it would survive their flight.

She returned to the lounge with it in tow, holding it by a frayed strap.

"Maybe you should just throw your things in with mine,"

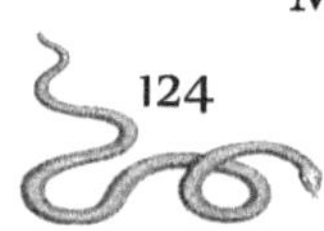

Noland said eyeing the bag with scrutiny. He opened his own rucksack and Achaia pulled out her things and added them to his pack.

"I'll carry the provisions bag," Achaia offered. Noland nodded.

Som Wang returned a little while later carrying two large duffle packs that looked heavy. She handed one to Noland and one to Adisa.

"I'll carry the provisions bag," Noland smiled, handing Achaia the smaller and significantly lighter bag of clothes. "Oh, and I brought you something." He reached in his pocket and pulled out a small folded up piece of photo paper.

Achaia reached out and took it, unfolding its soft worn edges. It was her father's copy of their family photo. It was marred by tear stains, and the oils from her father's hands. If there was ever a possession in this world that she treasured, it was this.

"How?" Achaia asked, feeling tears of relief well up in her eyes. She'd thought that everything from her apartment in New York had likely been disposed of by their landlord once the rent went unpaid and he hadn't heard from them.

"I packed up your apartment. I kept a bag full of things I thought you might want and donated everything else." Noland shrugged.

Achaia clutched the photo hard in her hand, as if she were afraid that some strange wind would swipe it out of her grasp. "Thank you." A tear escaped, gliding down her cheek. She swiped at it quickly and smiled. "I don't know what I did to deserve you …"

Noland shook his head, wiping away the compliment. "Gifts aren't earned Achaia, or deserved. They are just meant to be cherished."

"Is that what we are? Gifts to one another?" Achaia asked, meditating on the idea.

"I certainly hope that's how it feels when I finally give myself to you," Noland said in a low voice.

Achaia blushed, violent pink.

"I don't just mean that," Noland smiled. "I mean the promise, the oath, and the vow of it all."

Achaia nodded. "It already does." Achaia reached for Noland's hand, and laced her fingers through his.

"Well that's good." Noland smiled, and leaned down to kiss her.

Adisa cleared his throat. "Still here, my friends."

Noland stood back up straight with a tight-lipped smile, holding back a laugh. "My bad, bro."

Achaia smiled an apology at Adisa and nodded.

"I'm glad you got the girl," Adisa laughed. "But we should all be going."

"You're right." Noland agreed.

Chayan was standing in the doorway of the kitchen talking to Som Wang. He turned to them as they approached.

"We will meet again, soon," he said, confirmedly.

Noland and Achaia nodded. Chayan put a hand on Noland's shoulder, and Som Wang put a hand on Achaia's cheek.

"Go in peace, and may your journey be swift and fruitful." Chayan patted the shoulder he'd held and released Noland.

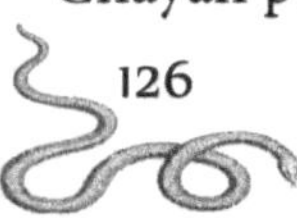

Som Wang nodded in agreement with her husband and rubbed Achaia's cheek ever so slightly with her thumb before dropping her hand. Achaia smiled, wondering if this is what it would have felt like if her mother had survived to see her off to college or something. She took a deep breath and sighed at the thought of no longer having any parents to send her off anywhere, and the thought that by the time she would have been leaving for college, there might not be any world left. In that moment, she no longer felt young. She felt like years had passed in the last eight months. She felt older, and jaded, and tired, and broken, and healed in ways she didn't think possible at only seventeen.

Amelia lay in her bed, a lavishly dressed platform in the guest room of Lailah's abode. She was concentrating hard, but it was taking less effort. She was getting better at talking to Emile and Bale in their dreams. She wasn't sure how well it had worked with Achaia, and she hadn't been able to get back in touch with her since. Achaia's mind worked fast, and it spun like a revolving door set to high speed. If Amelia didn't catch her at the exact right moment, she missed her entrance and hit a wall. Bale tended to meditate on things, which made him much more easily reached. Emile thought long and deep on everything, with great focus. If she could find where he was focused, she could insert herself in. She hadn't been able to reach Noland. His mind was complex. He seemed calm and collected from the outside, but she suspected the waters of his mind were much more troubled than she'd ever realized, and it made it hard to cross into his thoughts.

Knowing that Olivier and Yellaina were newly married, Amelia hadn't wanted to impose. She'd also been a little too scared of what she might see, trying to enter their dreams.

Bale however, had finally fallen asleep. As if emerging through a fog, he appeared before her in one of his dark grey suits, and a deep blue scarf. He sat on the roof of the Moscow Safe House, looking out over what looked like dawn.

"Nice view, tonight," Amelia said walking up behind him and taking in the city set on fire with orange and pink.

"Red sky in the morning, sailor's warning." Bale smiled down at her. "A storm is brewing. Spiritually, more than physically, I'd say." His smile faltered and vanished.

"Hasn't it been for a while?" Amelia asked, taking a seat on the ledge of the building and turning to look at Bale's face instead of the sky. His thoughtful hazel eyes squinted at the rising sun.

"I think it is finally upon us," he said seriously. As if on cue, Amelia heard thunder rumble in the distance.

"What is it? What do you know?" Amelia asked.

"I'm not entirely certain, but I fear the ramifications of drawing Joash out of feigning holiness." Bale looked down at her then, as if looking to read her reaction.

"Like, we forced his hand, so he's not going to bother trying to look good anymore? What do you think he'd do?" Amelia had been surprised at how comfortable she had been talking to someone as intimidating as Bale, before she'd known they were mates. He was a legend, and everyone looked at him as he was,

holier than all those who were fallen on earth. But to Amelia, he was just Bale. She wasn't sure the moment it had happened, but in addition to his gift of making people feel like they can trust him, Amelia also just found his presence comforting.

"I'm not sure, on his own. But I don't know who all is working with him. And as conniving as he is, he's no architect. Who's actually calling the shots?" Bale pondered aloud.

Amelia thought. "He hates Luc, so he wouldn't be working for him would he-"

"Maybe not for, but if he was arrogant enough to think he was keeping him in check and if they were working toward a mutual goal, I'm not so sure he wouldn't utilize Luc as a resource. I pray he's not that stupid. Lucifer is too charming and manipulative for him. Luc could take him in a heartbeat, already has, once."

"So, that would be our worst-case scenario. If that is true, what would that look like? What is the worst thing Luc could do with Joash in his pocket? I'm pretty sure if he just blatantly tried to give the council orders, they would see right through that. He'd lose their support. I'd hope he would anyway. There has to be some sort of line, that if he crossed it, the council would stop following. Right?" Amelia hoped she was right. As messed up as the council had gotten, she desperately wanted to believe that they genuinely thought they were right, and were trying to do good, and just going about it wrong. Once they realized how off course they'd gotten, they would repent.

"Before the fall, Joash had an impressive heavenly form. That is one of the reasons the council is so willing to follow him, now. He has not been able to take it since the fall. He has been bound to mortal flesh; I believe it is part of his particular bitterness toward their penance."

"If he can't take that form, then how could Luc use him?"

"Joash can't take that form. But Lucifer is a shape shifter, as well. If he were to take possession of Joash, he is more powerful. He may be able to force the shift. He would not hesitate at any pain it may cause to Joash, to force it."

"Possess him like a demon possession?" Amelia asked, fascinated and horrified at the same time.

"Luc has taken on the nature of demons; he is capable of all manner of evil." Bale frowned. "Let us hope Joash is not stupid enough to give him the foothold."

"For argument's sake, I think we should have a plan. Because I'm sorry, but I don't have enough faith in Joash to think he isn't that stupid," Amelia said casually. "Besides, don't your scrolls talk about a beast of some kind in the end? Could he be it?"

Bale nodded solemnly. "That's what I've been most afraid of. Joash and Luc together, hell bent on Achaia, and the power she possesses- she doesn't even realize yet the magnitude. That battle could end the world." Bale looked down at Amelia. He reached for her hand, and she stood letting him take it. Thunder rolled again, nearer and louder than before. "Here at the end of all things, I feel so much more peace knowing you are already freed from this world."

Amelia squeezed his hand back, and watched the sky grow dark before them, and the rain pour down in a sheet all

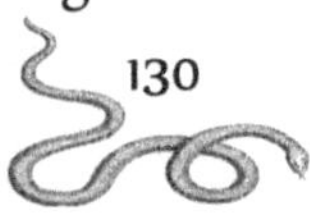

around. But on the roof where they stood, it was light and dry.

"I have to wake up soon," Bale said sounding disappointed.

Amelia squeezed his hand tighter. "Then, until we dream again," Amelia stood up on her toes, and kissed Bale for the first time. Bale stiffened in surprise before reaching his hand up and cupping the back of her head. He kissed her softly and gently as the rain poured down all around them, splashing at her boots as it bounced up from the ground.

Amelia woke and went downstairs. Naphtali was with Lailah in the drawing room, having tea.

"Hey," he said, as she entered the room and took up a chair.

"Hey," Amelia said, lost in thought, still thinking about the storm, and the possibility of Joash and Luc joining forces.

"What's going on in there," Naphtali asked, pointing at Amelia's temple.

"Just thinking about the conversation I just had with Bale. Lailah, what do you know about the end times? There's a beast. What is it? Where will it come from?"

Lailah's face grew pale. "Even I do not know."

"Could it possibly be Joash?" Amelia asked.

Naphtali and Lailah exchanged a look. "His form is impressive, but-" Naphtali looked doubtful. "He wouldn't. Would he?" Naphtali asked Lailah.

Lailah looked like she hated considering the thought. "He has fallen far, but I do not think he has that level of hatred in him," Lailah said, finally.

"What if he teamed up with Luc, or Luc…"

"Now that," Naphtali shuddered, then looked up sharply at Amelia. "Does Bale think-"

"I don't think he believes it far-fetched," Amelia granted.

"Perhaps it is time," Lailah said, looking inquiringly at Naphtali.

"I'll pay Hilmaya a visit and see what she knows." Naphtali stood. "We don't have time to waste. Not anymore, if this is true."

Lailah nodded, and squeezed his hand affectionately. Amelia looked away, feeling awkward for noticing. Wasn't Lailah Shael's mate? Naphtali left a moment later, leaving Lailah and Amelia alone.

"So, what do you know about the end?" Amelia asked. "Can you please tell me?"

Lailah sighed. "Perhaps I should. But," she stood, "for that we are going to need more tea."

8

"Our ability to reach unity in diversity
Will be the beauty and the test
Of our civilization."

-Mahatma Gandhi

Yellaina and Olivier walked through the massive front door of the Moscow Safe House, with all its many locks and latches, which were undone for the welcoming of the summit attendees. Veronica and Emile rushed forward to meet them, dressed diplomatically in a gray dress, and a navy suit respectively. "Welcome back!" Veronica hugged Yellaina tightly, and Emile pulled Olivier into a tight embrace.

"Sorry your honeymoon got cut short," he said quietly to them, so that the rest of the surrounding crowd didn't turn to register the insinuation.

"Looks like a good turnout," Yellaina said looking around hopefully, but also feeling a knot in her stomach at the thought of addressing the crowd.

"I don't even recognize more than half of them," Olivier said happily. "This is better than I imagined."

"Dina made some calls," Yellaina said to Emile, who was looking around the room, impressed. Out of the corner of her eye, she spotted Dace and Ivars from the Latvian safe house.

"Noland and Achaia have been recruiting on their way back, too," Veronica informed them.

"Achaia is coming home?" Olivier asked, as if asking if tomorrow were Christmas already.

Emile smiled widely. "Yes. She and Noland are good. She *knows*."

"And they've been stopping in villages and towns along the way through Europe. They should be here tomorrow," Veronica added.

Yellaina smiled. They were all going to be back together, finally. Well, save for Amelia. "Have you talked to-"

"She's good, too." Emile smiled.

"I wonder why she hasn't talked to me," Olivier said off handedly, but Yellaina knew better. He was hurt his sister hadn't turned up in one of his dreams. Since hearing from Emile that she was developing this new skill, Olivier had wanted to go to bed early most nights and sleep as late as possible in the mornings. Still, there had been no sign of Amelia.

"I'm assuming she figured you were both preoccupied,"

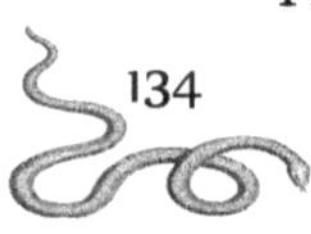

Emile said scrunching his face uncomfortably.

Olivier waved the comment away, "That's no excuse."

Yellaina agreed. There were definitely things worth interruption. Besides, their "honeymoon" had essentially been a work trip anyway.

"Have you eaten?" Veronica asked. "Come, the cooks have been working overtime to make sure the travelers have food when they arrive. There's lots to choose from. You should eat something."

Yellaina didn't argue. She and Olivier had eaten breakfast but skipped lunch since they were so close to reaching Moscow. They were ready to just get back. "That sounds good."

"I'll take our bags to our room and meet you there," Olivier said, hefting her duffle bag over his shoulder with his own. Butterflies tickled Yellaina's stomach at the words "our room." It was going to take some getting used to. Their honeymoon trip had felt like another life. Being back around friends and family in their normal surroundings, but not having separate rooms, this was going to be weird in the best possible way.

Olivier had rounded the corner out of sight, before Yellaina coaxed her feet to move. Emile kept his post to greet their guests with Bale, as Veronica accompanied Yellaina to the dining room. As they made it to the hall, and the voices of the crowd died away, Veronica smiled at her. "So how was it?" she asked.

"Exhausting," Yellaina replied, trying to recollect which safe houses they had visited, and the names of everyone they had talked to.

"Oh," Veronica's face fell.

"Oh, no." Yellaina said, catching the other girls meaning too late. "The mission was exhausting. Olivier was wonderful. It's been a surreal few weeks."

Veronica reemployed her smile. "Were you scared?" she asked shyly.

"No, maybe a little nervous. Maybe a little awkward," Yellaina laughed. "But there was nothing to worry over."

Veronica nodded and dropped the subject, her curiosities for the moment satisfied.

As they entered the dining room, Yellaina's stomach growled at the sight of all the food, and especially the smells- the crisp buttery scent of fresh baked pastry and the savory warmth of roasted meats. There were finger foods covering the entire dining table as well as the buffet, and the console on the other side of the room, up against the windows. Briefly, Yellaina recollected the day the bombings had blown most of those windows in.

Soon, they would all be together again, in this safe house that had become like a home. It had seemed foreboding at first. *Bale* had seemed foreboding at first. Yellaina lost herself in reverie, considering everything that had taken place and changed in the course of only a few months. Less than a year was all it took for an entire life to be upended. Amelia was no longer with them, but Veronica was. They had lost Achaia several times, but she was on her way home. Yellaina and Olivier had married, and Achaia had finally warmed up to Noland. Emile had found his mate, and Amelia, hers. Yes, the world was ending, but even so, there were still good things happening with the bad. A remnant was emerging. Faithful Nephilim were gathering from all over the world to come to humanity's aid. They weren't as alone as she had once feared. The Lord was knitting his troops together.

Yellaina picked up a *piroshki* and took a bite. She never imagined having this much hope at the end of all things. But maybe everything would turn out alright after all.

Jude lingered on the beach after teaching his yoga class, but he wasn't in his typical mood to chat. The simple truth was that he just didn't have anywhere else to be, or anyone to go home to. He smiled politely, though not really listening to what his few lingering students were discussing. His thoughts were elsewhere. He waved goodbye as the students finally wandered away, and took off his shirt to take a swim.

He swam laps along the shore until his legs and arms were numb and climbed back out of the surf toward where he'd left his shirt. He bent down to pick it up, and a pair of dark bare feet stepped into view, kicking up a little storm of sand. "What do you want?" Jude asked, standing back up, before even looking up to see who he was actually talking to.

Not his brother, but a woman stood before him. He was taken aback, and wished he'd taken note of the slightness of the ankles, before assuming Tobias had made a comeback.

The woman was startlingly beautiful. She had sharp angular cheekbones, and ebony eyes that glimmered in the afternoon sun. Her frame was slight but toned, and Jude knew she, like Achaia, was probably much stronger than she looked. She had long blue dreads streaked through with purple and pink, wrapped up into a huge knot at the top of her head. She wore no makeup, but her skin glowed with health. When she smiled, it reminded him of his adopted mom back in America. He hadn't spoken to her in months, but all of a sudden, he missed her like crazy.

"I thought you were someone else," Jude said in way of apology. "Are you here about yoga lessons?" he asked.

The woman shook her head. "I am here about you."

"Do I know you?" Jude asked confused.

"You may know of me, but maybe not." She smiled humbly. "I am Hilmaya."

Jude swallowed. "You're Tobias' mother."

Hilmaya nodded. "That is one identity that I don't mind owning up to."

Jude nodded politely. "What can I do for you?" he asked, unsure of why she was there, and kind of wanting the conversation to end as soon as possible.

"Word has reached me of a summit I thought you may be interested in. A remnant of Nephilim, not Council, and not Luc. I thought this new option may interest you?" Hilmaya smiled. "You may accompany me to the summit if you like."

Jude shrugged in disinterest. "Where is it?" he asked, if for no other reason than to appear like he was considering it, to placate the woman.

"Moscow," she answered.

Jude's stomach dropped and a wave of nausea crashed in

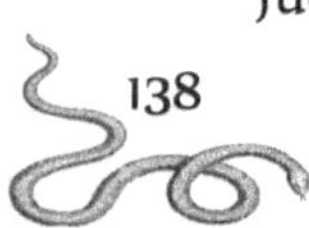

his stomach. "Uh, no thanks. I'm never going back there. I had a bad experience."

Hilmaya frowned. "How will you ever vanquish your demons if you refuse to face them?"

"I prefer to ignore them, and hope they go away," Jude answered sarcastically, not appreciating the woman's assumption that she knew him well enough to make such a comment.

"Demons make a habit of inviting friends into places from which they are not evicted. I urge caution-"

"I have plenty of experience with demons, thank you." Jude said shortly, cutting Hilmaya off before she could continue treating him like her child. He wasn't. He most definitely wasn't. He felt a rage rising in his chest.

"You are worth so much more than you give yourself credit for, despite what Lucifer would have you believe."

"Look, I'm sure you mean well, but this little pep talk, or whatever this is, really isn't helping or doing me any favors. If it's your own conscience you're worried about, you're good. You did your duty, you checked in on the poor bastard of your husband. Now, as I have told your perfect son on several occasions, I'm good right here. Have fun at your little conference." Jude turned on his heel, feeling mildly guilty about his tone, and walked determinedly down the beach back toward his cove and his hut. Once there he threw himself down on the bed and stared at the leafy ceiling. The other half of the bed was still unmade and looked as if Achaia had just climbed out of it. A week had passed, and her sweet, lemony scent was beginning to fade from the sheets.

Noland hung up the phone after touching base with Bale as promised. He had informed Bale of their plan to fly as far as they could tonight and then cloud-camp, so they could get back earlier tomorrow, lest they not make it back in time for the summit.

Noland missed having the resources of the council, being able to just board a plane and go wherever he wanted. But at least his conscience was clear. "You ready?" he asked Achaia, who was polishing off a croissant. They sat at a table on the sidewalk outside a café, re-caffeinating and stocking up on food for the flight.

Achaia nodded. "Who knew we'd be flying by night through France again so soon?" she joked. "This is becoming a ritual of ours."

"You're sure you're okay with cloud-camping?" Noland asked, skeptical. It sounded a lot more romantic than it actually was. There wasn't anything glamourous about a mattress of tiny freezing-cold water droplets.

"Yeah," Achaia nodded, wiping her buttery fingers off on her jeans. "We know how I can be warm now." Achaia shrugged casually. "Besides, as far as dates go, how many girls can say they got to go sleep on a cloud?"

This time, Noland blushed, remembering when he had transferred some of his ability to her, before she had fought Lucifer, and won, if you could call it winning.

"Alright then, let's head out," Noland said, strapping their

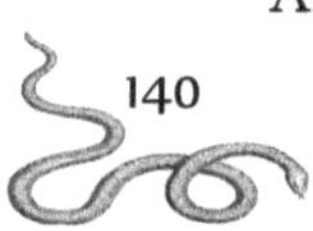

provisions bag over his shoulders snuggly. They disappeared down a dark alley to take flight above the roof tops and into the lower hanging cloud cover.

The sun was sinking in the sky, bathing the clouds and the city below in gold. Above the cloud line, everything was bathed in light. It was blindingly beautiful, and Noland wondered for a second if this was at all what Heaven looked like.

"This is incredible," Achaia yelled over the wind, soaring a few feet away. Her flying skills had vastly improved since the last time he had flown with her. She had obviously been practicing in Thailand. It made him happy to think she had been training, and maybe always planning on returning. The note she'd left him had made no such promise. But clearly the goodbye wasn't forever.

As gold turned to pink, they stopped on a cloud to rest and have some dinner. Noland dug through their provisions bag for some fruit, cheese, and bread. Achaia giggled.

Noland smiled as he looked up at her, curious as to what was so funny.

"Do you remember the first time you brought me up onto one of these?" She laughed.

"Oh, how could I forget?" Noland laughed. "You'd tried to take off and ran straight into a horde of demons. They tried to rip you up into barbeque."

"Mmm barbeque sounds good," Achaia said, taking the loaf of bread Noland handed to her.

Noland rolled his eyes and huffed a laugh. "If I remember correctly, you got pretty pissed at me for saving you."

"Then you remember incorrectly," Achaia chided him.

"I wasn't mad you saved me! I was quite grateful actually." She nodded. "I was mad you never told me we had *wings*." She cocked her head at him, making her point crystal clear.

Noland barked a laugh. "That's right. I never made it come up in conversation, like I *should* have," he said mockingly.

"I mean *wings*?" Achaia said raising her eyebrows and spreading her hands out as if her point were undeniably right.

Noland chuckled. "That was the moment I *knew*. Did I ever tell you that?"

Achaia stopped laughing and stared at him. "No, you didn't."

Noland smiled at her and popped a grape in his mouth.

"Wait." Achaia thought for a second and stared at him. "That means I had just yelled at you for withholding information, and then you immediately repeated the same mistake." She rolled her eyes in annoyance.

"Oh, don't ruin the moment by yelling at me again." Noland scoffed.

"Apparently I yell at you in all of our best moments." Achaia smirked.

"Only on clouds." Noland mirrored her smirk and popped another grape in his mouth. "Can I ask you a question?" Noland said after swallowing.

Achaia looked up at him, registering his change of tone. Her eyes were curious if not slightly wary. "Of course."

"Why? Why did you leave with him? Why didn't you just talk to me?" Noland took a deep breath, glad that the question was finally out there, but nervous about the answer. Things were

good, now. He didn't want to risk messing that up, but he also couldn't just let it go.

"I know *now* that I was wrong. But," Achaia took a deep breath and let it out slowly. "I guess at the time, I wasn't really thinking logically. I think- I guess-" she took another breath to slow herself down. "It's like I was so angry at myself, and I believed *so hard* that you guys should be angry at me, that you should hate me… In that head space it never really occurred to me to consider that that was how I thought you guys should feel, and not necessarily what you actually felt. If that makes sense? It took me weeks to get my head on straight. I was just so full of self-loathing; I couldn't see that I was the only one who hated me. I just assumed everyone did."

Noland nodded. It sucked, but it made sense. "Did it have to be with Jude?" Noland said sarcastically, trying to lighten the mood.

"It was him or no one. And call me cautious but I didn't think running away on my own was the wisest choice."

"Agreed."

"Amelia called me out on it, in my dream," Achaia said, grabbing a handful of grapes.

Noland studied her face, trying to see how she felt about that. Her expression was relaxed, if not amused. She had been crying in her sleep. He'd wondered what the conversation had been.

"I miss her calling me out on my crap." Achaia smiled.

"What did she say?" Noland asked, through a bite of cheese.

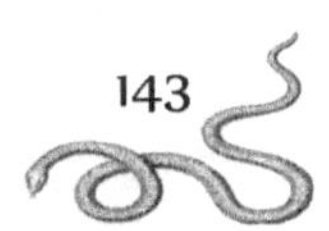

"She told me I can't exile myself, that I was just running away."

Noland smiled. That definitely did sound like Amelia. "What else did she call you out on?" Noland laughed.

Achaia's eyebrows raised and her eyes widened in recollection, "Well when we were in Rome, after-" Achaia choked on her words, but pushed through quickly, "after my dad disappeared, she told me I liked you. I thought I was just annoyed by you." Achaia laughed.

Noland nodded cockily, "Smart girl. Should have listened to her."

Achaia slapped his shoulder, and he reached up grabbing hold of her hand. "*Kaya*," Noland looked Achaia in the eye, making sure she knew he was being serious, now. She nodded for him to go on. "From now on, no matter what it is, just talk to me. I suck at guessing. If you need space, I can give it to you. If you need comfort, I can try." Noland shrugged his shoulders, knowing that wasn't really his strong suit. But he was willing to dive headfirst into the messy process of learning, if it meant they would be stronger for it.

"Nole, I promise, I am not running away ever again. I am here." Achaia squeezed his hand. "I am in this, and I am for us, as terrifying and as weird as that is for me. There's no one I could see myself opening up to, but you."

Noland swallowed, and smiled, feeling his breath catch in his chest.

"You make me feel safe. You push me to be better, not because you require me to be, but because you see potential in

me. And you accept me, as the mess that I am in the meantime." Achaia laughed, a tear escaping down her darkly freckled cheek. "I can't begin to tell you what that means to me. Now, more than ever."

"You're my family Achaia. You, Emile, Olivier, Yellaina, even Ronnie. It might not be conventional, but we are a family. And we are stronger together."

Tobias was waiting down the beach, and as Hilmaya saw him, his mother shook her head in defeat. He hung his head in anger, and frustration. He didn't want to give up on his little brother, but he appeared to be determined to not pledge allegiance, which Tobias expected would result in his being claimed by Lucifer. He hated the possibility, which he was convinced of, more than the frustration at his brother's willful ignorance.

"Come, we have to leave if we are going to be able to catch a ride with the Dawei safe house," Hilmaya said, tugging on Tobias' arm. He could tell she shared his disappointment, but their purpose was bigger than just Jude. This summit would affect the outcome for the whole world. This could change the tide, or at least the way the end times occurred. They couldn't wait for Jude to wake up and realize sense.

"Alright, to Burma." Tobias gestured for his mother to take off first.

Hilmaya unfurled her wings and took off into the lower

hanging clouds. Tobias was grateful for the cover and wondered if perhaps the Lord had ushered clouds all over the earth to provide passage for Nephilim today.

Naphtali had landed in Burma, where his friend Nyan ran a safe house in Dawei. He had encouraged him to reach out to Hilmaya about the summit and invite her to join them. Nyan was perhaps the wisest of the Nephilim on Earth, excluding Bale. He usually kept his head down but kept tabs on, if not in touch with, big players, even ones who had been excommunicated.

Naphtali had spent the last several hours catching Nyan up on the news in Heaven and being caught up on the news of Earth. The war had escalated with the humans, with successful bombings in several countries. Terrorism had taken the opportunity to plant attackers in cities worldwide. It was almost to the point of people no longer knowing or caring who was responsible. If a country got hit, they retaliated on whoever they were prepared to pepper with bombs. The world was burning. Diplomacy had been abandoned. Countries who were ill-equipped were simply cowering, hoping the other countries forgot they existed or wouldn't think them worth the fire power. America, China, Russia and the UK were the main targets, but were also the best defended. Smaller European countries had taken the worst of it so far, and the smaller Asian countries had been the most successfully overlooked. The middle east was a riot of blood.

It was getting late when a knock came on the door. Naphtali was beginning to wonder if Hilmaya had gotten lost. The Dawei safe house was an unassuming two-story rectangular house painted a muddy red, like many buildings in the city. It could easily be and often was, overlooked.

"Evening," Nyan said, welcoming Hilmaya in. Someone was with her, a tall broad-shouldered man. A young man, Naphtali realized, getting a closer look at him in the dark of the room. "Come and be refreshed."

Nyan led them into the sitting room where he and Naphtali had passed the last several hours in conversation. The cook brought out a tray of tea, and bowls of tea leaf salad topped with chickpeas. "How do I find you?" Nyan asked warmly, leading Hilmaya to a chair.

"Far better than I deserve," Hilmaya answered. "This is my son, Manasseh."

"Please, call me Tobias," the boy said. Naphtali had followed them into the room.

"Pleasure to meet you." Naphtali and Nyan both reached out their hands in turn. Tobias looked surprised.

"Is it?" he asked, genuinely.

"Indeed," Naphtali responded, handing Tobias a cup of tea, as Nyan waited on Hilmaya.

"I should have known you were behind this invitation," Hilmaya smiled at Naphtali.

They drank and ate, and Hilmaya and Tobias voiced their frustrations about Jude, surprised to learn that Naphtali already knew who he was.

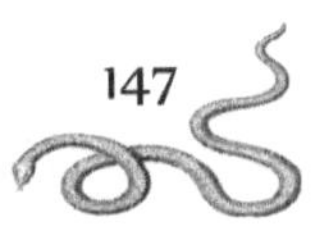

Nyan smiled sadly. "Are you in Burma or Myanmar?" he asked, a seemingly random question. Tobias looked confused, but Naphtali watched Hilmaya smile sadly. "My country is just an example of identity being harder for some to find. One must wait patiently while they search and be prepared to not like what they find. But it is not for us to point out. True identity is between each one, and God."

Naphtali watched Tobias frown further. He didn't appear to like this lesson. Naphtali took the break in conversation to change the subject. "Hilmaya, when was the last time you saw Luc?"

Hilmaya flinched as if he'd pinched her. "Not since shortly after Manasseh's birth, when I told him he would never see us again."

"In all your years of still- well- visiting him," Naphtali pushed through awkwardly, "did he ever speak of his plans for the end?"

Hilmaya looked thoughtful for a moment, as if trying to recollect. "He mostly bragged and made grand promises. Most I dreaded he would keep. He never was good at reading a room." She sighed.

"Namely," Naphtali went on, "did he ever mention the beast?"

Hilmaya's eyes shot up, clear and bright, and hesitant.

"He did, didn't he?" Naphtali coaxed. "Is it a form he can take? A beast he keeps locked away?"

Hilmaya swallowed.

"What is it mom?" Tobias joined in the questioning. "You

know, don't you?"

"It's a beast he keeps in plain sight, and perfectly placed. He always intended to use Joash. I've prayed Joash's disdain for Lucifer has kept him out of reach."

"I wouldn't hope too hard." Naphtali frowned.

9

Reformations and Rifts

"To err is human,
To forgive, divine."

-Alexander Pope, An Essay on Criticism

It was late when Achaia and Noland stopped flying. They had chosen a thick dark cloud hovering over the boarder of Belarus and Russia. It smelled like fresh rain and was damp and cold like a winter storm. Their return trip had been a huge out of the way arc flying west over Europe and back east to Russia, but Achaia thought that if half the Nephilim they had met along the way showed up for the summit, it would be worth it. She stretched out her back muscles as Noland unrolled a sleeping bag out of the provision sack.

Achaia no longer had a phone to check the time. With her father no longer around to pay the bill, the service had been cut off, and at some point, in Thailand she had stopped charging it, and eventually misplaced it. "What time do you think it is?" she asked.

Noland eyed the stars, "My guess, about two in the morning, give or take."

"You can tell that from the stars?" Achaia asked in wonder.

"Well, that and estimating about how many hours have passed since the sun went down." Noland laughed.

Achaia smiled and dropped Noland's bag down on the cloud with a small splash and watched it sink into position until it was about a quarter embedded in sopping wet fluff. At least Noland's ruck sack was water resistant. She hoped they would have dry clothes in the morning.

Noland flung out the sleeping bag and pulled out the second. The first lay unevenly over lumps and tufts of cloud. Achaia knew as soon as she laid down in it, the clouds would conform to her shape, and she, too, would sink down a little into the form.

"Have you done this a lot?"

"Oh yeah, loads. We used to go cloud camping over the New York safe house all the time after Emile first moved there. It was our version of building sheet forts I guess." Noland smiled at the memory. Achaia wondered, not for the first time, what it would have been like to grow up knowing about her abilities, about her wings and her heritage.

"That sounds awesome," she mused, rummaging around

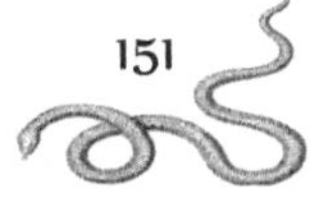

the ruck sac for their pjs.

"It was and it wasn't," Noland said, spreading out the second sleeping bag next to the first. "New York smells terrible."

Achaia laughed and tossed Noland his pajama bottoms. She pulled out her own, and a sweatshirt. They changed back-to-back and climbed into their bags. Achaia was physically exhausted, but her mind was a riot of thoughts that wouldn't slow.

"What are you thinking about?" Noland asked her, curled on his side, with his head propped on his arm.

"So many things," Achaia said, rolling onto her side to mirror his position. "What's going to happen, what did happen, what could have…" She looked up at the stars and shook her head as if mocking herself. "I feel like my brain has been in overdrive and I can't get it to shut off or slow down. It's like a high-speed train that just keeps picking up momentum and can't be stopped."

"I think it's probably a normal reaction to be anxious right now. I mean, if ever there was a time to be uncertain, or even to freak out. These are the days."

"But it doesn't help." Achaia shook her head, "Normal reaction or not."

"No, it doesn't," Noland granted. "Maybe you don't need to slow your thoughts or stop them as much as you need to focus them and do something with them. Sort of like, funnel them through a drain, so they might be spinning, but they eventually pass out of mind."

"Ooo," Achaia scooted a bit closer, "I like the mental image of that idea. Funnel them through, and out."

"Yeah, you just say, 'I see you, thanks for stopping by,' and let them go," Noland suggested with a smile. "And the heavy ones, try saying a quick prayer over them, and hand them off to God."

"I still don't really think I understand prayer," Achaia said, thinking of when Olivier had spouted off in ancient Greek over Noland's seemingly lifeless body after the bombings in Moscow, before Noland had come to. "I mean I know there's power in it. I've seen it. But it isn't magic. It's not like an incantation."

"No!" Noland shook his head. "Think of it more like a really important conversation. It's just a conversation. You're just talking, in your head or out loud, but you're addressing-" Noland paused, "you're addressing a king. One with the power to make things happen, change things, fix things, grant things. But he isn't a vending machine for requests. He knows the whole big picture from beginning unto forever. He knows what needs to happen and when. So, you're not always going to get the answer you want, but it doesn't hurt to ask."

"A lot of the thoughts we have, we can't really do anything about. But if we hand it over to someone who can, we recognize that that is where our role ends; that we don't have a say in it after that, but that it is in good hands. We just need to let it go. Easier said than done, but it helps me release things to be able to sleep." Noland looked up at the stars. "He created each one and knows them by name. I can't even actually use them to tell what time of night it is." Noland laughed. "It isn't my job to know, or to fix everything. My job is to know my place and submit to the one who is much more powerful, and good."

Achaia nodded. "I talked to Him, when I was in- wherever I was."

"Did it help?" Noland looked back at her, studying her eyes, as she thought.

"It did. I felt a peace I had no right to feel, under the circumstances." Achaia remembered how cold and scared she'd been, how broken and devastated. "It was like, I felt his response rather than heard it. Granted, I wasn't really expecting a voice to come out of nowhere and give me all the answers. But I wasn't really expecting to feel, I guess it was like a presence. Like I wasn't alone anymore."

Noland smiled and reached a hand out of his sleeping bag. He wiped a strand of hair away from her temple that was blowing in the wind. At his touch, she warmed. "You're never alone."

"I know that now, even if I still don't understand." Achaia smiled.

"Sometimes I wonder if God intended us all along, or if I picked you first, and he thought 'awe, yeah. That's a great idea kid.'" Noland smirked.

Achaia huffed a laugh. "You're always picking me first."

"Damn straight." Noland smiled.

"Language," Achaia reprimanded in jest.

"No one is around to hear," Noland laughed.

"We're never alone, remember."

Noland shook his head in mock annoyance. "He's not like Santa. He's not a creepy stalker."

"Thank God," Achaia laughed.

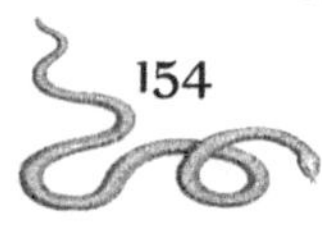

"You should," Noland winked.

"I've heard that before." Achaia nodded, smiling. "In Moscow, after the bomb-"

Noland nodded.

"I thought you were dead, and Olivier prayed the- What do you call it again?"

"The *Katallagé*."

"Right, do I need to learn it?"

"If you want to. It's a powerful prayer." Noland looked back up at the stars. "I'll teach it to you."

"I'd like that." Achaia followed his gaze; the stars were bigger and brighter up closer.

After a moment of silence Achaia spoke again, "What do you think is going to happen?" Achaia turned back to study Noland's face.

Noland sighed and thought for a moment before answering. "I'm not really sure." He turned back to face her, "But I expect there will be a battle, a big one. Mankind is already fighting theirs, but ours is yet to begin. I think heaven and hell will each be emptied, and the fate of it all will be decided here."

Achaia's eyes grew wide in wonder and horror at the idea, and the mental images it conjured. "How are we supposed to sleep on the edge of that?"

"With the knowledge that it isn't happening yet, and we will want to be rested when it does," Noland said, his voice low, and soft. He cupped her temple with the hand he'd used to wipe her hair aside and leaned forward and kissed her. It was a gentle brush of his lips, but it sent warmth radiating through her. "We also already know the end, remember. We win." He smiled against her mouth and kissed her again. She kissed him back, before he pulled away. "Sleep, Achaia. Tomorrow the sun will rise, and so will we."

In Moscow, Naphtali, Nyan, Hilmaya and Tobias exited the plane they had slept on. The airport was a deserted wasteland. Restaurants and shops were closed, and only the necessary handful of employees needed to run the place with so few travelers remained. It was eerily quiet. The few employees present eyed them in wonder, perhaps trying to figure out who they were that they were important enough to be allowed to fly in these distrustful times. Naphtali had never made it through customs faster, even with the heightened level of scrutiny every bag received. They took a cab to the safe house, arriving on the front steps just in time for breakfast.

Yellaina was there to greet them. "Naphtali!" She exclaimed excitedly.

"Greetings!" Naphtali laughed as she threw herself on him with a tight hug.

"I am so glad you're here!" She released him, and took in his companions. "Hello, I am Yellaina bat Jacob."

"I am Hilmaya bat Yahweh, and this is my son Manasseh Tobias ben Lucifer."

Yellaina froze, staring at Tobias.

"This is my trusted friend Nyan ben Yahweh," Naphtali

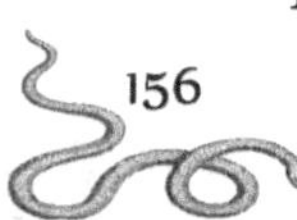

added, presenting Nyan. Yellaina spared him a polite glance, and a small smile before her eyes were locked back on Tobias'.

"Hello," Tobias said with an awkward smile. "You can call me Tobias."

Yellaina nodded, still staring. "I'm sorry, I didn't know-"

"I understand. I assure you, the only father's way I follow is Yahweh."

Yellaina nodded, "Of course. Please, do come in. We have breakfast laid out in the dining room. And several are passing their time in the library. The summit will take place in the chapel in a few hours, after lunch."

Naphtali clapped a proud hand on Yellaina's shoulder. "Will your father be in attendance?" he asked quietly as the others filed inside. "What of your mother?"

Yellaina's eyes fell to the ground. "I'm not actually sure."

Naphtali nodded. "Achaia and Noland are on their way. We passed them on the way in." Naphtali smiled. "I saw them out the plane window," he laughed.

Yellaina smiled widely at that.

"I'll see you in there," Naphtali said following his party inside and toward the promised breakfast.

Veronica made herself useful by helping out the staff carrying trays of food to the dining room, and trays of coffee and tea to the library. There had to be at least a hundred Nephilim already in the safe house and more were arriving every minute.

157

There was an excited hum of energy in the halls that had never filled the house during her time there. She wondered how long it would be, before the council got wind of what was happening, if they hadn't already.

Veronica entered the library, carrying her third tray of coffee that morning and dropped it to the floor. The shattering of china resulted in the immediate halt of every conversation in the room, and every eye turned on her. Her eyes, though, were glued to her mother's.

"Ronnie?" Alexandra asked, in disbelief.

"Mama?" Veronica responded automatically.

Her mother rushed across the room toward her and wrapped her arms around her in a tight embrace, that made it difficult for Veronica to breathe, though she wasn't sure that was the only thing that had caught at her breath.

Over her mother's shoulder she saw her twin brothers Vito and Vidal- one, wearing a look of pure loathing, the other one of baffled confusion.

"What are you doing here?" Veronica asked.

"We are here for the summit," Alexandra answered as if it were obvious. "What are you doing here *mijah*?"

Veronica's eyes dropped to the floor in instant shame. "I came here for refuge."

When she looked back up into her mother's eyes they were full of hurt. "Tell me what happened Ronnie. I will hear your side. Did you think I wouldn't? I have longed to know." Her mother's hands frantically grabbed at her own.

"Not here," Veronica said, looking around the room at

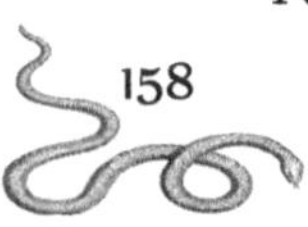

half of the people still staring at them, though trying to pretend they weren't.

"You." Vidal stood before her, full of rage.

"Not here, *mi hijo*," Alexandra said in a hushed, but desperate whisper. "May we go speak, as a family?" Alexandra asked, looking around and placing a hand around each of her son's wrists, but looking at her daughter.

Veronica swallowed hard, her stomach doing a sort of heavy nauseating dance. She nodded and stooped to pick up the tray of broken dishes, cutting her finger on a sliver of coffee cup. Blood pooled on her fingertip.

"The hands of a murderer will always be coated with blood," Vidal spat down at her. Veronica looked up sharply, hurt.

A maid knelt down beside her, shooing her hands away as if to say "I've got this. You go."

Veronica stood, not breaking eye contact with Vidal. There was no shame he could heap on her, that she had not already dowsed on herself. "Come," was all she said, and she led the way out of the room.

Veronica led them down into the old kitchens, which was now her forge. Here they could raise their voices without being overheard, tucked away from the rest of the house. She turned around, already emotionally worn. Three pairs of eyes stared at her with varying degrees of expectation, some mingled with hope, some as if daring her to speak. Her mother's were full of eagerness.

"Long have I waited for the opportunity to hear from

your lips what has passed," Alexandra said taking a tentative step forward. "Will you tell me?"

"There is nothing she can say. She has no excuse!" Vidal yelled.

"*Silenció!*" Alexandra swatted at her son. Vidal bit his lip and stared at Veronica with a hatred she had never seen in him before.

"You don't understand," she said to him, with pity. "You cannot hate me, more than I have hated myself."

Vidal rolled his eyes as if to challenge that idea.

"I have gone over many times how I would explain this matter to you. But I have found no words." Veronica felt a painful lump take up residence in her throat. It choked her, and tears formed in her eyes. "I cannot excuse my actions. I swung the sword. But the desire to do so was not born in my heart. Papa asked me to. He made me swear it."

Vito's eyes went wide in half surprise. "I knew there had to have been something. That you would never, but-"

"He feared the council, and desired escape. I thought he meant for me to help him run away, so I promised. I realized too late that the escape he sought was death." The tears poured down Veronica's cheeks. "He said they would blame him for the weapons. But he wasn't just selling them to the council. He furnished Lucifer with blades that could kill angels. And more than that," Veronica paused, and looked into Vidal's cold glare, "Papa was the one who was killing those charges."

Alexandra took in a sharp breath as if she had just been bathed in ice.

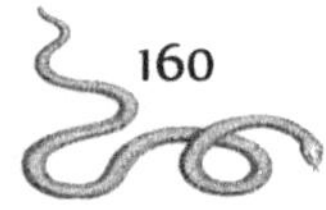

"Papa was the killer," Veronica stated plainly, still looking Vidal in the eye. He looked determined not to believe her, to hold to his belief that she was the disdainful daughter of a righteous father. "Vidal, our father loved us. But he was not a good man."

A scowl, the likes of which were worn by demons spread across his face, flushed with hatred. "Shut up!" he yelled. "You're a liar!"

Veronica shook her head sadly but made no other response.

"Papa killed those kids?" Vito asked, painful recognition registering on his face. "Papa worked with Lucifer?" He looked like Veronica had taken away every precious belief he'd ever clung to and crushed it.

"I believe you," Alexandra said.

Veronica looked at her mother in shock.

"Your father made many mistakes." She turned to look at Vidal, "How do you think we become fallen? Not as a result of righteousness. Your father always preferred to dig his way all the way through holes instead of doing the hard work of climbing out." Her voice was not without compassion, and full of sadness for a man she obviously still loved in spite of his shortcomings. "He had too much pride to admit defeat, or error. Everything he made had to be perfect, and also, his decisions."

Veronica let out a breath she hadn't realized she was holding. Her mother believed her. Her mother didn't hate her.

"Can you forgive me mama?" Veronica asked, taking a step closer.

Vidal looked at Alexandra as if daring her to commit

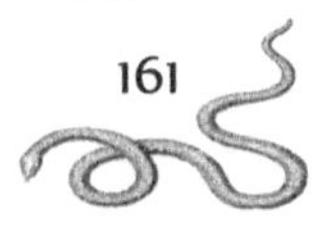

such a sin. "Of course, I can mijah. I only hope that someday, you can forgive your father. I do not think he thought of how his actions would affect others. He sought freedom; I do not think he thought beyond that to see that he would be sacrificing your peace in the process."

"How can you just believe her?" Vidal shouted, his face turning red with rage.

"Because he asked me first, and I denied him," Alexandra said. "Centuries ago, when we first fell, he asked me to end him, but I could not, even if I had known how. I told him that the Lord knew best, and His punishment would fit our crimes, and we would pay for them with honor and dignity. We would make right what we had broken. I thought that he had eventually found peace in our penance. I see I was wrong." She looked to the floor overcome with grief. "I was always blind when it came to your father. When I looked at him, I saw only what God had intended him to be, not what he had actually become. I saw only how much I loved him."

Veronica closed the few steps between them and wrapped her arms around her mother. She had never clung to her so tightly as she did now. Vito's arms were around them in an instant. But Vidal stared on incredulously. As Veronica and Vito released their embrace, Vidal looked Veronica deep in her eyes, "I will never forgive you for this." His voice was full of thick savage disdain.

Veronica felt as if he'd smacked her. She wished that he would just hit her. "I hope for your own sake that you someday change your mind and lay that burden down. I can assure you; it is a heavy load to carry. Rest assured I still carry it myself."

Achaia and Noland landed in the alley behind the Safe House, but walked around front to enter with the rest of the arriving Nephilim, to be seen and checked in. Achaia stood behind a tall broad man, thinking that his size could not possibly be common. She nudged Noland's shoulder and gestured in front of them, "is that who I think it is?" she mouthed.

Noland eyed the man and peeked around to get a look at his face. He made Noland look childlike-small. Noland's eyebrows raised, and his mouth contorted in amused confirmation as he nodded. The man was none other than the bailiff from Achaia's first introduction to the council. She had been interrogated about her father's disappearance. And this man had intimidated her. However, if the end was nigh, she was happy if he was choosing the same side as her.

As the man moved into the room and stepped aside, Achaia heard a familiar voice cry out. "Frenchy?" Achaia's eyes snapped up to see Olivier pushing his way through the crowded room. "Excuse me, you're very much in my way." Olivier pushed men aside without regard for manners. "Achaia!"

Achaia made her way up the last couple of steps just in time to be scooped up and spun around in the most welcoming hug she'd ever experienced.

"God, I missed you," Olivier mumbled in her ear before placing her back on her feet.

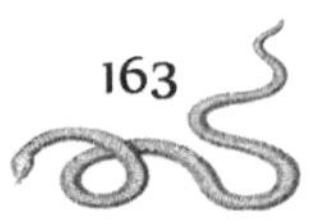

She hadn't registered tears stinging the backs of her eyes, but they were streaming down her cheeks now. "I'm so sorry." She was smiling and relieved, and happy, and guilty, and sad, and everything all at once. And she was reaching back out to hug Olivier again. He squeezed her tightly.

"No more leaving me, bestie," he said lowly in her ear.

"Mm-mm," Achaia confirmed, tightening her hold on him. They released each other again, and Achaia realized her cheeks weren't the only ones that were wet. Her hands slid down his arms to grasp his hands, when she felt the ring on his finger. "You're *married-*"

"I am," Olivier smiled.

"I missed it-" Achaia looked back up at him, regret filling her chest.

"I know, I had plans of putting you in a suit made of comic book pages and calling you my best hu-man."

Achaia barked a laugh. "I'm sorry I missed that opportunity."

"Me too." Olivier smiled sadly, but squeezed her hands as if to tell her he was happy she was home *now*.

War Council

"Patience is waiting. Not passively waiting. That is laziness.
But to keep going when the going is hard and slow- that is patience.
The two most powerful warriors are patience and time."

-Leo Tolstoy, War and Peace

Tobias sat in a pew between his mother, and the largest man he'd ever laid eyes on. He wasn't used to feeling small. All around them, Nephilim were taking their seats. There were stragglers standing along the perimeter of the room and filling the back and the balcony. He was pretty sure there were still Nephilim standing in the hall. He hoped their gift was super hearing.

In front of him, the pretty Russian girl he'd met on his arrival took the stage. She was slightly fidgety with nerves but carried herself with a shocking amount of confidence for one so young in front of a crowd so old. When she began speaking, he was shocked. It took him a moment of extreme focus before he realized that he was understanding her in all four languages in which he was fluent. She was speaking every spoken language at once, as well as signing. The occupation of her hands seemed to have steadied her nerves, and by the time she was done introducing herself and welcoming them, she was speaking quite comfortably, and had commanded the attention of the entire room.

Looking around, Tobias was sure he wasn't the only one who had deduced that they were understanding her in multiple languages. The Nephilim who looked like they weren't expecting to be able to understand, or for her to be speaking their language, were rapt in awe. Tobias was impressed. He'd never met a polyglot who had so developed their gift as to be able to speak every language at once. It was quite a thing to behold.

Yellaina, that was her name wasn't it, paused and took a deep breath before she began to address the corruption of the council, and the importance of unity. She made it clear that the objective of the Remnant was not to prune the council, or engage them in any way, but to fulfil the mission that they were all called to, as Nephilim, in protecting humanity. And when the time came, meeting evil on the field of battle to put it to an end once and for all. Nephilim all around grunted and shouted "Amen" in their agreement.

Once she had finished explaining their objective, Bale ben Yahweh took up the stage next to her. He spoke in Russian which Tobias didn't understand, but Yellaina translated for the crowd.

He explained his anxieties about what he understood of the end times, and what lay ahead of them. He suggested strategies that needed to be developed and put into place for when the time came and divided the group into units. He assigned generals, and then opened the floor up for questions.

Tobias watched in wonder. They were actually efficient. They were respectful when others were speaking; they were concise and relevant in their remarks and questions. Tobias had imagined getting this number of Nephilim together to be pandemonium. He'd been an outlier for so long, he'd always imagined the worst of organized Nephilim. However, if they could keep this up, Tobias understood why the enemy didn't stand a chance.

If humanity could accomplish the tower of Babel, then unified angels really could vanquish evil. Tobias sat up straight, and wished Jude were here to see this. He felt for sure that if his brother could see what the Nephilim were really like, then he, too, would change his mind about them.

Olivier had never been prouder than when he listened to Yellaina speak. Sharing her gift now, he heard her for what she was really speaking, the language of God; it was unlike anything he had ever heard before. He deduced that those in the audience who weren't polyglots only heard Yellaina speaking their own language. Olivier was grateful to be able to hear the glorious truth. Next to him, along the side of the stage, stood Noland,

Achaia, Emile and Veronica. Olivier imagined Amelia standing with them in spirit. How had a group of kids found their way into the center of the throng? How were they the ones pulling all of this off, with the help of Bale, and Naphtali, of course.

Olivier looked out into the audience and saw his parents sitting a few rows back with a dark-skinned boy, about his age, he thought was named Adisa. When he looked out over the crowd, he was blown away by the beauty of it. All of the colors, the vibrance of backgrounds and perspectives all coming together in one room to see love win. He felt, more than he knew, that the end was close, and yet he'd never felt more hope. That, in and of itself, felt like a victory over Luc, having visited his hope-sucking prison. Hope was a formidable weapon against evil and despair. One little ray of hope was like a candle lit in a dark room; no matter how small the light, darkness could not exist in its presence. And the hope in this room shone like the sun.

There was a sort of reception planned, after the summit. The units convened together and discussed plans and strategies for their respective areas of the world. Emile however took the chance to talk to Veronica. She had come in at the last moment, looking troubled. He hadn't been able to talk to her before the summit had begun. "Are you alright?" Emile asked. Out of the corner of his eye, he saw his parents approaching them.

"My mother and brothers are here," she told him, quietly.

"What?" Emile was shocked. Throughout the entire

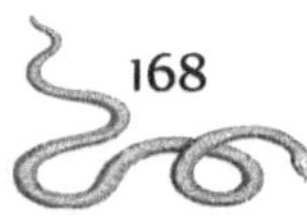

meeting he could feel her mix of emotions even over the collected growing optimism of the crowd.

"I invited them," his mother said, giving him a light side hug and kissing the top of his head. She reached out a hand and squeezed Veronica's hand. He could feel her pride. She was proud of them all. "Your mother loves you, Veronica. She needed the chance to see you, to talk to you."

Veronica nodded. "I understand."

"Perhaps I should have let you know beforehand?" his mother said, as if she'd really not thought of it before, and she felt a little sorry. But he could still feel how pleased she was that they had come.

Emile smiled at Veronica. "Have you spoken to them yet?"

"Yes." Veronica scanned the room, looking for her family. "It went better than I would have thought, but," her eyes turned downcast, "I fear Vidal will never forgive me, and I can't blame him."

Emile's mother wrapped Veronica in a warm embrace. "Give it time. For yourself and for Vidal. It's going to take time."

Veronica nodded, but Emile felt a sadness rise up in her, threatening to overcome.

"You might have more time than you think," he said guessing the cause of her distress.

Veronica smiled sadly and nodded again.

"There is no easy cure for anger, especially where forgiveness is withheld. But each day there is an opportunity for advancement, in yourself." Emile's father smiled gently, joining in their conversation.

Veronica smiled and nodded. Emile was acutely aware of how hard she had been working toward processing and forgiving herself. She had a long way to go, but she'd already come so far.

"If you'll excuse us, I must go scold your bother for wedding his mate without us." His mother frowned as she bowed her goodbye. Emile huffed a laugh, and side stepped for his mother and father to walk toward Olivier and Yellaina who were chatting with Bale still up on the stage.

"Noland!" Noland turned toward the voice calling his name and saw Dina striding toward him. Behind her, he spotted Chayan and Som Wang waving at them. Noland nodded at them, before turning back to Dina.

"You made it," he said, turning Achaia around to face Dina with the hand he held on her back. "This is Achaia. Achaia this is Dina,"

"Hello," Achaia said, offering a hand.

Dina shook it, smiling. "It's a pleasure to finally meet you."

"That might be a first," Achaia smirked. "But, likewise," Achaia smiled.

Dina's smile faltered. "So, I think I need to speak with you and your unit," she said looking back up to Noland.

"My- unit?" Noland stammered. He didn't recall Bale assigning him a unit.

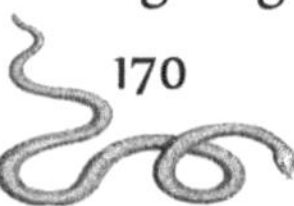

"Of course. Yours was the first, the one that brought us all together. Your unit." Dina spoke as if it were obvious.

Noland nodded. "Right," Noland scanned the room, laying eyes on Emile and Veronica talking to his parents, and Olivier and Yellaina stood just behind them talking to Bale. "My unit."

"Is there somewhere quieter we can go?" Dina asked.

"Bale's office should be empty," Noland said.

"Gather your troops and meet me there. Fifteen minutes," Dina said, walking away.

"Alright then," Noland nodded at her back.

"You heard her General. Assemble your avengers." Achaia elbowed his side smiling.

Emile met his eye across the room, and Noland nodded out toward to door. Emile nodded, and took Veronica by the elbow, and whispered something in her ear. She looked up at Noland and followed Emile out. Noland turned to see Emile's parents had joined the crowd over by Bale. Olivier was looking hesitant when Noland approached. "Bale, might your office be available for a clandestine meeting?"

Bale eyed Noland and Achaia.

"For all of us," Noland clarified, gesturing to Olivier and Yellaina and Bale himself.

"Oh, thank God. Sorry mom, I'll have to catch you later. Duty calls." Olivier whisked Yellaina away before Bale gave his affirmative answer.

"You go ahead. I'm going to just go grab Naphtali, and we'll be right up," Noland said, taking Achaia's hand in his. She followed him through the crowded, chatter-filled room to where Naphtali stood with a beautiful blue haired woman and a broad-shouldered young Nephilim whose apparent age surprised Noland.

"Hello," Noland said as he approached the group. "I was coming to see if we could steal you away for a moment."

Naphtali looked up, smiling hesitantly. "I'd like for you to meet some people first."

Noland nodded, and noticed the guy was staring at Achaia.

"Achaia, I've heard a lot about you," he said in a low voice.

Achaia looked surprised. "I assure you, I'm not as bad as they make me sound," she laughed.

"I have not had dealings with the council," he answered, nodding that he'd gotten her meaning. This made sense to Noland, because judging by his age, he should be the leader of their generation instead of Noland. "My brother holds you in the highest regard."

"Brother?" Achaia asked, looking thoroughly confused.

"Jude."

"Jude is your brother? Then, is-"

"Luc is my father as well. My mother," the boy gestured to the beautiful blue haired woman with him, "is his mate Hilmaya."

Achaia looked as astonished as Noland felt. "I'm Noland ben Nathaniel." He reached out a hand to the two new recruits. "We are happy to have you with us."

"Thank you, my name is Manasseh Tobias, but I go by Tobias." The guy had a very firm handshake. "I am sorry my brother would not join us. I hope he may yet change his mind."

"I hope so, too," Achaia said sadness tainting her voice.

"Well, I hate to cut this short, but Dina wants to speak with us," Noland said, addressing Naphtali.

"Of course. And what Dina wants, Dina gets," he laughed, waving goodbye to Tobias and Hilmaya. "We'll catch up later."

Achaia entered Bale's office last, behind Noland. Bale stood behind his desk which was surrounded by Emile, Veronica, Yellaina, Olivier, Naphtali and Dina. A few discarded coffee cups sat on the desk in front of their owners. Achaia wished she'd grabbed a coffee. She was going to need some soon. She was riding an adrenaline wave but wasn't sure how much longer it was going to last.

"Okay, shall we just dive right in?" Noland suggested looking across the room to Dina.

Dina nodded, and took a steadying breath. Achaia felt like this was it. Once Dina started talking, they would officially be planning out battle strategies. The war had started a long time ago, but this was the preface to the final battle. Well, maybe. Achaia shrugged inwardly at the thought. "I have some bad news, or at least a bad theory. And I think we need to go ahead and assume it's true and put a plan in place." She took another deep breath. "I am fairly sure Lucifer has taken possession of Joash. I'm not sure what his move is, or what he is waiting for-"

Dina looked around the room, studying everyone's

reactions. Achaia assessed their expressions in suit. Veronica, Emile, Yellaina and Olivier seemed the most surprised. And Bale and Naphtali the least. Ever since her conversation with Luc at the waterfall, Achaia had wondered how he would make good on his threat, and what he could possibly have meant. Now, she guessed she knew.

Achaia cleared her throat, her dread thickening. "I think it has to do with me, as egotistical as that sounds." She nodded and cocked her eyebrows at herself. "Lucifer told me he would come after me. And he alluded to using 'another form' and said something about shaking the foundations of the earth." She felt the weight of all the eyes in the room come to settle on her.

"Oh, is that all?" Olivier replied. "That only sounds mostly definitive to me." He nodded and gestured casually with his hands in his typical form of physical sarcasm.

Achaia nodded, a humorless smile tugging on her lips.

"Wait, what? When did he say that?" Yellaina asked. Her cheeks were flushed, and she looked supremely uncomfortable with the information. "What a creeper."

"When I was in Thailand, he would visit me. He wanted me to come back to him," Achaia said, hating how normal it had become, talking to Lucifer. They were on familiar terms now, to say such things to each other. How had that happened? Achaia was drawn from her reveries by Bale.

"But you refused," Bale added almost in question.

Achaia fought back an eye roll. "No, I ran off into the sunset with him, but changed my mind later," Achaia said not able to contain her sarcasm.

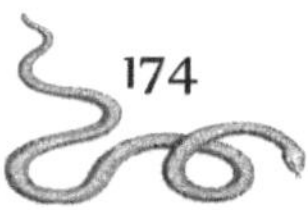

Bale rolled his eyes, a gesture Achaia didn't think she'd ever see in all her life. It made her smile.

"If he wants you that badly, maybe we should assume that is his goal. We could lure him away from humanity where there could be less casualties," Dina posed.

Achaia had to give Dina props for her compartmentalization, even if she was to play the pawn on her chessboard. Achaia nodded and stared at her feet, thinking through what all that would mean. "So, I'm bait." Achaia paused, formulating how that would play out. "I fly out to the middle of nowhere, and what? Let him take me back to Hell? Let him kill me? Is that really the best way to use me?" Achaia said bluntly. "Let's not waste an opportunity. If we are going to draw him out and away, let's end him. We have access to someone who could make us a weapon to do the job." Achaia nodded toward Veronica.

Veronica rallied at the opportunity. "I could! I have some ideas-"

"Engaging him in battle could kill anyone within a hundred-mile radius or more." Dina shook her head, uncertain of this suggestion.

"As opposed to handing over the angel of death for him to do with as he pleases?" Achaia asked bitingly.

"So, we draw him far, far, away from people. Let's start there," Noland suggested, ending the glare between Achaia and Dina.

"Out to sea?" Emile suggested.

Bale looked up at him and nodded. "At least there, everyone would be at some sort of disadvantage."

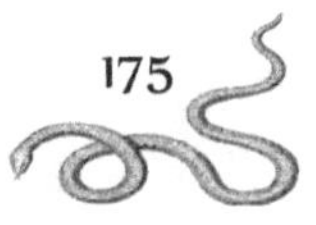

"Level the playing field," Achaia concurred, nodding. "And knock out the risk of other casualties."

"So, we need a ship," Olivier said. "Man, I bet Tony Stark could build-"

Yellaina touched his arm lightly, cutting him off. But Achaia met Olivier's eyes over the desk and shared a smile. Her mind had gone down a similar rabbit hole just as quickly.

"Who do we know with access to a vessel?" Bale asked looking to Naphtali and Dina.

"Vessel sounds so much cooler than ship," Olivier said under his breath. Yellaina nodded with a placating smile on her face. Achaia stifled a laugh.

"The Tjøtta safe house in Norway used to have a ship, back in the day," Naphtali offered.

"Like a Viking ship?" Olivier asked excitedly. Achaia imagined a huge wooden ship with an ornately carved figurehead.

"I'll see if they have anything we can use," Naphtali went on, ignoring Olivier's enthusiasm.

"Okay so we make a weapon, acquire a vessel, and then what?" Dina asked, taking up Noland's line of questioning.

"Achaia and I will set sail and lead him away from shore, as far out as we can, and hope he comes after us."

"At which point, I become who I was always meant to be, and murder him." Achaia shrugged nonchalantly. She didn't feel as confident as she hoped she sounded. But if she was going to be the angel of death, she guessed it was about time to figure out what all that meant.

"No offense, but angel of death or not, I'm not sure you're

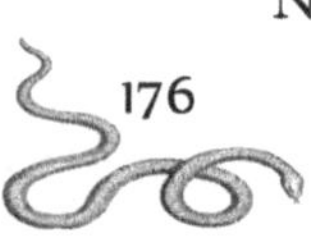

prepared to singlehandedly take on a seven-headed dragon." Bale said. "Even with help," he added, with a nod toward Noland, "you're going to need a team."

Noland nodded in agreement. Achaia agreed, but didn't feel like giving Bale the satisfaction of showing it.

"Well of course I'm going," Olivier said, eyeing everyone in the room as if daring them to tell him to stay behind. Achaia smiled.

"Where you go, I will go," Yellaina added. "Besides, none of you speak Norwegian, and I am fast now," she said proudly. Achaia felt anxious about Yellaina joining them, but she wouldn't dare to ever take away her choice. Amelia had already laid into her for that.

"I can teach you some moves on the road," Olivier offered.

"No one needs to hear this," Noland cut in. Achaia's attention snapped back to, with a flush to the cheeks. She nodded in ardent agreement with Noland.

"Not those kinds of moves!" Olivier clarified.

"I'm in," Emile said, surprising no one.

"Then I am, too," Veronica said resolutely next to him. Achaia smiled. She looked forward to getting to know Emile's mate. Noland had told her a lot about Veronica on the road, but she wanted to get to know the girl behind the stories.

"No," Dina said. "We need you here, making weapons." Achaia frowned, more because of the disappointment on Veronica's face, than from her own dismay.

Bale and Naphtali nodded their agreement with Dina however, sealing the verdict. Emile squeezed Veronica's hand reassuringly, but he looked relieved.

"So, we set off as soon as you can make us a weapon fit for a dragon," Achaia said wanting Veronica to remember how important she still was to this whole plan. "Agreed?" She eyed everyone in the room, waiting for someone to disagree, but no one did.

"Amen," the chorus echoed.

The group dispersed and broke into their own side conversations. Veronica made her way across the room to where Noland and Achaia stood, just as Yellaina grasped Achaia's hands. "We are going to need some appropriate sailing clothes," she was saying.

Noland was laughing and rolling his eyes.

"Can I have a word?" Veronica asked quietly. Noland nodded and followed her silently out into the hall. "I finished this, and I'm almost done with your other order." Veronica smiled, and pulled a small box out of her pocket, handing it over. It was an ornately carved wooden masterpiece, but she wasn't half as proud of it as she was of what was inside.

Noland took it, smiling. He cracked the box open and took in the ring. Veronica watched anxiously, studying his face to see if he liked what she'd done.

Noland took the ring out of the box, turning it over in his fingers, sliding his finger over her design. "Veronica, this is even more than I hoped. It is exquisite."

Veronica felt a balloon of pride take flight in her chest, and her cheeks flushed with pleasure. "I am so glad you like it."

"It is perfect." Noland smiled, putting the ring back into its box, and tucking it in his pocket, eyeing the door to Bale's office.

Veronica smiled. "I think you're going to like the other piece as well."

"I am sure I will. I am sure *she* will," Noland said, cutting off as Achaia and Yellaina came out of the office.

"Apparently we need supplies," Achaia said smiling.

"We're going shopping. We'll be back before dinner," Yellaina amended.

Noland nodded.

"Do you want to come with us?" Achaia offered, looking to Veronica.

Veronica felt a twinge of something. She appreciated the offer, but she didn't really feel like bonding with anyone new at the moment. She was socially exhausted from the meeting with her family, the summit, and then their strategizing. But she also felt bad turning it down. "Um, I should really get to work in the forge. I've got a dragon slaying weapon to make." She said, happy for a valid excuse to get away, and be alone to process her thoughts on the day. "I'll see you at dinner," she said addressing the group at large, before making her way down the hall.

"Ronnie!" Emile's voice called out behind her.

Veronica stopped.

"Hey, where are you off to so fast? Have you eaten?" His eyes were sharp, and full of concern. They studied hers.

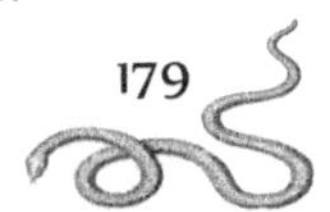

"I'm not really hungry. I just really want to get started on figuring out the weapon."

Emile nodded, but also looked like he wasn't buying it. "Today's been-"

"I'm fine really. I just need some alone time. I rest best while working."

Emile cocked an eyebrow. "I don't think that word means what you think it means."

"Which one?" Veronica cocked her head, smiling. "English is my second language."

"Rest," Emile said smiling. "Do you ever really do it?"

"In my own way," Veronica laughed. "Besides, it isn't physical rest I require right now. I think getting to work and having some time to just process is really what I need right now."

"Okay, but I'm coming to get you before dinner. Because you need food, too."

Veronica nodded. "Take your own advice." She eyed him up and down. He'd lost so much weight over the last few months. Emile nodded in concession and turned to let her go, but she reached out grabbing his sleeve. "Hey."

Emile stopped and turned. His hair was as dark as her own, if not darker, since hers was lightened by her days in the Chilean sun. But his eyes were bluer than the ocean and kinder than any she'd ever known. "I know that it can't be easy to-" Veronica stopped, questioning her word choice, nervous all of a sudden.

Emile took in the vulnerability on her face and softened even more. "What?"

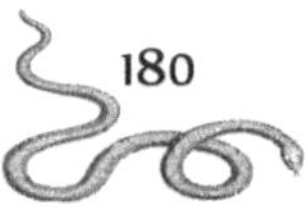

"To love me. At least right now," Veronica went on. "But I want you to know that I appreciate all the ways you try. And I am here for you, too." Veronica smiled, embarrassed.

Emile's eyebrows knit together, and he looked more hurt than happy about her show of gratitude. Veronica looked up at him puzzled. "Ronnie," Emile said bringing a hand up to cup her cheek. His thumb slid back and forth across her skin, gentle and light. "Loving you has never been difficult. It is easier than breathing." He looked her in the eye, more serious than she'd ever seen him, as if he was bent on making her understand. "The ways in which I show my love may sometimes be a work in progress. But loving you is anything but difficult. Don't get that confused."

Veronica nodded, her eyes stinging with unshed tears. She stood up on her tippy toes and pressed her lips to his. Emile's hand slid around into her hair, gently holding her face to his. His kisses were soft, and gentle. He pressed his forehead against hers and met her eye to eye. She watched his long dark eyelashes brush his cheeks as he pinched his eyes shut. "Don't ever doubt I love you."

Veronica pushed her forehead slightly harder against his in response, running her fingers through his hair.

"If we were married and you could feel my love, it would overwhelm you."

Veronica leaned in, kissing him again, harder this time. Emile was always so gentle, but she wanted him to know that if his feelings were as powerful as he said, he didn't need to keep them bottled up. With her, he could always find an outlet. She knew he must be overwhelmed, himself. On the precipice of the end of all things, feeling the hopes, fears, and anticipation of all men, demons and angels, it's a wonder he wasn't going mad. If she could offer him peace, she would give it to him, if only through a moment of distraction.

Noland tucked the ring into the top drawer of his chest when there was a knock on his door. "I want you to meet someone," Naphtali said, as he turned around. Behind Naphtali stood a tall thin girl with ivory skin, curly white blonde hair and the brightest blue eyes Noland had ever seen. "This is Kylie, Kylie, Noland." Naphtali introduced them.

"Hello," Noland walked over to the doorway and reached out his hand. Kylie took it in a firm handshake.

"Kylie helps her parents run the Tjøtta Safe House. She heads up their nautical division."

"We have a retired ship I think may suit your needs," she informed him. "It will need a few preparations to make it sea ready, but I will get started as soon as I get home."

"Thank you," Noland said shocked at how quickly their plan was coming together. "We have a few preparations to make here as well, before we head your way."

Kylie nodded. "What else will you require? A crew? I will have the ship stocked with provisions, and weapons."

Noland looked to Naphtali, wondering how much he had divulged to Kylie. "Um, keep your crew. My unit will man the ship." It hit Noland, just how small the odds were that he would

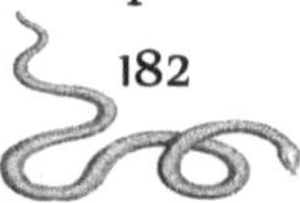

be returning her ship, let alone any crew she sent with him.

"Do you know how to sail?" Kylie asked skeptically.

"I am hopeful we can learn quickly." Noland took a deep breath. Naphtali nodded at him solemnly.

"I am confident they can learn," Naphtali vouched.

Kylie eyed them both. "This is what you call a 'suicide mission,'" she guessed.

Noland looked at Naphtali then back at Kylie and nodded, "Most likely."

Kylie nodded at them resolutely and Noland appreciated her efficiency despite the fact that he could tell she didn't like the idea. "Whatever you require, our unit is at your disposal."

Contingency

"Success can be insured only by devising
A defense against the contingency plan."

-Charles P. Boyle

Achaia browsed through the racks of jackets with Yellaina. It wasn't the season for jackets. Summer in Moscow wasn't as warm as Achaia was used to, but she still didn't need a coat. However, going out to sea was sure to be wet and windy, and Yellaina insisted they needed the proper garb.

Achaia watched Yellaina and wondered if she was afraid. She hadn't hesitated to volunteer her presence on the journey, but she was definitely the least equipped. Yes, she shared Olivier's gift for speed now, but it wasn't as if she could run away on a

ship. How long would she be able to dodge attacks before she would fall? Achaia shook the thought from her mind. Yellaina was determined, but determination didn't necessarily cancel out fear.

"Can I ask you something?" Achaia ventured, as Yellaina held up a pale pink raincoat.

"Of course." Yellaina didn't look up from the coat but checked the price tag.

"Don't get offended. I'm sure I am going to word this all wrong." Achaia paused, as Yellaina finally offered her full attention. "Why do you want to come?" Achaia looked down, sure that this was an insensitive or offensive way to ask how Yellaina was feeling. Truth was, Achaia wasn't gifted with talking about feelings. She was better at ignoring them in pursuit of what needed to be done.

Yellaina sighed.

"I mean. It's your choice, and I would never take that away from you. But are you scared? You've rejected and avoided training and combat your whole life. This can only end in blood. You know that."

Yellaina sighed again and nodded. "I do."

"So," Achaia shook her head, perplexed. "Why do you want to come?"

"Because I've been left behind before. Twice." Yellaina looked incredibly sad. "It sucks. Not knowing what is happening. Who is being hurt, who is coming home- And if none of you come home, I don't want to be the only one left. I would rather die beside my friends than to be left without any."

"Veronica isn't going," Achaia offered. "What if something happens to Emile?"

"My loyalties lie with Noland and Olivier and Emile first. And with you. Veronica still has her family." Yellaina looked as if she was trying really hard not to sound selfish, but knowing she was being just that. "Without all of you, I have my father. And I would rather die with you, than live with him."

"You hate your father that much?" Achaia asked. She knew that Yellaina didn't like her father and avoided him at all costs, but she had never asked why.

"I don't hate him. I just struggle to love him," Yellaina said flatly.

"Why?" Achaia asked, unable to understand that level of disdain for someone so close. Even Veronica didn't seem to hate her father, even after everything he'd done.

"Because I will always fall short of what he wants me to be, and he can't accept me as anything less. Because I don't want to be what he wants, but what God designed. He refuses to see that God's will may be different to his own." Yellaina took a deep breath and looked down at her hands, which at some point had started to fidget. "He isn't here, Achaia. He didn't show up. Even though I asked him, he sided with the council. See, my father wouldn't choose me either."

Achaia couldn't fathom their relationship. How could anyone look at Yellaina as being a disappointment? She was incredible- kind, patient, compassionate, intelligent, and look at how she had united the Remnant, how she had moved them with her words into action. Yellaina was a force all her own, to be reckoned with. How could Jacob be blind to all of that? Thinking about Yellaina still having her father, but not having the relationship she wanted with him caused Achaia's chest to ache. She wondered if that was even harder than having loved your father and lost him. Achaia missed her father in a way that left part of her feeling hollow and empty.

"Achaia, if you're wondering if I fully understand my choice and its risks, I do. Am I scared? Yes. Do I understand that I may not come home? Yes. But, to me, it's worth it. If I perish, it will have been entirely worth it. Not just to fight with you, but for creation."

Achaia nodded. "This is insane."

Yellaina smiled. "This is life." She shrugged, shaking her head.

Bale sat in his office long after everyone else had left. A few other Safe House Directors had stopped by to bid him farewell before getting back to their posts. He now sat alone in silence, contemplating the plan they had made. Would he leave these young Nephilim to head out to sea alone? Was there any hope of their return? Yes. He had to believe there was. Achaia was the angel of death, and Noland the very fury of Heaven. Together with the help of Emile and Olivier, they stood a chance of vanquishing the dragon, which led him to a new thought. What if there was no dragon? Or what if the dragon didn't take their bait? What if the dragon unleashed its terror, instead, on humanity? How were they to fend it off? The more Bale thought, the more he was convinced they weren't done planning. He stood up from his chair and went to find Dina and Naphtali. They needed more lines of defense.

Bale found Dina in a corridor outside of the old sanctuary turned war council. "Dina," he called, grabbing her attention away from the Nephilim she was talking to, a huge man with ebony skin.

"Bale?" Dina said, turning to him.

"Abayomrunkoje ben Chetachi," the huge Nephilim reached out his hand, "but my friends call me Omi."

"Welcome," Bale reached out a hand. Large as though his hands were, they were swallowed by Omi's.

"You look like there's something on your mind," Dina speculated.

"You have the gift of foresight. How sure are you that Joash and Luc will pursue Achaia?" Bale studied Dina's eyes, trying to read her level of confidence. "What if he does not? I think we need to be prepared in the event he directs his attentions on humanity. Achaia is important to Luc, but if Joash is able to resist?"

Dina's eyes were dark and contemplative. "Joash might want Achaia dead more than Luc wants her alive. I think either way they will have their eyes on her," Dina said, but she shrugged at the persistent look Bale leveled on her. "You're right, of course, that we should be prepared for any number of scenarios, just in case." Dina nodded. "It would be foolish to ignore other possibilities."

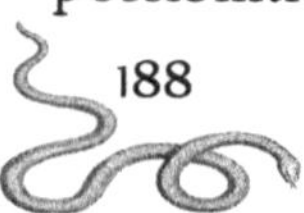

"What needs to be done? If there's any service I may-" Omi offered.

Bale nodded. "I think if we create another unit to support and aid Noland's… Where is Naphtali?"

"Last I saw him he was with Kylie from Tjøtta," Dina answered.

"Probably went to introduce her to Noland," Bale deduced. Nephilim were finishing up conversations all around them before heading back to their respective corners of the world. Among them he spotted the original DuBois. "Korban, Oriel, can I steal you for a moment?" They nodded and followed him.

Bale led them toward the library, shooting Naphtali a text to meet them there. When he arrived, he led them over to the armchairs by the fireplace and poured each of them a brandy.

As he handed out the drinks, Naphtali entered the room, Kylie in his wake. "I'm here," he said closing the door behind them. "Do you ever get your fill of planning?" he asked lightly.

Bale shrugged, eyeing Kylie and debating if he should offer her a drink. He poured her a club soda. She cocked an eyebrow at him and grabbed the glass of brandy out of his other hand. She smiled up at him coyly as she took a sip. Bale shook his head and drank the club soda. "It has occurred to me that we have left some bases uncovered. In the event that Luc and Joash do not move as we anticipate, I think we should be prepared with a backup plan."

"Like what?" Naphtali asked.

"That is what I'd like to figure out," Bale said, abandoning

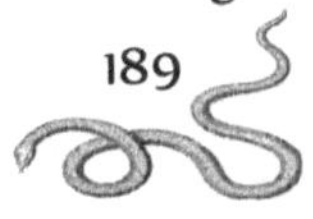

the club soda on the drink cart and pouring himself another brandy.

"So, let us ask the right questions," Omi offered.

"Like, if Joash and Luc don't go after Achaia, what would their plan be?" Dina offered.

The group stood in silence, staring at each other. "Any ideas are welcome," Bale offered.

Korban cleared his throat. "I have not tampered with the ways of the dammed. So, I know not, but is there a way- is it possible-" he took a steadying breath, "could Lucifer resurrect Shael?" Korban looked apologetically across their circle at Naphtali. "Could he wield him as a weapon?"

"I do not think that power exists beyond Christ," Bale answered. "Any life that entered Shael's body, would not be Shael's soul."

"That's what I fear," Korban mumbled.

"I have searched extensively, and there's no sign. Lailah has felt herself freed, at last," Naphtali confirmed.

Bale looked closely at Naphtali, seeing something other than sadness there behind his expression. However, he dared not suspect Naphtali of desiring Shael's mate. "I think that would, in part, explain why Lucifer would stoop to possess Joash, if in fact he has."

"What about a demonic possession of Shael's body?" Korban continued.

"At this point that would pose no more threat than any other human possessed by evil spirits, other than that it would be off putting for it to wear Shael's face," Bale said.

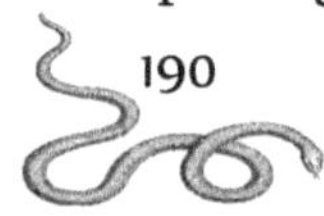

"I don't think Luc is interested in a false representation. He would want Shael himself." Naphtali stopped, thinking for a moment. "At least- well, I suppose that depends on how desperate he is for a companion."

"I am fairly certain of Joash's possession," Dina interjected bringing their conversation back to the point, "however, it has not been confirmed. And that want for a companion, I think, is what makes Achaia so desirable. Easier to capture her, than to try anything with Shael." Dina gave Korban a consoling nod. Omi and Kylie looked alarmed at the thought.

The group stood for a moment in contemplative silence. "Do we force his hand?" Omi asked.

Bale looked at him in a way that bid him go on.

"Do we make an attempt on Joash's life? Kill him while he is in his human-sibilance form, before he has the chance to shift? We have the means now, to accomplish this." Omi elaborated. "In defense of his life, surely he would reveal- or better yet, we would just eliminate him."

"That's a thought," Kylie agreed.

Something inside of Bale clinched at the direction of this conversation. Oriel looked just as uncomfortable, as she reached unconsciously for her husband's hand in shock.

"We don't have confirmation," Dina said, logically, though sounding disturbed by the consideration.

"But if we did?" Naphtali asked, "Just to play devil's- well, *not* advocate."

"If we knew for a fact, and it would prevent the loss of who knows how many lives?" Korban pondered aloud.

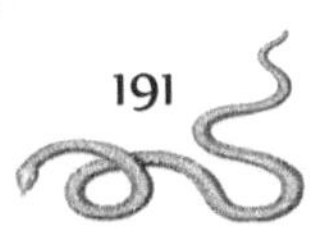

"At the very least it should be a consideration," Omi shrugged. "If we are truly weighing all of our options."

"To take the life of our brother is no small verdict." Oriel's voice shook, the gravity of their conversation weighing on her.

"Then let our first step be to get confirmation," Bale said, looking to Dina, who was in the best position to ascertain if they were indeed right in their suspicions, "without life-threatening tactics."

Dina nodded resolutely. "Everyone agreed?"

"To be clear, if we receive confirmation, the plan is to kill Joash before he can shift?" Korban asked, sounding stern and rational.

"Yes," Bale said looking around the circle and meeting each of their eyes. Most of them took no joy in this verdict, but there was no arguing that if it came down to that, it was the path of least devastation.

Oriel swallowed hard. Kylie was the first to agree, Omi just after. Korban nodded solemnly. Dina and Naphtali looked at one another, then at Bale. "Agreed," Dina said, though sounding reluctant.

"Agreed," Bale spoke with a nod. "And may the Lord stop us if it is not His will."

Noland made his way to the weapons room to blow off some steam, and to have the room and privacy to think. However, when he opened the door, the room was not empty. Admiring the walls of weaponry was Tobias. Upon hearing Noland's entrance, he turned. "Hello," Tobias said, wearing a pleasant expression.

"Hey," Noland said with a nod.

"I hope it's okay that I am here." Tobias gestured around the room.

"I don't see why not," Noland said, coming inside, and allowing the door to close behind him.

"Were you hoping to have the place to yourself? I can go. There's still much to explore in this safe house. It is quite grand." Tobias looked up at the vaulted ceilings as if he'd never been in a building this size.

Noland shook his head but said nothing. He made his way over to a rack of swords, inspecting them.

"Or would you like a sparring partner?" Tobias offered.

Noland looked up at him, intrigued, and gave him a nod. Noland picked up a longsword, while Tobias selected a broad sword.

"Who trained you? You didn't grow up in the council, right?" Noland said, beginning a slow circle, and swinging his sword through the air to warm up his wrists.

"My mother trained me, in warfare, in many languages, and in service." Tobias swung his sword now in a way that made it look light, even though Noland knew how much the broad sword weighed in hand.

"Why did she hide you? Why are you coming forth now?" Noland parried Tobias' genial, half-hearted attack.

"We have never abandoned the call. I believe my mother has been attempting to work off her guilt of not abandoning my

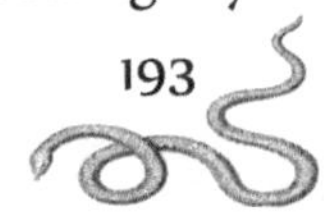

father sooner. She betrayed the council, and didn't feel the right to continue- well, once I came along her transgressions were obvious." Tobias shrugged. "We have worked tirelessly to protect the vulnerable, and aid those in need. We merely avoided the society of the council, but not all Nephilim. My mother knew who she could trust."

"Clearly," Noland raised an eyebrow, looking Tobias over.

"How do you think she learned her lesson?" Tobias cocked his head with a smile. Noland gave him props for not being at all concerned with what anyone thought of him, and nothing Noland threw at him seemed to faze him in the slightest. Maybe he would have made a better head of their generation. Would Tobias have let Joash push him to the point of losing his temper? Would he have been wise enough to not get himself exiled?

Noland lunged forward in his first assault. Tobias deflected him, but with some effort. He laughed and nodded at Noland, impressed.

"I have heard a lot about you. Not only because of the fate of your parents, but because of your own merit. You are thought of highly by many. Further proof that we were right not to trust the council, if they would exile one so competent in the Lord's work," Tobias added.

Noland shrugged. He couldn't deny that the council as an entity had been proven untrustworthy, but he was hopeful that over time Nephilim could undo the impression of their collective. "We aren't all bad."

"I am growing in confidence of that fact." Tobias lunged

again.

Noland hadn't battled anyone who'd made him work this hard in a long time. "Do you mind me asking, what is your gift?"

"In my experience, everything that needs to be, is revealed in due time." Tobias winked and lowered his broad sword. "You're a worthy opponent, and the destined leader. Don't ever doubt that."

Noland lowered his sword and scrutinized Tobias' face for any sign of irony or sarcasm. It wasn't there.

"By all rights, my brother and I should never have been born. Legitimate though I am, I was born out of weakness, not love. And Jude-" Tobias frowned. "No, you are the one the Lord intended to lead this, the final battalion."

Noland gave Tobias a nod, and they returned their practice swords to the weapons rack. "Should you not be taking rest, while you can?" Tobias asked, heading for the door and noticing that Noland did not follow.

"That all depends on how you define rest," Noland smiled, taking up an axe. Tobias gave him a quizzical look. "I do not require physical rest, but mental, and spiritual rest. I find both in my practice."

Tobias gave Noland another nod of understanding and left.

Finally, alone, Noland closed his eyes for a moment, taking a deep breath and bathing in the silence. Then, he moved.

Luc sat with his back up against Shael's altar. "He always was a pompous bastard. I knew that." Luc shook his head and waved a hand in the air, knowing what Shael was thinking. 'He should have known better than to venture inside of Joash's head.' "I know, I know. I asked for this," Luc agreed. "It's just so tedious, the meetings, the lying," Luc scoffed. "He's not even good at it!" He spat contemptuously, his chest filling with loathing for Joash. "I'm going to have to work on that." He cocked an eyebrow making a mental note to lie through Joash for him, to make sure it was done right. Yet another thing he had to do! Add that to the list of 'everything'- That of course would mean taking even more control, which he hardly had the energy for. Joash was fighting him, hard. But unfortunately for Joash, he wasn't actually committed to God. So as annoying as Joash was being, Luc had his claws in deep, and there was no way in Hell he was letting go.

Luc jumped up to his feet and looked down at Shael's lifeless face, letting out a deep exhausted breath. "Okay, I have to go hold a war council, but I'll be back later. You're not going to believe what the council thinks my plans are. You're going to laugh when I tell you. But it'll have to wait!" Luc opened the door and looked both ways to make sure the cavern was clear, before sneaking out of the room and drawing the door shut quietly behind him. He needed some help, preferably someone more competent than demons. He would find a way to make Achaia join him. He was constantly scrolling his list of options in his mind. Offer her something she wants? Threaten someone she loves? Those seemed crude... She was a difficult girl to force into doing anything. She was incredibly stubborn. He couldn't deny

196

that that was actually a huge turn on. It was a shame he had been overzealous and pushed her too fast in trying to persuade her to see things his way. He'd been so close to having her. A shiver ran down his spine at the thought, and desire coursed through him like an electric shock. Yes. He would have her, whatever it took.

Veronica sat at the former kitchen island which had been repurposed as her current work bench, sketching out idea after idea for a dragon slaying weapon. She wrote out lists of possible stones and gems and other elements she could possibly combine to kill a dragon. She dreamt of brutality and scale rending sharpness. What weapon could end such a beast?

A design both savage and beautiful began to take form. It would have to be large, yet easy to wield, something that could multiply its momentum and the strength of its wielder, long and slender, but that could pierce deep past scales, into the residing heart of the beast, if a heart it held.

When she leant back to look at what she'd created, it was a long handled broad sword, the blade lined with backward facing serrations. If this sword was able to stab into its target, then if it were removed, it would rip and tear away even more tissue on its exit. She smiled, then consulted her list of elements.

"Hey," Noland stood in the doorway. "How's it coming?"

Vernoica smiled up at him, excited to share her concept with the one who would wield it. "What do you think of this?" She held up the sketch, and Noland joined her at the bench to inspect it. His eyebrows raised in admiration and surprise.

"Brutal," Noland said, cocking his head to the side, and taking in all of its detail.

"That's kind of what I was going for," Veronica admitted.

"Well, I think you were successful." Noland studied the design closely.

"How do you feel about wielding it?" she asked.

"If there was a counterweight here," Noland pointed to the end of the handle on the drawing. "That would balance the blade, but also make it rotate at regular intervals if I needed to sling it. If it's heavy enough that should help its momentum to pierce deep on impact."

Vernica nodded and added the weight to the sketch. "How heavy of a blade can you handle?" Veronica looked up, and saw a smile spread across Noland's face.

"Don't worry about weight. Make it heavy." That grin was the least humble look she'd ever seen on Noland. "What will you make it with?" Noland asked taking a seat on the stool next to Veronica's.

"That's what I've been trying to figure out. I don't really know anything about dragons or their weaknesses."

Noland nodded. "Maybe consult with Bale. He may be of assistance. He is ageless and has committed much of his time to study. His knowledge is extensive on most subjects."

"Good idea." Veronica folded her sketchbook closed and tucked it under her arm. "Is he in his office?"

"I'd try the library first," Noland offered, smiling, and standing to follow her out.

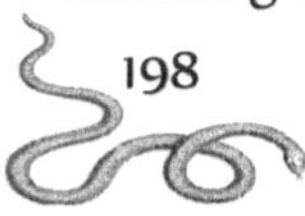

Noland had been right. Veronica found Bale in the library. He sat in an armchair in front of the fireplace, with an old book. He looked up at her over its pages as she entered and cocked his head in attention.

"I was wondering if you could tell me anything about dragons, or their weaknesses. I am trying to determine the materials I will use to craft the weapon."

"There are many scrolls that mention dragons. Come." Bale stood and walked over to a table littered with old scrolls and flipped through them for the right ones.

"Thank you." Veronica crossed the room eagerly, laying her sketchbook down on an empty corner of the table, so as not to crush any of the fragile parchment, or papyrus.

"So have you determined the type of weapon?" Bale asked.

Veronica nodded and opened the book to her sketch.

Bale studied it and cocked an eyebrow. "Yep, I think that will do." He gave her a look as if realizing she was more dangerous than he'd realized. But he looked pleased about it. Veronica had come to admit there was a darkness in her. It had grown in its depth since she'd killed her father. But she wouldn't allow it to swallow her. She would temper it with light and would wield it as she would a weapon. Any rage she had would be a righteous anger, and she would use it to fight for the innocent. And any savagery in her would be directed toward the enemies of the Lord. A weapon was designed to end life. But weapons were controlled and utilized by those who wielded them. In the right hands, weapons could also save lives.

Precipice

"I am terrified of this dark thing
That sleeps in me."

-Sylvia Plath, Elm

Achaia sat on Yellaina's bed folding all the new clothes they'd bought and washed. There was a brisk knock on the door.

"Hey," Kylie stood in the door. Naphtali had introduced her to them a couple of days before as their contact for a ship in Norway. She had joined Bale's unit and had stayed a few days longer than the other summit attendees for whatever planning meetings they were focusing on. She'd spent her evenings hanging out with Achaia and Yellaina, and occasionally Veronica when she surfaced from her forge.

"I'm heading out tonight. I've got to get everything prepared for you to set sail. Veronica should be done with the weapon in the next week. So, I need to make sure the ship is sea ready."

Achaia frowned. She knew it wasn't goodbye, but Kylie had proved to be a breath of fresh air. She was kind, but hilariously bold. "When do you leave?"

"In like an hour?" Kylie said shrugging with her mouth. "But I'll see you guys in like a week."

"Yeah, but then we are just going to be leaving soon after we get to you," Yellaina said sighing.

"Still, not goodbye. We'll see each other again after that. On either side of life, it's never goodbye." Kylie smiled casually. "I've enjoyed hanging out. You have been so welcoming. There's something to be said for being surrounded by allies and feeling less alone. I thank you."

Achaia stood up and before she knew what she was doing, she was wrapping her arms around Kylie. Apparently, she'd been spending too much time with Yellaina, and it was rubbing off on her. Yellaina joined them in a group hug. "We'll see you soon," Achaia said, releasing them.

"Yeah," Kylie said, straightening her shirt. "I can't wait to see the finished weapon. Veronica has been working like crazy on it."

"Yeah, and I have barely seen Noland in days. He's been having to keep the fire heavenly hot." Achaia shrugged.

"It'll all be worth it, if it works," Yellaina said, nodding at Achaia.

"When it works," Kylie corrected. "Still, I hope I get to play with it before you leave." She smiled mischievously.

"I'm sure that can be arranged," Achaia laughed.

"Well, I need to go throw my crap in a bag and get ready to go. I still need to pop in and say bye to Noland and Veronica, too."

"If you can even bear going in the room. I have to knock and wait outside," Achaia smiled.

"Yeah, I'm pretty sure it singed my eyebrows yesterday." Kylie ran a finger over her pale blond brow. Her blue eyes sparking with silent laughter.

Yellaina giggled. "They look fine."

Kylie nodded, then turned for the door. "See ya!"

"Bye Ky!" Achaia called. "I'm going to miss her," she said after the door closed.

"Me too," Yellaina agreed. "She's sweet."

Achaia sighed and laid back against Yellaina's lush pillows. "I wish my dad were going with us." Achaia hadn't actually been planning on speaking out loud, and it surprised her that she had.

"Yeah, me too. It's kind of crazy that we are the ones going. Like when did we become old enough to be the ones responsible for leading revolutions, or battling beasts? When did we stop being the kids?" Yellaina looked deeply contemplative.

"Right? I think it was the second my dad was taken, for me." Achaia stared up at the ceiling, at the ornate lighting fixtures that lit all the rooms of the safe house. They didn't make them like that anymore, she thought absently. Out of the corner of her eye she could just see Yellaina nod.

"The end feels close, doesn't it?" Yellaina said quietly.

Achaia felt the truth of it in her chest. Like a looming cloud of darkness, the wind was pushing closer and closer. Each day felt darker and darker, and heavy. Sleep had been hard to come by. No matter how much she tried to rest, the exhaustion ran deeper than fatigue. It was a spiritual restlessness.

"I'm ready for this to be over, I think," Achaia mused. "I'm not so much dreading it, or afraid of it, as much as I'm afraid it will never come." She sat up and looked down to where Yellaina was sitting cross legged on the floor, her back leaned against her chest of drawers. "Does that make sense?"

Yellaina nodded. "Yeah, the looming is worse than the actual event, because then at least you're in action, and something is happening that you can see. But waiting on the edge of it, picturing worst case scenarios and not ever really knowing what to expect is ten times worse. I can't relax. I don't think I'll be able to really sleep again until all of this is over. I've just been tossing and turning."

"Me too," Achaia sighed. "I just feel like if my dad were here, I would be so much more relaxed. He knows Luc and the way he thinks better than anyone. He would know what to expect and how to combat him, what to be doing to prepare. And I always felt like he could take anyone. I just can't believe-"

Yellaina nodded, "I know."

"It's not even that he's gone though. It's that-" Achaia swallowed back the lump in her throat, her voice catching. But she choked the tears back. "It was so easy." She let out a deep breath. "They killed him like it was nothing, when he wasn't even looking. It was so fast, and that was just *it*." Her breath shuttered, as she tried to steady herself against the onslaught of tears that wouldn't help. It was past the time for tears. It was time for reality. She could die just as easily as her father. It would be nothing at all. If she did fall, she prayed it was just as fast.

Dina walked into her office and could just tell. It was by no means messy, as if it had been ransacked, but items were just enough displaced that she could tell it had been searched in her absence. She didn't leave anything for them to find, though.

"And?" She turned around to see Joash standing in her doorway.

"What?" She feigned misunderstanding.

"You went to the meeting of the rebellion," Joash accused calmly.

"I did." Dina didn't bother denying it.

"And?" Joash looked at her expectantly.

"No one had seen him." Dina had formulated her story on the plane home.

"Who?" Joash looked confused, and irritated.

"Harlem. I thought that maybe, maybe someone there would know something about what happened to him." Her mate had disappeared years ago. Joash wasn't the most feeling Nephilim, but he might write it off as an excuse that he wouldn't understand.

"I don't care about your mate. He's been gone for what?

Years." Joash waved this away. "What are they planning?"

So, he still believed she was on his side, that she had gone on his behalf to spy for him. This was good. "Nothing of consequence. They are rowdy and directionless. They don't stand a chance of organizing to actually accomplish anything. They can't even understand each other."

Joash nodded. "What about the Rosanov girl?"

"Running around frantically trying to translate every conversation between everyone? Yeah, she'll exhaust herself and give up hope soon enough. Her efforts are futile and pointless."

"How many were there?"

"Not a great multitude, mostly the smaller safe houses that have more limited resources. I think they were mostly looking for handouts. Now that they've seen they don't have the financial resources to help them like we do, I don't think they will give it any more attention."

Joash nodded, looking victorious. He was so proud, and way too quick to acknowledge any lie that suited his wishes. He would have had a harder time believing the truth. Dina tried not to roll her eyes at his vanity. "The end times have been in play for centuries. Nothing new is happening. They are just trying to stir up political riot."

"So, you don't think the end is near?" Dina probed.

"Of course, it gets nearer every day, but it is not so very close. People are always looking for signs. This is foolishness. The Lord has said we will not know the day or hour. We need only keep our head down and complete the task at hand." Joash patted her on the shoulder in an almost fatherly gesture.

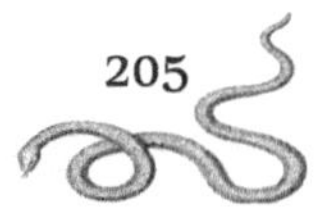

"And what do you think Lucifer is planning? He seems more active as of late?" Dina ventured, watching him closely for any sign.

Joash's eyes narrowed and darkened. "What makes you say that?"

Dina's eyes widened in surprise. "I mean, the entire world is at war."

The darkness of his eyes dissipated into humor. "Yes, well that has happened at least twice before. Nothing new."

Dina shrugged and nodded. "So, you don't think we have anything to fear from him?"

The darkness returned to his glare, as well as a sharpness. She felt the look cut straight through her. "Only idiots don't fear Lucifer."

Dina shuddered and nodded. "Well, I should get back to work."

"Indeed." Joash's voice was icy. He turned and she closed the door behind him as he left.

It wasn't confirmation, but Dina was surer than ever that Lucifer was present in that man. She was also sure that the old Joash would have said Lucifer wasn't to be feared but kept in check. But he would have been wrong. Lucifer was to be feared indeed, especially if he was as close as she dreaded.

"Emile!" Emile turned to see who had called his name and saw Vito running down the hall to catch up to him. "Have

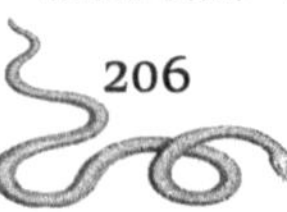

you seen Veronica?" Emile shook his head. "I checked her room and the forge and the dining room, but she isn't there."

Emile shrugged. "I haven't seen much of her lately, but she is *usually* in the forge."

"I thought she'd be spending all her time with you, and that's why she wasn't-"

"She's been working pretty constantly," Emile said, hearing the disappointment in his own voice.

"I thought she was avoiding us," Vito said, as if his suspicions were confirmed.

"I don't think it's that." Emile looked at Vito and felt pity for him. He was trying so hard to understand, but was so confused, and hurt. "I think she is trying to work toward earning forgiveness." Emile had tried to explain to her that that isn't how it works. But Veronica deeply felt, differently.

Vito nodded as if he understood. "We were hoping to spend time with her, but mother says that if our presence is disturbing her, we will leave."

"No, don't leave," Emile said hastily. "As soon as she finishes that weapon, me and my unit are leaving, and she can't come with us. She will need you guys when we are gone, even if she doesn't realize that yet."

Vito nodded.

"What about Vidal? Where is he?" Emile invited Vito with a wave, to walk with him in the direction he'd been heading.

Vito sighed. "He is still here, but he doesn't want to be. He hasn't forgiven Ronnie. He won't even try to see things from her point of view. He refuses to believe our father would have done the things Ronnie said he did."

Emile nodded. He was familiar with denial. It was a deceptive comfort.

"Where are we going?" Vito asked, looking around at the hall that they'd just turned down.

"The kitchen. I was heading to get a snack."

"The kitchen?" Vito asked excitedly. "I've been looking for it all week!"

Emile laughed. "Well, here we are. Are you hungry?" He asked, opening the fridge.

"Oh, always." Vito's eyes brightened looking at the fully stocked pantry and fridge.

Emile took out some cheese and grapes and found a box of crackers that had already been opened in the pantry. He laid them out on the bar and pulled up a stool for Vito before grabbing one for himself. "So, how are you doing with all of this?" Emile asked, concerned.

"Don't you already know?" Vito smiled at him.

Emile shrugged and gestured for Vito to go on anyway.

"It's been a lot, ya know?" Vito placed a piece of cheese on a cracker and popped it in his mouth, thoughtful as he chewed. He swallowed before speaking again. "I mean, I've had a lot of time to think. It wasn't normal, or right, my dad taking us to those crime scenes as young as we were, forcing children to study death so closely. I guess it was easier if we joked about it, dehumanized the victims. But that isn't right." Vito shook his head. "I guess it isn't much of a stretch to believe Ronnie when she said dad is the one who killed them all." Angry tears formed in his dark brown eyes. "It's all so sick. I just keep thinking of those kids." He shook his head, clenching his jaw. "Manipulating my sister into killing him, wouldn't be a far leap for someone who could do that." Vito swallowed hard, rolling a grape between his thumb and forefinger, without really registering it. "I don't want to hate him, but I think I might. So, I kind of get why it's easier for Vidal to be angry at our sister who is still with us, than to hate our father who- made us into what we are. If he was shaping us, like one of his creations, what was his design for us?" Vito looked up at Emile, wiping away an escaped tear before popping the grape into his mouth, and chewing it tensely. "God, what were his plans for us?" Vito thought for a second. "It's almost enough for me to be glad he was stopped. But what kind of son does that make me?" He looked up at Emile guiltily.

Emile could feel all Vito's emotions swirling around like they were rushing toward his mouth, like it was an overflow valve. It was better for him to get them out. Emile didn't want to interrupt, but he was pleased to find Vito so introspective. He'd been worried in Chile that he was emotionally stunted by his early exposure to such graphic scenes of death. "I don't think there's really a right or wrong way to feel in this situation. I think it's probably a good sign that you feel a little bit of all of it."

Vito sighed. "Well, that's good. Because I think I feel more than a little bit of all of it. If the math made sense, I would say I am one hundred percent sad, one hundred percent angry, one hundred percent-" Vito stopped short.

"You can say it. It stays right here. And I can feel it anyway." Emile smiled at him encouragingly.

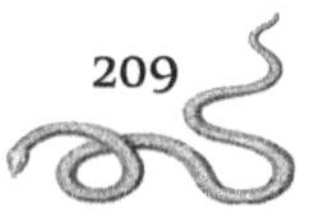

"One hundred percent relieved."

Emile placed a hand on Vito's shoulder and squeezed. "Feels better to let it out, doesn't it?"

Vito nodded. "It's just, Vidal doesn't want to hear it. He sees it all so differently, and we can't understand each other. I know we are just handling it differently, but he thinks I am handling it *wrong*."

Emile clenched his jaw a little at the wave of frustration coming off of Vito. Some of it might have been Emile's to own. He hated the idea some people held of feelings being right or wrong.

"We're so used to agreeing on almost everything. To disagree this strongly over something this important…," Vito shook his head sadly.

"You can disagree with someone and still love them. And still treat them with respect. That is important to remember. You can't control what he does, but as long as you remain responsible for your side, that's all you can do." Emile patted him on the shoulder again. "Pain can bring out the worst in all of us. There's going to be a lot, for a long time. Don't try to run this path like it's a sprint. You won't get through it any faster. You have to set a pace for the long haul and approach this grief for what it is, a lifelong journey. It will eventually subside, and become a dull ache, and then someday you'll find it has become like emotional room noise. Always around, but something you learn to live with. Trust me." Emile sighed, trying to remember to take his own advice. "Talking about it is important. All of those emotions swirling around in there," Emile pointed at Vito's chest, "they are all valid, and they have merit. Keep looking closely at them and figuring them out. Ignoring any one of them won't make them go away."

"How far down the path are you?" Vito looked up at him curiously.

Emile huffed out a breath, "not as far as I'd like. I'm still in the really painful part, too."

"I'm sure you have other people to talk to, but if you ever need it, I'd love to return the favor." Vito smiled, reaching again for the cheese and crackers. "This really helped."

"The chat, or the food?" Emile smiled, eyeing how much of the cheese had disappeared while he'd been talking.

"Both," Vito nodded with an encouraging smile.

Jude laid on his bed, watching the golden sun turn to pink outside the cut-out window of the shack. The sun was setting. How long had he been lying here? Did he get out of bed today? He sat up, feeling a little lightheaded, and knowing he was probably dehydrated.

A thump drew his attention back to the window, where Winston had just jumped to sit on the sill. Was it his imagination or did the monkey look worried? "I'm fine Winston." Jude laughed at himself, without humor. "Like you're actually worried about me, you're probably just mad I didn't give you any bananas today." Jude rolled his eyes at himself and stood out of bed. Winston jumped inside, and grabbed Jude by the hand, pulling him toward the door. "What?" Jude asked, following the monkey outside.

The monkey pointed out over the water, making all kinds of high pitched squeals.

"That's a bit much," Jude said gesturing for Winston to take it down a notch. "Here." He handed the monkey a banana to shut him up, but he wouldn't settle.

"What?" Jude asked, looking out over the horizon. It was a beautiful, clear night approaching. Winston grew more agitated and threw the banana back at Jude. "Hey! It's not my fault you can't speak English." Winston pointed and flailed his arms in the direction of the sea.

"Is something out there?" Jude asked. He was pretty sure the monkey rolled his eyes. A thought occurred to Jude. "You want me to go after her?" he asked. "You want me to follow Achaia?"

Winston hit himself in the head, as if to say "duh".

"Not happening buddy. She's not coming back, and I'm not going to go be a third wheel where I'm not actually wanted."

Jude was sure the monkey had just huffed an exasperated sigh. Clearly, he needed a drink, some food, and to get out of the house more tomorrow. "I'm going to go for a jog. Do you want to come?" Jude asked. Winston shook his head, and turned his back on Jude, galloping off toward the trees, but not before taking back his banana.

Achaia sat alone in her room, staring at the fireplace. A cold front had come through with the setting sun, and the staff had come through to tend the hearth. Achaia stared at the dancing flames, dwelling on dragon fire. She was meditating on the sobering thought that she likely had little over a week before she could potentially be face to face with a beast from myth and legend. She was a skilled fighter, but she had yet to learn to tap into whatever it really meant to be the angel of death. What was she going to do against a dragon? Especially one with seven heads.

There was a faint knock on her door, and it cracked open. "Hey." Noland slipped inside and closed the door behind himself. Something about the way he did so, had Achaia's nerves singing, his movements so smooth and concise.

"Hey," Achaia said, smiling.

Noland joined her on the bed and stared into the flames with her. She was acutely aware of how close he was, the mattress sinking down under his weight, leaning her against him. After a moment, he spoke. "There are so many conversations I want to have, and things I'd like to do, and our days are toiled away in preparations," he said sadly.

"We don't really get the luxury of being able to just hang out," Achaia agreed. "It seems selfish to want to, with everything going on."

Noland nodded and reached for her hand. "But there's nothing left that has to be done tonight." He looked at her. "Can we be a little selfish?" He smiled.

Achaia's breath hitched, and she felt her stomach break

into summersaults. "Please, I could use the distraction. I don't want to think about dragons, or weapons, or death."

Noland turned to face her, tucking his knee in and up onto the bed. "Then, let's just not." He shook his head, and he pulled hers toward him, kissing her mouth. "Let's talk about a future, regardless of whether or not it exists." He kissed her again and she leaned into it, letting her mind focus on mundane things, like the freckles lining Noland's jaw, that were now covered in scruff, the way the fire brought out the gold flecks in the green of his eyes. She breathed in deeply the comforting scent of him.

"Like what?" she asked, laying her hand on his chest, and looking up into his eyes, which were more dilated now. She counted the beats of his heart, which were strong and steady.

"Like, what side of the bed do you want? How many kids? If you could live anywhere, where would you want to go?" Noland looked her in the eye, studying her face intently.

"Oh, is that all?" Achaia laughed leaning against him. She pulled her legs onto the bed to turn completely toward him and rested her forehead against his collar as she thought, taking hold of his hands in hers. "I want the right side of the bed." Noland smiled and nodded, as she leaned back to look him in the eye again. "I want four kids," she smirked. Noland's eyebrows shot up in surprise. "And I don't care where we live as long as we're a family."

"I promise you all of those things," Noland said in a low voice, leaning forward and sliding his hand back into her hair to pull her face to his.

Achaia broke the kiss, putting her hands on his shoulders.

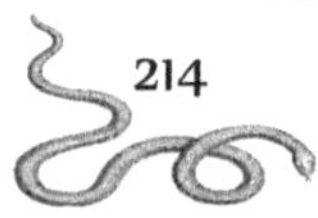

"What do you want?"

Noland thought for a second before sighing. "Time," he whispered, brushing a kiss along her temple. "But we can't have everything."

Joash stood in his office in the dark, looking into the mirror on his wall. "You're an idiot if you think that woman is loyal to you." His reflection rebuked him.

"Dina is like a daughter to me; she wouldn't betray me." Joash argued back.

"And Shael was closer than a brother to me. Relations mean nothing to Nephilim who were born individual and remain so to the end. None of us are linked so close as to be above betrayal. We fight for ourselves." His reflection rolled his eyes.

"You're so broken, I wouldn't expect you to understand loyalty." Joash huffed.

"Look in the mirror." Luc's voice grew cold, coming from his own lips. "Oh wait, you are."

Joash punched the glass and drew back a bleeding fist. "Get out!" He pounded his own chest, covering his shirt in blood. He clawed at his flesh, ripping the layers of clothing that got in his way. "GET OUT!" He screamed. He dug trenches in his skin beneath his nails, pulling away layers of flesh.

"Stop that!" Luc's voice chastised. "There's no use." Luc's voice spoke now in his mind. "I'm not going anywhere. But if you're so bent on destroying this form, we could take another."

"No," Joash said, his voice sounding fearful even to his own ears. He stopped clawing at himself and looked down at his bloodied hands. "I wouldn't be able to retake a human form. The Lord forbade me."

"Convenient then, that you're no longer bound to Him." Luc's voice snickered.

Dina listened to the screams coming from Joash's office with chills racing up and down her spine. She stiffened in her chair, breathing deeply. Joash went silent. She was tempted to go check on him. But she didn't want to alert him to the fact that she'd heard what she had. She took three deep steadying breaths, then picked up her phone.

"Bale, it isn't actually confirmation, but it's just shy of. I have to admit, I am scared to push him any further." She relayed everything that she had witnessed and heard. "The way he screamed," she shuttered. "It's almost enough for me to think killing him would be a mercy."

"Do nothing. Keep your head down, and don't provoke him. Don't wake a sleeping dragon. I'll talk to the others. Do nothing without talking to me first."

"I've got the DuBois and Omi here. You inform Kylie and Naphtali," Dina said before hanging up and dialing Korban's number.

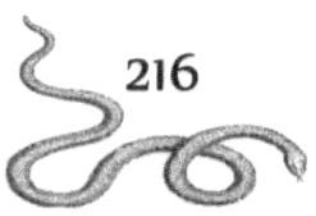

That night as Dina walked back to her apartment, she had the heavy feeling that she was being watched, followed. Her fingers brushed the dagger she wore in a thigh sheath under her skirt. When a feeling like ice cold fingers tracing her spine caused her to sidestep into an alley out of the main lights of the street, she drew her dagger, and took a few deep breaths, listening. "I know you're there. Come on out," she called, in no particular direction.

Demons, with a multitude of legs, like a band of spiders scaled down the walls of the buildings. Some leaped from the roof tops, in an eerily controlled decent. Of course, they'd been following her from the roof tops. There were more of them than she had realized though, and when they reached the street, she would be surrounded. Dina tucked the dagger to her chest and cursed under her breath, sprinting back for the light of the street.

Just before she reached the cobbled road, her ankle was yanked back, dragging her into the darkness.

Irrevocable

"I do not see why I should e'er turn back,
Or those should not set forth upon my track
To overtake me, who should miss me here
And long to know if I still held them dear.

They would not find me changed from him they knew-
Only more sure of all I thought was true."

-Robert Frost, Into My Own

Dina slashed through the thin brittle bone of one of the demon's legs. It screeched and drew back as the others closed in. She wished she had carried a larger weapon, like a sword. It would have been much more effective against these skuttling demons. Their twitchy movements, so inhuman, were difficult to predict and with only a dagger she had to be incredibly precise. She spun, and kicked, and slashed at the creatures, which withdrew, and broke on her like waves. There were too many, and as she looked up, she saw still more crawling down the sides of the surrounding buildings. She sighed and kicked an oncoming demon-spider hard in the face, which was somewhat humanoid though covered in eyes, making them all the more disgusting.

Dina's hope was dwindling. She was out of practice in physical combat after centuries of being bound to a desk. "Dina!" A voice called.

Dina turned in time to see a glittering sword being tossed in her direction. She caught it and spun, slicing her nearest adversary in half. Korban and Oriel DuBois stood back-to-back, slaying demons at the entrance to the alley. Omi was running parallel up the walls, cutting down the demons who were still in descent. Dina smiled and breathed a quick sigh of relief before returning to battle. Few hordes of demons would be enough to take on four trained Nephilim. The creatures were soon dispatched, the alley baptized in blood.

"I think it's safe to say your cover is blown," Korban said.

"You're bleeding," Oriel said, straightening Dina's shirt, and noting a couple of deeper cuts along her chest and stomach.

"It's nothing," Dina said, checking herself over.

"Maybe it should be," Omi said, coming over, wiping his blade clean on his pants.

Dina looked up at him sharply.

"If the council believed you fallen, or dead, would that free you up to be of more use elsewhere?" he suggested.

"It may give Joash a false sense of security as well. If we aren't ready to move against him, it might be good for him to settle," Korban agreed.

"Here." Oriel took off her blouse, standing in her

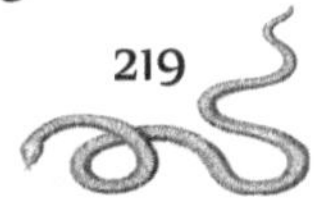

undershirt, and pantsuit. "Wipe yourself off with your shirt and wear this. We can take your shirt back with us, covered in blood and convince the council you've been slain."

Dina looked around at all of them. She considered going back into work tomorrow, but Korban was right. Her cover was blown. Joash or Luc had put a hit out on her. There was nothing more she could do in the council.

"Go back to Moscow," Korban suggested. "Bale could use your help."

Dina took Oriel's shirt and nodded. Korban and Omi stood with their backs to the alley, as Dina took off her shirt, and sponged up as much of her blood as she could, from the cut on her chest. She handed her shirt to Oriel, and put the button down blouse on, covering her wounds.

"Go quickly, pack what is necessary. We will inform the council that we need to go back to Paris for an emergency, and we will fly you to Moscow." Oriel squeezed her hand. "Omi can go with you to pack."

On hearing his name, Omi turned. Seeing her dressed, he and Korban rejoined them. "Let's go, give our excuses. Omi, tomorrow, you bring in Dina's shirt saying you found it on patrol. Give her a head start."

Omi and Dina nodded. "Peace go with you." Oriel leaned forward, kissing Dina's cheek. "We will see you soon at the airport."

Korban and Oriel disappeared around the corner back down the lighted street. Omi took Dina's arm, leading her back deeper down the alley, taking the darkened back paths to her

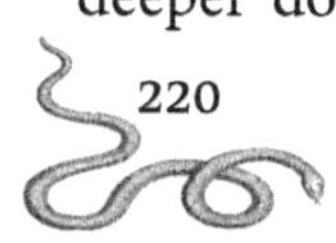

apartment.

Noland sat up alert and braced himself for news as Bale entered the dining room at a brisk pace.

"Luc or Joash has made an attempt on Dina's life. Her cover is blown. She is coming back here," he said, before he'd even made it to the table.

"Oh my God, is she okay?" Achaia asked, tensing next to Noland, dropping her croissant back on her plate.

"She escaped, but only just. Your parents and Omi came to her aid just in time," Bale said looking to Emile and Olivier. "How close are you to finishing the weapon?" He turned his attention to Veronica.

"Another day. I can have it finished tonight," she said, standing, and immediately leaving the room to head back down to the forge. She grabbed an apple on her way out, abandoning the rest of her breakfast.

"Got to love her can-do spirit," Olivier smiled.

Achaia smirked back at him; Noland suppressed his grin before speaking. "So, we ready ourselves, and the moment the weapon is finished, we leave for Tjøtta."

The group nodded. "I'll go inform Kylie," Bale said, pouring a mug of coffee for himself, and grabbing a *vatrushka* before leaving the room as quickly as he'd entered it.

"Man!" Olivier eyed the tray of pastries morosely. "That was the last cheese danish."

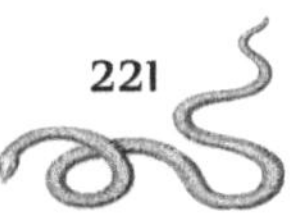

Yellaina shook her head, smilingly at him, patting his hand in mock comfort.

"Alright, is everyone already packed?" Noland asked, looking around the table.

"We are," Achaia said looking over at Yellaina.

"Well, I just want to sneak some Russian tea out of the kitchens, and then I'm set," Yellaina amended.

"All set," Olivier smiled.

Emile's jaw was clenched as he nodded, and Noland didn't need his friend's gift to tell Emile was anxious.

"If you're prepared, why don't you go down and help Veronica finish. Spend time with her before we go," Noland suggested.

Emile sighed, stood from the table and silently left. Noland and Yellaina exchanged a look of concern for him. Without realizing it, Noland had taken Achaia's hand in his on the table. She flipped her hand over, so their palms were touching, and knit her fingers through his.

"Last breakfast at this table," Olivier said with a dramatic flair. "And no cheese danish."

Jude stood on the clifftop looking out over the deep, a growing sense of dread spreading through his chest. He felt insane for being paranoid because of a monkey. Was it a trick of the fading light? A sandbar? A whale? Something was moving beneath the water's surface, darkening the denim blue waves to

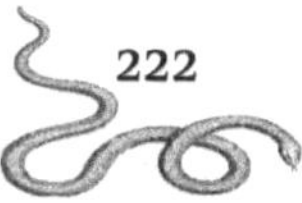

almost ebony. Then, it was gone. Jude remembered the stories he had grown up on, from his adoptive American family. "Leviathan?" he mused nostalgically.

"You missed a good meeting. It went well. The Nephilim are not what we feared."

Jude released his breath, his mood dropping. He turned to see Tobias landing behind him on the rocks. "I should care, why?" Jude shrugged carelessly.

"They have a sound plan. I think we stand a good chance. Join us. You don't want to be on your own. There will be a reckoning. You can't remain unpledged."

"Neither side wants me. I doubt either of them will come knocking. My strategy is to just stay out of the way when they have at each other." Jude shouldered passed Tobias, heading back toward the beach.

"Jude, you know that's not how it works. Why must you be so stubborn!" Tobias yelled. "You'll be damned brother. Does that mean nothing to you?"

"As little as it means to me, I'm surprised you should care so much." Jude lashed out, his tone sharp. Tobias, with all his righteous self-possession, was finally showing a crack in his perfect façade.

"This is eternity we're talking about Jude, not a stint in dad's cells." Tobias' voice dropped to a vehement whisper. "Everything in all of creation has been leading to this moment. Will you throw your will away so carelessly?"

"Did I ever *really* have a say to begin with? A lesser son, of the father of the damned?" Jude cocked his head sarcastic

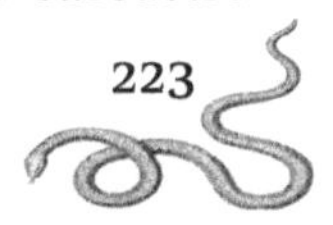

contemplation.

"You have every bit as much say as I do. More so because you have human blood. You have all the say. Father cannot take command of you unless you submit to him, unless you refuse to pledge allegiance." Tobias closed the space between them and put his huge, warm hands on Jude's shoulders, shaking him gently. "You have light in you, brother. Do not forsake that for darkness."

"What do you know of darkness?" Jude said with a sneer, brushing his brother's hands off his shoulders. "No one has ever chosen me. My mother didn't want me, father doesn't. I was nothing but trouble for my adoptive family. Achaia-"

"Achaia was taken before you ever even met her. She did choose you, as a friend. She asked you to go with them. It broke her heart that you didn't." Tobias' eyes were on fire with anger. "For you to even speak of her. If anyone knows what it is like to not be wanted, it is Achaia, and yet look at her fight! She chose a side, and she is giving her all for this war. She is willing to sacrifice herself!"

"What?" Jude froze. "What do you mean sacrifice herself?"

"Father has taken possession of a shape shifter who shifts dragon. He will be hunting her. She means to sail out to sea and draw him away from humanity."

Jude felt as if his veins had turned to molten rage. "And they are going to let her? Noland is just going to let her?" Jude yelled.

"Noland is going with her. As are her friends. There is a

small chance they can defeat him."

"Chance? There is no chance," Jude fumed.

"This is her choice. She volunteered because she has hope that her sacrifice is worth it."

"While what? Everyone else just sits back and lets her die and hope she takes him down in the process. You all make me sick," Jude spat.

"And what would you do?" Tobias asked, exasperated.

"I am going to stop father before he can go after her." Jude turned for the beach, already developing his strategy, weighing his options.

"Jude, you can't stop him. He wants her more than he wants anything. He will not hesitate to go through you to get to her."

"Yes, well luckily for me, father has always severely underestimated what I can do," Jude shot back over his shoulder before unfurling his wings and flying back to the beach.

Luc sprawled himself on one of the ice sofas covered in layers of furs, running a frigid finger around the rim of his brandy glass.

"Hello, father."

Luc sat up straight. "What the hell are you doing here?" Luc said in surprise, as Jude strode into the room, his dark skin a stark contrast to the white-blue icy walls. It was a bit like looking at the sun, one of the many things Luc found disappointing about his offspring. "Did I abduct you again?" Luc asked, confused. He didn't remember bringing Jude here…

"No." Jude rolled his eyes. Luc smiled. Maybe there was some hope for the boy after all. "You look terrible. How many people are you trying to control right now because no one will volunteer their services for your cause?" Jude asked, cocking his head.

"Enough," Luc spat. He took a large gulp of brandy. Truth be told, which he wasn't in the habit of doing, he was stretched a bit thin.

"How many people can you possess before you crack and lose all control? How much can you try to accomplish with incompetent demons, and diminishing strength?" Jude stepped closer, scrutinizing him.

Luc clenched his jaw and tried to drown out all the voices in his head: the staff meetings, the coffee orders, all his unwilling subjects living their daily lives. "Is there a point to this visit?" Luc asked, annoyed. "You know, I didn't really know your mother, but I'm assuming your long-windedness comes from her side of the family. Get. To. The. Point," Luc said exacerbated.

Jude's jaw clenched. Luc smiled; his son looked a bit like himself just then.

"I've weighed my options." Jude sat on the sofa opposite Luc's.

Luc cocked an eyebrow, and sat back down, gesturing for Jude to get on with it.

"The option with the highest likelihood for success is for me to make you a deal."

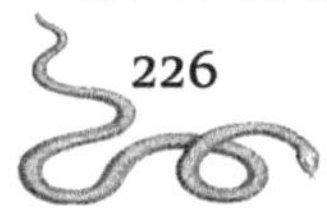

"A deal?" Luc scoffed. "Problem is, I don't want anything from you. What have you to offer?"

"My allegiance," Jude said flatly.

Luc perked up but knew there had to be a catch. "You hate me."

Jude nodded, not denying it. "But I love Achaia," Jude said plainly.

"So, the deal would be?" Luc asked, intrigued.

"I will pledge you my allegiance in exchange for Achaia's life. You will not kill her."

"Deal," Luc said before Jude had hardly finished speaking. He stood, offering a hand.

Jude eyed him warily. "Just like that?"

"Just like that," Luc said cocking his eyebrows again toward his extended hand. "As you said, I could use the manpower." Luc smiled inside but did his best to not appear eager of face, until the deal was done.

Jude stood, and haltingly took Luc's hand.

"You're mine now, son." Luc smiled, Jude gasped, and fell to his knees, struggling to breathe. As Jude slumped struggling to catch his breath, Luc tilted his chin back up toward him, smiling. "I was never planning on killing Achaia. I *want* her *alive*." Jude's face dropped. "Welcome to the team." Luc smiled, cherishing the look of betrayal on Jude's face. He watched the dawn of realization on his son's face. He'd miscalculated.

Noland knocked on Achaia's door. She answered it, smiling when she saw his face, which made something in his chest hitch a little. "Want to go train and kill some time?"

"Yeah, just let me change." Achaia shut her door back, and a few minutes later, returned in yoga shorts and a t-shirt.

"How are you feeling about all this?" Noland asked, accepting that he wasn't great with subtlety when it came to talking about feelings. He looked sideways at Achaia as they walked the halls to the weapons room.

"I don't think I've let it sink in yet. Honestly, I think if I think about it too much, I might change my mind." Achaia huffed a halfhearted laugh.

"No, you wouldn't," Noland smirked. "It's danger. If you had stopped to think on it for too long, we'd already be on the ship."

Achaia laughed as she slapped his shoulder. "You're probably right."

Noland opened the door to the weapons room and stood aside for Achaia to enter first. Achaia went straight for the weapons rack to choose a blade. Noland watched as she swung a rapier and put it back on the rack, pensively. He wondered if she was thinking of Amelia. She was fiddling with the dagger strapped to her thigh sheath as she ran her other hand along the handles of the other swords. "You know what, I think I need to branch out," she said, walking over to the long table to the right of the room. She picked up a mace. "What do you think?" She turned smiling.

"I think you look terrifying with a pencil in your hand,"

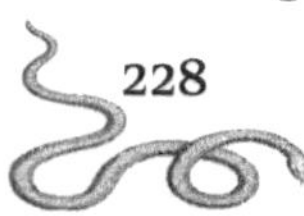

Noland joked, smiling. "But branching out is a good idea." He reached in his pocket fidgeting with two boxes, the gifts Veronica had forged for him.

Achaia laughed. "Do you know what Veronica is making? What does someone take to battle a dragon?"

"Harry was only allowed a wand." Noland cocked his head.

Achaia laughed again, walking over to him. "I'm being serious. As gnarly as this looks, it wouldn't do anything against a dragon. Neither will Akakios." Achaia looked down at her diemerilium snake whip affectionately but shaking her head.

"Veronica's weapon stands as good a chance as we could hope," Noland finally answered. "Though, I will have to wield it, it's about the same size as you." Noland took up a flagrum.

They paced a slow circle in the middle of the room. Noland struck out first. Achaia spun out of the way, her hair flying out behind her, hitting Noland in the face. He spit the hair out of his mouth. Achaia laughed. They trained until both were out of breath and red in the face.

"I got you something, or rather, I had Veronica make you something," Noland said as they put their weapons away. He led her over to one of the alcove window seats and pulled the larger box out of his pocket.

"What?" Achaia smiled. "But it's not Christmas, or my birthday." She took the box out of his hand, eyeing it nervously.

"I just missed you," Noland said, cocking his head and shrugging a shoulder.

Achaia smiled up at him and opened the box. Inside were

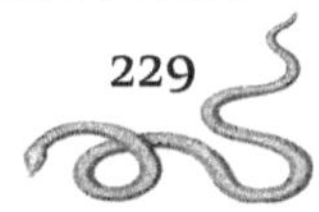

seven beaded rings, each with a tiny hook blade on them. Achaia cocked an eyebrow and grinned. "They're for your hair." Noland chuckled. "So, it really can be its own weapon."

Achaia lifted one of the beads out of the box and inspected it closer. The hooks were jagged. With enough momentum, they would tear flesh, no problem. "These are savage. Thank you!" She put the bead back in the box and leaned forward to hug Noland. Noland squeezed her close, breathing in her lemon soap. "Yellaina is going to have so many ideas about how to style my hair with these." Achaia leaned back smiling widely and clutching the box to her chest.

"Well, why don't you go figure that out. It's probably time for me to reheat the fires for Veronica. I also want to see her progress. Unless you want to come with me?"

Achaia raised her eyebrows. "Is that a real question?"

Noland laughed, and stood, offering her his hand. She grabbed it excitedly, jumping up from her seat, to go check out the dragon blade.

Bale stood in the entry hall waiting to greet Dina and the DuBois on their arrival. It was in this very room that six months ago he had seen Achaia for the first time. The power that radiated off of her had shaken him. Now, he was comforted that such a force was on their side. He would be lying to himself if he didn't acknowledge that he had grown to care for her, especially since Shael's death, and Naphtali had been more absent. Bale didn't know what it felt like to have a daughter. But if they survived this war, and it wasn't the end of Earth, Bale would take Achaia in as his own. Though, if he continued in his honesty, he wasn't sure she would survive their plans for Joash. He regretted this more than anything. And Noland, who had become like- Bale shook the thoughts away of what lay ahead for the young Nephilim. More than regrettable, but also, he feared, unavoidable.

Korban walked through the door hefting a large suitcase up the step. "Bale," he said in greeting.

"*Zdravstvuyte*," Bale said, stepping forward to grab the case.

Oriel and Dina entered behind Korban. "*Bonjour*, Bale," Oriel smiled.

"Dina," Bale nodded toward her.

"*Ehi*," Dina smiled.

"Are you well?" Bale asked, eyeing the cut across Dina's chest. There were blackish webs spreading from it toward her neck.

"I haven't seen a healer yet; I think it might be infected," Dina said looking down but shrugging it off casually.

"Inessa is a miracle worker," Bale said, gesturing for Dina to follow him at once.

Bale led the way to Inessa's rooms, where Dina was instructed to strip and get into a bath immediately. Bale smiled and left her in his healer's capable hands.

Korban and Oriel had gone in search of their sons. Bale made his way down to the forge to check on Veronica's progress, as he had taken to doing every hour, much to Veronica's annoyance.

231

This time, Noland and Achaia were also there. The weapon had taken shape, and Veronica was at work sharpening the many bladed edges.

"You'll want to stab and twist to inflict maximum damage when you pull the blade back out," Veronica was telling Noland.

Bale eyed the blade unable to mask just how much Veronica had impressed him with this creation. "If brutality were a blade," he smiled.

"Well, it is now." Veronica smiled. Emile was helping her by holding some of the weight of the handle while Veronica sharpened the blade on the spinning stone.

"What did you end up using?" Noland asked, studying the shimmering darker green blade, which was also splattered with red, as if already bloodied.

"Dragon's blood jasper," Veronica answered. "I don't know why I didn't think of it first!"

Noland nodded.

"It's also laced with emerald along the core, and of course tipped in diamond along each point." Veronica held the blade up into the light, and eyed the point, to make sure it was satisfyingly sharp.

"How much does that thing weigh?" Achaia asked, reaching her hand out to grasp the handle. Emile and Veronica released it into her hand, and it clunked to the floor with a ringing thump.

"Thirty-five pounds," Veronica answered. "Mostly because of the added counterweight, but otherwise it wouldn't have been balanced. And now it will also sling well if Noland

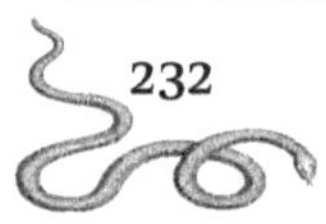

needs to throw it."

"Can you throw it?" Achaia asked, looking up at Noland.

Noland scoffed, "Can I throw it?" He rolled his eyes in answer.

"Stupid question." Achaia rolled her eyes at Noland.

"Germans are known for their heavy swords, like the *Zweihänder*. Granted, those were closer to nine pounds." Noland eyed the blade, appreciatively.

"Um, just a thought," Achaia prompted holding up a finger. Bale looked back to her, waiting. "But is there a case for this thing," she said pointing to the blade that stood as tall as she did, "or are we supposed to parade down the streets with it, and just trot right onto the plane?" Achaia gestured up and down the five-foot-long weapon.

The group looked at each other.

Right, Bale thought. "I'll find something," he assured them, racking his brain for what he could possibly put a weapon that size in. He might have some deer hides in the attic he could wrap it in-

"What are we going to call it?" Achaia asked.

Veronica looked at Noland. "I leave it to you to name your blade."

Noland thought for a moment, before a smile spread across his face, "*Olethros*." Bale smiled.

"Destruction?" Emile asked. "Appropriate."

"But that particular variation lends itself to the positive connotation of leading to renewal," Bale expounded. "Optimistic," he added with a nod.

"You've truly out-nerded yourself," Achaia said smiling at Bale, and nodding at Noland.

"We'll see what happens." Noland took the blade from Achaia, stepped back, and spun it, slashing the air. He ended in a side lunge with the blade outstretched behind his back.

"If I ever doubted your gift of strength, I'm now convinced," Achaia laughed.

Bale felt a tiny blossom of hope bloom in his chest.

"I made these too, since you can't all wield the blade." Veronica brought over a basket of daggers and arrows all made from the dragon blood jasper. Emile picked up the arrows, studying the arrowheads; their shafts were ebony black with blood red fletching. Achaia grabbed a dagger. There was a slim, slightly prettier blade that looked more like a letter opener to Bale, that must have been designed with Yellaina in mind.

Bale wasn't excited about *her* resolution to attend the group. Her skills would be better served staying behind. But Bale knew she'd been left behind twice before, and he would not be the one to order her to stay, though he prayed she would change her mind.

"Your parents are here," Bale said, remembering, to Emile. "You should go find them." Bale didn't have to finish his thought for Emile to nod. This was his chance to say goodbye to them, in case things went poorly on this mission.

"Everyone has a darker nature. Everyone.
Good men fear it, and evil men embrace it."

-James Islington, The Shadow of What Was Lost

Amelia stood at the window of the bedroom Lailah had given her to use as her own. Once Bale returned, she would reside in his house, their house. But it was lonely there, without him, and didn't feel like home. The streets of gold below were full of angels rushing back and forth, brushing past, and not stopping when they collided. They were preparing for war, and there was no time for polite sentiments. Amelia had never seen so many angels on mission the way they were here in heaven. If this is how they were meant to work together, then no wonder the Nephilim on earth were fallen.

She looked out over the golden city. Houses, also of gold, reflected the light from the Lord, like a river of gold leading to the pearly gates. They were densely packed together with only narrow alleys separating them. A winding street wound around them, with no rhyme or human reason behind it. There was no grid system, no multiple streets, but one winding road that meandered around, seemingly aimless, but somehow would eventually land you at the door of anyone you needed to visit. The air around the city shimmered, similar to when Amelia used to watch heat rising off of asphalt in the summer. She didn't think you were supposed to be able to see heat. Likewise, she was stunned by her ability to see and feel the holiness rising off the city itself. Everything was bathed in the shimmer of the holy light. At first it had been nearly blinding, even to her angelic eyes. Now that she had acclimated to heavenly life, she found that the one thing she could never adjust to was the state of awe. Looking out at the city, she could feel her proximity to God. His presence filled all space. The air she breathed unnecessarily into her lungs was full of Him. To exist in Heaven was to be constantly in awe.

She saw Naphtali cutting his way through the crowd toward Lailah's door. "Lailah, Naphtali is coming," she said, running down the stairs just as the door opened, admitting him into the house.

His eyes were franticly searching until they came to land on Amelia. "How have you been progressing in developing your gift?"

"Pretty well. I was able to talk to my mom," Amelia

smiled.

"Can you reach people when they're awake?" Naphtali asked.

"No, it's still a struggle to maintain a connection longer than a few minutes when they are asleep." Amelia cocked her head at Naphtali, silently bidding him to explain the reason for these questions.

"I have news," he began, looking at Lailah as well. "We believe Luc has taken possession of Joash and is going to use him to shift dragon."

Lailah's eyes widened. "Oh," her voice was a faint whisper.

"Excuse me, did you say dragon?" Amelia butted in.

Naphtali sighed. "Yes, Joash hasn't shifted since ancient days, but he is a shape shifter. His *alterform* is a dragon. That is likely why the fallen have followed his lead for so long. They know the power that lies within." Naphtali looked down shaking his head. "I don't think they ever thought to consider whether his other qualities might prove to be dangerously weak."

"So, what's the plan?" Lailah asked.

"That's the thing. The earth has grown too crowded. There is no place to battle dragons without the serious loss of human life. So, they are going to draw him out to sea."

"How do they plan to do that?" Amelia asked.

"Bait," Lailah answered.

"Achaia," Naphtali said, meeting Amelia's eye, his full of regret.

"What?" Amelia was outraged. "You're going to let them send her out to sea to tempt the beast? What is this? Greek

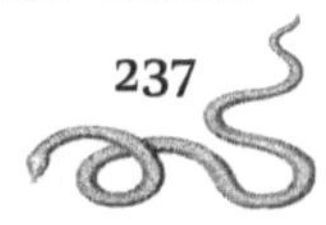

Mythology? We don't do that crap in real life!"

"She won't be going alone," Naphtali said calmly. "They are all going."

Amelia's stomach clenched and dropped. "No."

"I come to give warning. Because this likely will not end in life." Naphtali looked to Lailah. "You may want to prepare room." Naphtali stepped forward gently taking Amelia by the shoulders. "You're going to want to train hard."

Lailah cleared her throat. Naphtali turned his attention back to her. She cleared her throat again, as if she was struggling to find her voice. "You know who else you need to tell."

"Yes," Npahtali nodded, understanding her meaning, though Amelia did not. "Amelia, if you can, I want you to try to get a glimpse inside of Joash's mind. We desperately need confirmation. If we can get it, we may be able to eliminate him before he brings destruction on humanity."

"Eliminate him, as in kill him?" Amelia asked, nausea bubbling up in her stomach. Based on what she could or couldn't find out, they were planning to kill Joash? Amelia didn't know if she could live with that, no matter how much she couldn't stand the man. Lailah, as if sensing her turmoil, grabbed hold of her hand.

"Naphtali, go, find her." Lailah's voice cracked, and Amelia questioned whether Lailah was trying to give her strength or borrow some.

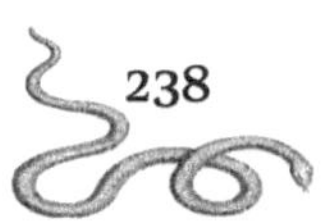

Jude sat in his room, not a cell, but a room lavishly though frigidly decorated in furs and things that looked like they should offer more warmth than they did. He took a deep breath, trying to think, to strategize. He could smell the sea salt in his dreads. It reminded him of the sunshine that used to kiss his skin, and the waves, the sand, warmth. All of that was behind him now, a former life that had ended. This was going to be a chapter of ice, and loathing. If this was the part he was to play in this war, he would have to set aside the lighthearted boy of his youth and don the cold hardness of disillusionment. This was his lot. There'd never been an escape. This was his end all along. He was the son of a pagan witch and the devil himself. He never stood a chance of being good.

Jude looked over to his bed, where a dagger lay, glimmering with its diemerilium blade. He took it up and looked at his reflection in the glimmering ice walls. He took the first dread in his hand, and raised the dagger, slicing it off, close to the root. He felt the weight of his old self falling away, dread by dread. If he was to forge himself into something new, he would become someone hell itself would grow to fear. He would make his father unfortunately proud.

Tobias landed on the deck of the houseboat he shared with his mother. She was waiting for him, just inside the door. "He has not come." She sounded mournful.

"I'm afraid it's worse than that," Tobias said, entering the house, and leaning against the kitchen counter, which was little more than a rickety salvaged table. He was finding it hard to breathe, not from the flight back, but the realization that he had failed his little brother. He couldn't fathom or process how Jude could see things so differently than he himself.

"He hasn't gone to Luc. He wouldn't." Hilmaya raised a shocked hand to her mouth. "No."

Tobias nodded. "He thought he could stop him from advancing on Achaia. He means to save her, but he will only lose himself."

Hilmaya collapsed onto a floor cushion, her head in her hands. "That poor boy."

"What do we do now?" Tobias asked. His mother looked up at him, as if trying to shake off her sorrow, to refocus on her purpose.

"There's nothing now that can be done for Judas. He has made his choice. Let us hope something good may yet come from it." She stood back up, and handed Tobias a packed bag and a woven satchel of food. "We are needed elsewhere."

"Where are we going? We've only just gotten back."

"I fear that if Joash shifts dragon, he will not be the only beast. There is one that sleeps in the deep. If it wakes, we will be fighting a beast on two fronts."

"What beast?" Tobias asked, his chest clenching, making it still harder to breathe.

"I fear the waking of Leviathan."

Emile stood in the grand foyer of the Russian Safe House, his duffle bag slung over his shoulder, his sheathed, bladed bow digging into his back, prodding his since of urgency. He was ready to be off and doing something. He was growing anxious waiting on the edge of battle. He would rather be fighting, than waiting for it to start. His hands were shaking slightly, and his legs were restless. He shifted his weight impatiently, waiting for Yellaina to come down with her bags. He knew that not all of the anxiety he felt was his. He was feeling Noland's impatience, Achaia's nervous anticipation, Olivier's dread, Veronica's- resentment. He would rather her be resentful than dead. Besides, Bale was right. They needed her to make weapons. Her duty was here.

He looked down at her, where she stood near enough to touch him, but she wouldn't. She was angry. Emile couldn't help that. He was relieved she would be staying behind. He reached his fingers toward hers hesitatingly. But Yellaina came in, dragging a suitcase, and an additional duffle bag.

"What is all that?" Olivier asked, stunned.

"Necessities," Yellaina said shrugging, "and healing supplies," she said hefting the leopard print duffle bag into Olivier's arms.

"I'm not walking through the airport with this," Olivier said, holding it out by the straps as if it was somehow contagious.

"Oh, come on, no one will see you anyway," Achaia laughed.

"Airports are vacant these days," Noland nodded in agreement, smirking.

Emile took in the moment of laughter like a breath

before a plunge. He risked another look down at Veronica. She looked back up at him, her eyes glistening with unshed tears of frustration. He pulled her aside, into one of the room's many alcoves. She took a deep breath and let it out, as if bracing herself for rebuke.

"If I should fall," Emile started.

Veronica's eyes widened in surprise, "No."

Emile shook his head, silencing her refusal to have the conversation. He felt her dread. "If I should fall, hold fast to Vito. He needs you." Veronica nodded, the tears escaping her eyes now and cascading down her cheeks. "Make peace with Vidal. But give him time. He holds more anger than he knows what to do with. And for Heaven's sake, forgive yourself. Lay down the guilt and allow your mother to love you." Emile pulled Veronica into a firm hug. He kissed the top of her head, hard. "You deserve so deeply to be loved."

Veronica hugged him back, burying her face in his chest. He felt the tremors of sobs reverberate through him. "Don't go where I can't follow."

"You will follow someday. And on the other side you will find me waiting." Emile kissed the top of her head one more time before releasing her.

"I pray my arrows protect you." Veronica's words were hiccupped. "I love you Emile Alan DuBois."

"I love you too, Ronnie." Emile kissed Veronica's forehead, before turning quickly, being the first of the others out the door. If he turned back, or looked into her face, he might change his mind. He felt her heart break on top of his own, and it caught his

breath, and made him forget everything that happened between kissing her face and standing at the base of the stairs leading up to the plane.

Achaia sat by the window, and Noland next to her. Yellaina and Olivier were across the aisle from them. Emile sat up front by himself. His head leaned against the window. Achaia had prepared for this. She looked across the plane to Olivier. They had specifically curated a playlist of funny videos, mostly cats, and people falling, for the four of them to watch. Emile had enough of his own feelings to sort through today. He didn't need the added weight of their anxieties and dreads. Olivier pulled out his phone, and elbowed Yellaina. She looked up at him and smiled before looking down at the phone.

Noland leaned in close, to share Achaia's phone screen and ear buds. Before take-off, the four of them were in stitches, laughing. Emile looked back at them, curiously, and took in the phones in their hands. Achaia looked up at him and winked when they made eye contact. He smiled at her appreciatively. After the first hour, he got up from his seat, and came back to join them. Their abdomens and cheeks were sore from laughing.

Achaia needed the mental and emotional shut down just as much as Emile did, and she was happy that her idea was working. By the time the plane landed in Norway, they were in unreasonably high spirits.

Kylie was waiting for them at the airport. She cocked

243

her eyebrow in curious expectation when Noland descended the stairs carrying the sword wrapped in leathers and tied with tanned straps. "I want to see it!" she said, reaching impatiently for the blade.

Noland pulled it back out of her reach. "Not here," he said, shaking his head but smirking.

"Ugh, fine," Kylie said turning on her heel, and leading the way to the SUV she'd brought to pick them up.

Omi clutched Dina's bloodied shirt in his clenched fist, outside the door to the council chamber. This had the potential to be as the breath of God prompting a tidal wave. How would the council members react to this news? He didn't feel the least bit guilty lying to them if it would prompt them to right action. He thrust the door open. His physical presence usually prompted a hush, because of his size, but this time, his countenance was just as sobering.

Those closest to the door he could hear whispering, "What is that he's got?" "Is that blood?" "Who's is that?"

Omi didn't stop until he reached the center of the room. Joash looked up at him as if he didn't know whether to be annoyed or curious. "Abayomrunkoje ben Chetachi, what purpose bids you?"

Omi threw the bloodied shirt up onto the dais at Joash's feet.

"Dina is dead," he said, telling himself it was true, so that

his voice carried the weight of such news. He was no natural liar.

Joash stood abruptly to his feet, almost diving for the shirt. He studied it closely. Murmers broke through the crowd. "How has this come to pass?" Joash's voice was broken. Omi was taken aback, surprised by Joash's honest emotional distress.

"She was hunted down by a horde of vengeance demons. They were too many." Omi lowered his face to the floor but kept his eyes on Joash.

As if he had forgotten the crowd around him, Joash fell to his knees with a wail that wrenched through Omi's chest. Joash tore his robe with sobs that tore out of his throat.

The crowd went silent, staring on in sympathy, shared mourning, and in some cases morbid fascination. "NO!" Joash wailed, looking down at the shirt in his hands. "I told you no!" Joash yelled.

The crowds' compassion turned to confusion, as they whispered to one another, "Who is he talking to?" "He is beside himself."

"She was loyal to me, like a daughter," Joash sobbed into his hands.

Another voice sneered, "Shut up, you idiot. They are watching." Omi leaned closer, realizing the second voice was also Joash's.

"NO!" Joash screamed. "I told you to stay away from her."

The crowd was staring. Some had risen to their feet.

"Sit down you fool." Joash rebuked himself, snapping his head to the side, his face shifting from grief to rage.

"NO!" Joash stood to his feet. "Get out! GET OUT!" Joash

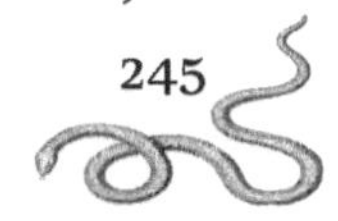

screamed, standing to his feet, clawing at his chest, ripping his robes further. The crowd was all on their feet now, most making their way toward the exits, running to clear the room. "GET OUT NOW!"

As Omi watched, Joash's skin, red with irritation from his clawing deepened to burgundy, the bloody welts turning into scales beneath his clawing fingertips.

Omi, with the last of the stragglers, turned to run for the door. One last glance over his shoulder showed him Joash had grown three times in size, and his fingers had turned to claws. His eyes were slitted, and dancing like flames. "RUN!" Omi yelled at those still standing in the halls. "He is shifting dragon!"

As the crowds of Nephilim made it out to the street, the roof of the basilica exploded upward showering stones and debris on the onlooking pedestrians. Mortals screamed, as the dragon burst forth from the ruins beating its football-field-spanned wings like a hurricane and turning its seven heads to take in its surroundings before launching itself into the sky.

Omi looked on in horror, waiting to see what direction the beast would take. To his relief instead of attacking the city, the beast flew to great heights, into the skies beyond view. He took out his phone and called Bale. "Joash did not take well the news of Dina's demise. He has shifted. The Vatican is destroyed."

Naphtali raced through the city street, colliding with angels who hastened away too hurried to offer apology. Everyone

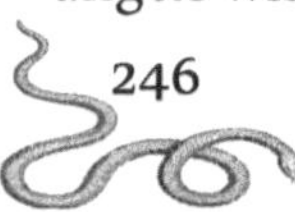

was hastening the coming end. He came to what he thought was the right door, and took a deep steadying breath, looking it up and down. He took another breath before knocking. The golden door opened. Curious eyes met his, then widened in surprise. "Naphtali?"

"Hello, Anna."

To the Depths

"My course is set
For an uncharted sea."

-Dante Alighieri, The Paradiso

Noland stood in the Tjøtta safe house, staring at a news channel reporting in a language he didn't understand. He didn't need to understand the frantic reporter. The footage playing on repeat on the screen showed an enormous seven headed dragon exploding out of the Vatican in a cloud of stone dust, before launching into the sky and disappearing. The wind outside was beginning to sound like the beating of wings, as Noland's mind turned on him. He fought off paranoia and panic. This was the plan. This is what they wanted. "We don't have time to wait. We need to set sail tonight. He could be upon us any moment."

Kylie nodded, eying the setting sun outside. "I'll have the ship made ready."

Noland's phone rang. Seeing Bale's name, he answered it "I know. We're watching it on the news. We set sail tonight."

"Noland," Bale's voice was heavy with regret or something like it. Noland wasn't sure. "This isn't the path I would have chosen for you. For any of you." Bale's voice was quiet. "You are strong. I am convinced your gift is not just of physical strength, but mental, and spiritual as well. You have borne more than most, with incredible integrity, and drive."

Noland swallowed but said nothing. He could hear the pride in Bale's voice and wondered if his father would have spoken similar words if he were still alive.

"You can do-" Bale paused, and the shift in his voice drove home the true meaning to his words, *"all things-"* Bale's voice broke off.

Including die, Noland thought. "You have been a faithful and true friend," Noland said, knowing Bale probably felt guilty allowing them to go on this mission at all. "Knowing you has in part prepared us for what we must now do. We will not fail you, any of you," Noland said, hanging up before Bale had a chance to respond. He thought of Shael, wondering what words of wisdom he would have had to offer them. How angry would he be that Achaia was here? How proud? Noland had made him a silent promise as he'd watched Shael fall and carried Achaia to safety; he would protect her. He was coming to grips with the fact that that might not mean "keep her alive." Protecting her might mean giving her the space to fulfill her purpose, defending her against those who would prevent her, including himself. He wouldn't leave her to walk that path alone. He would go with her. If Achaia had to be the angel of death, then they would meet it together, if it came to that. Noland hoped it wouldn't. Was he crazy to hold so tightly to hope now when it was most evasive?

"So, when you first said dragon, was I naïve to only picture one head?" Achaia asked, coming up next to him hugging a mug of coffee in her hand.

Noland scoffed. "Maybe a little. I'm trying to decide whether or not I am actually surprised, myself." Noland shrugged his mouth, tucking his lips in, and biting the inside of his cheek. "I don't think I am." He shook his head.

"No, I don't think I am either," Achaia said pensively, offering him a sip of her coffee. She drank hers black, which Noland was a little impressed by. He preferred his with cream and sugar, but he took a large gulp, shocking himself.

"Hey! That's my dragon slaying juice," Achaia said reaching for the mug back. "I thought you'd just take a sip, not half the goods."

Noland handed the mug back, wincing a little at the strength of the brew. "What kind of people our age drink coffee black?"

"The same ones who battle dragons in real life." Achaia smiled up at him, a glimmer of mischief in her eyes, making them look more green than usual.

Noland smiled. "*Real life…*" he mused, remembering the day he'd kicked down the door to her apartment and incurred

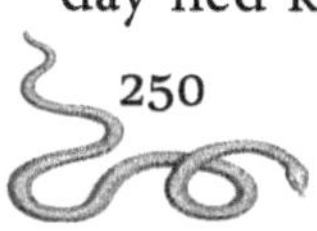

250

her wrath. "I still don't think I understand that concept."

"It's easy. Real life is apparently the one with dragons." Achaia chuckled. "Where people kick down doors and slay demons with their bare hands. I think I was actually the one who was confused all along." She nudged him with her shoulder, laying her head against him. "Are you ready?" She tucked her free hand into his arm and squeezed it. He didn't need Emile's gift to tell she was nervous but trying to make light of what they were about to do, all the while watching the enormity of the dragon on tv.

Noland nodded and kissed the top of her head. "Yeah, I'm ready."

"Me, too." Achaia took a deep breath, and released it, as the last bit of sun disappeared behind the horizon, turning the sky to blood orange and pink.

"It's time," Kylie announced, peeking her head around the door behind them.

Noland looked over at the tv one more time, catching a last glimpse of the beast, launching itself into the sky. He braced himself internally for whatever was going to come next.

"I don't think Joash is sleeping. I haven't been able to reach him at all." Amelia was sorry that she wasn't sorrier. In truth she was relieved to be taken out of the equation, if they were determining whether or not to end an existence.

Heaven quaked. Lailah grasped the table Amelia was

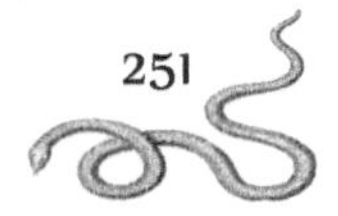

sitting at and looked to Naphtali. "It has begun," she gasped.

Amelia looked to Naphtali. "What is happening?"

Without answering, Naphtali ran for the door, Amelia followed, meaning to follow him to look down on the earth. When he opened the door Iesou stood there, as if He'd just arrived. Amelia knew Him immediately from the feeling of peace rolling off of Him in waves. His skin glimmered like the gold of heaven itself, and his dark hair curled down to his shoulders.

"Lord," Naphtali fell to his knees. Lailah followed, and so Amelia, too, knelt.

"What grief shakes Heaven?" Naphtali asked.

"These are just few of many things that must come to pass," Iesou said calmly, as the rest of them stood. "These are but the contractions of new birth. Lailah, it is time to bring forth the scrolls to be read. Naphtali, the steeds need readying."

Lailah and Naphtali went pale, but launched into motion, both leaving the house, and Amelia alone with Iesou.

"What do you require of me, Lord?" Amelia asked, unsure of whether or not she should be making eye contact, or not; should she be kneeling? Iesou's eyes were warm and kind. And the peace that washed over her gave her confidence enough to hold his gaze.

"Child, you need only rest." Iesou looked at her gently and brushed a hand across her forehead. Immediately Amelia felt sleep fighting for her. Iesou led her over to the daybed in the drawing room, and she lay down on it. "Rest makes you ready," she vaguely heard Him say before she fell into a deep and peaceful sleep.

Yellaina stood on the dock staring at the ship, listening to it creek eerily on the waters. Noland walked the boarding ramp onto the ship first, followed closely by Achaia, then Emile. Olivier stood at Yellaina's side. "If you want to change your mind, there's no shame in that," he offered hopefully.

"There's no getting rid of me now," Yellaina smiled. She grabbed his hand and squeezed it, just as her phone vibrated in her pocket. She pulled it out and was surprised to see her father was calling. "Hello?" She answered hesitantly.

"Yellaina, where are you? It's time to come home. Joash has-"

"I know." Yellaina cut him off. "But I can't come home, I'm- I'm on mission, dad."

"What mission? Yellaina, come home, right now." Jacob's voice was bordering on frantic.

"No, dad. I am finally doing what you always wanted. I'm joining the fight." Yellaina's voice faltered.

"Yellaina, what are you talking about?" Jacob's voice was progressing toward hysterical. Yellaina had never heard her father sound afraid, and knowing that he was now, and for her, moved her in a way she hadn't expected.

"I'm sorry dad, but I'm going to make you proud. I promise."

"Yell-," Yellaina hung up the phone, and shoved it back in her pocket. Her throat was tight, and her vision was blurred with unexpected tears. She choked them back, clearing her throat, and adjusted the strap of her bag over her shoulder.

"Let's go," she said to Olivier, who wrapped his arm around her firmly. They boarded the ship together, and if that was how they parted this life, then that was just as well to Yellaina. They all had to die eventually. She might as well go out fighting, just like her father had always wanted.

Kylie gave them a tour of the ship and gave them a quick lesson in hoisting the sails. "We don't really need to know how to steer. We don't really have a destination other than out." Achaia shrugged.

"What about coming back?" Kylie argued.

"I doubt that we will be coming back," Noland said, his words falling heavily on the group.

Kylie looked at him with fire in her eyes. Yellaina knew it wasn't so much anger at Noland as much as it was anger that they were in this situation to begin with. "Not with that attitude you won't," she said in an almost motherly tone.

"Kylie, you've given us everything we need. Thank you." Noland put a solid hand on her shoulder, but then nodded for her to get off the ship.

They worked together to get the ship out of harbor. The waves lapped against the side of the ship, and the night air was crisp and cool, a bitter chill in its gusts full of sea spray. Yellaina shivered, staring out over the vast endless dark. The reflection of the moon danced along the water's surface, showing her glimmering glimpses of the waves that rocked the ship back and forth.

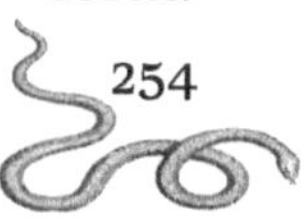

"What are you thinking?" Olivier asked coming up next to her. She looked up at Achaia who was sitting watch in the crow's nest.

"That the calm before the storm would be beautiful if it wasn't packed full of dread." Yellaina was fidgeting with her fingers on the ship's railing. "More than I hope this doesn't work, I hope that it does. But I'm ready to know one way or another."

"We'll know soon enough. Try to enjoy the quiet while it lasts." Olivier grabbed hold of her fidgeting hands. "We have the last shift. Come down and try to get some sleep."

Yellaina scoffed. "Sleep? Yeah, I don't see how that's going to happen."

"Rest then." Olivier cocked his head at her, as if there were no point in her arguing further.

"You're probably right."

"Can you say that one more time?" Olivier smiled. "I really liked the sound of that sentence coming out of your mouth." He chuckled.

"Shut up." Yellaina slapped his arm, but followed him to the captain's quarters below.

Achaia perched herself in the crow's nest, wrapped in a blanket against the wind. She strained her eyes against the expanse of dark, listening over the wind for the beat of wings, scanning the skies, and trying not to be distracted by just how much of nothing else she could see around them. As far as the eye could roam all she could see was the reflection of moonlight on rising waves. At the same time, she was in awe of just how many stars freckled the sky. She'd never seen so many stars. There was less space free of stars than she'd ever suspected. Layers of stars big and small, in varying shades of white, blue, even a pinkish purple painted the sky like it had been photoshopped. The night without the light pollution of humanity was infinitely more beautiful than she'd realized.

It had taken her some time to get used to how much she swayed up in the crow's nest. At first it had been unnerving. But she'd settled into the rhythm, and stopped trying to brace herself against it, and just relaxed into the motion. "You've got this, right?" she asked the air around her. "You're with us?" She hugged the blanket closer and felt a sort of resolve flood her heart. "I knew you were." Achaia smiled to herself. "Whatever happens, I'm with you. Whatever needs to happen, I'm in." Achaia promised as much to herself as to God. "But if I can be a little selfish in asking," she paused, thinking through exactly what she wanted to ask for. "Never mind, you know best. And I think I'm finally learning to trust that. So, I don't know what it looks like, but your will be done. Whatever it takes. Give us the strength to stand. There's no turning back now. Help us to succeed."

Achaia looked down to where Noland and Emile were pacing their respective sides of the deck. Something about Emile seemed darker than usual. She couldn't imagine the weight of these days, and everything everyone was feeling. Leaving Veronica had been hard, she knew. But she had no idea how he was functioning, bearing everyone's feelings. She resolved in

herself to be strong for him, if not for herself.

Noland, steadfast as ever, diligent, and vigilant. She smiled to herself, thinking how far they had come since they'd first met. She couldn't believe she had ever thought him full of himself or lacking compassion. Knowing him now, there was no one else who's side she wanted to stand by in battle or any other scenario. She trusted him more than anyone else on the planet. She hoped that she could be worthy of, and earn, his trust in return. She didn't deserve it, not after leaving him the way she had. She hadn't really been thinking straight at the time, but she regretted not talking to him first.

Her thoughts wandered to Jude. She wondered what he was doing now. Hanging out with Winston, eating bananas by the fire? Was he lonely without her? Would he be lonely enough to change his mind, and join their company? Well, the company that remained without them. Achaia tried to process what it meant that they likely wouldn't be going home. The end was a lot easier to accept than process. Achaia shook her head, trying to focus her thoughts. She was supposed to be looking out for a freaking dragon. She scanned the skies again, with a heavy sigh.

"Want some company?" Noland peeked his head up over the crow's nest floor.

"Hey," she smiled, scooting over to provide him just enough room to sit next to her, dangling their legs over the side.

Noland wrapped his arms around her, warming her instantly.

"Mmm, I don't think I'll ever get sick of that." She laid her head back against his chest.

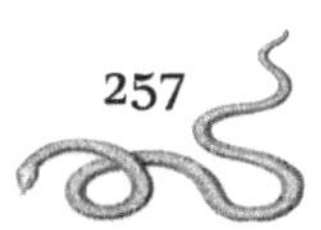

"I have one more gift for you." She felt the deepness of his voice reverberate through her chest from where her back rested against him.

"Are you trying to spoil me?" Achaia asked, looking up at him, his chin brushing her forehead as she did. He was scruffy, and his chin was scratchy against her face.

Noland smiled, and she felt his jaw work against her temple. "I have a lifetime of words to say, and maybe only one night left to speak them. Be patient with me."

Achaia felt a lump rise in her throat and burrowed back deeper into Noland's chest. She felt the warmth of tears filling her eyes, but she took a deep breath and begged them to hold their ground.

"Achaia Connolly Cohen- wait." Noland took Achaia by the shoulders, and started to turn her, "I need to look you in the eye." Achaia crouched precariously and scooted around to face him, putting a foot on either side of him, and sitting between his knees so they sat facing one another. He placed a hand on each of her knees and leaned against them as he spoke again. "Achaia Connolly Cohen, daughter of Shael ben Yahweh, here at the end of all things, I promise you this: That whatever the rest of this life or the one after have to offer, I am yours. Whatever time, whatever love, whatever strength, whatever loyalty, whatever life I have left-" Noland leaned forward taking her face in his hands, and looking her so intently in the eye, she couldn't look away. Her arms tingled with gooseflesh. "I love you, and if eternity holds such a thing as marriage, will you allow me the privilege of binding myself to you?"

"You're asking me to marry you?" Achaia said in disbelief.

"Oh, right," Noland leaned back, and dug in his pocket, pulling out a whittled wooden box.

"Oh my go-" Achaia caught herself.

Noland opened the box. Inside was a beautiful diemerilium ring. He lifted it out of the case and held it out to her. There was a regal looking sort of eagle, intertwined with a serpent.

"Noland, I-" Achaia paused, looking up into his eager eyes. "I don't deserve you." She shook her head.

Noland cocked his head to the side, eyeing her curiously. "Love isn't about deserving, Achaia. It's about giving. Being willing to lay down your life for someone. And as quick as it is to die for someone you love, pledging to live for someone, and to lay down the rest of your life every single day, that is nothing more or less than a gift. I offer you all of my days on earth, and whatever measure of time will be used once this life ends; it will never be vast enough for me to have my fill of you."

"I think you're forgetting how annoying I can be," Achaia smiled, taking Noland's hands in hers, her hands feeling insanely small next to his. She took the ring out of his hand and studied it. "I don't understand eternity, and I know nothing of Heaven, but if such a thing is possible, I want to belong to you in forever." She handed the ring back to him, and Noland smiled as he slid it onto her finger. "And in case it was ever in question," Achaia held Noland's face in her hands, his ring glittering on her finger against his cheek, as he smiled at her. "I love you more than I have ever loved anyone." Noland smiled and leaned in to kiss her.

"Even if we get killed by a dragon tonight, I'm the luckiest guy on earth," Noland smiled.

"I need to get you a dictionary, so you can look up the word *lucky*," Achaia laughed.

"It won't change my mind," Noland smiled, kissing her again. "I should get back down there and stop distracting the look out."

"Yeah, that's probably a good idea." Achaia blushed. "Hey Nole," Achaia called, stopping Noland in his descent. He looked up at her curiously. "I think my dad would have approved." She smiled.

"Of course he would," Noland scoffed. "Your dad freaking loved me."

"He didn't at first," Achaia said laughing.

"Neither did you, if I remember correctly. But I won you *both* over, trust me." Noland smiled sadly at her. She nodded at him, and he continued climbing down.

"You pierce my soul.
I am half agony, half hope."

-Jane Austen, Persuasion

Bale spent the night in his office, drinking copious amounts of coffee, and staring obsessively at his phone. Consciousness had at some point begun to feel surreal.

"Have you gotten any sleep?" Dina asked, coming to stand in his doorway.

Bale shook his head without tearing his eyes away from his phone.

"Any word?" Dina's voice lowered as she came to lean against the other side of his desk, her eyes also falling on the

phone.

Bale looked up at her and sighed before shaking his head.

"You need to eat something, and we need to figure out what happens if Joash comes back, should they fail." Dina snapped her fingers. "Come on, snap to."

Bale scoffed and smiled up at her placatingly as he stood to follow her to the dining room.

"Any sightings of him? Do we even know what direction he went?" Bale asked.

"I've contacted Adisa to see if he can track a dragon. He is on his way to Rome." Dina was nothing if not efficient. Bale wondered if that, as well as foresight, was her gift.

"What do you see happening?" Bale asked, as they turned onto the hall.

"That's the thing, nothing. I have dreams and I wake fearing fire," Dina shrugged, "but I don't know what that means." Dina sat at the table, once they entered the dining room. It was covered in breakfast pastries and there was a carafe of coffee, and a samovar of tea. "Your mate," Dina started, "Amelia." She poured herself a coffee, black. "She is in Heaven. Have you spoken to her to see what she knows?"

"I haven't slept," Bale stated. "She is learning to enter dreams, but I haven't slept."

Dina nodded. "After you get some food in you, you need to get some rest. Talk to her. She if she knows anything." A thought seemed to occur to Dina, "you don't know if-" she looked down at her plate, her cheeks tinted with pink. "Harlem-"

Bale nodded understanding her curiosity. "I will describe

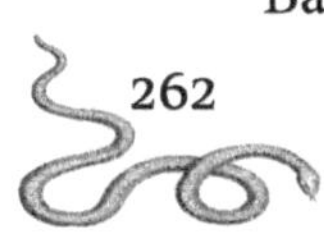

him to Amelia and ask her to keep an eye out for him, if he is there."

"It's just, Amelia is the first we know of. I don't know if it is because we aren't of the original fallen generation- Maybe Harlem?" Dina looked like she was fighting off hope, but hope was fighting just as hard to be held.

"It stands to reason," Bale nodded, encouragingly. "And if he wasn't blessed to visit dreams, he wouldn't be able to reach you."

Dina nodded, smiling, hope winning the fight. "I can't wait for all of this to be over."

"Agreed." Bale pushed his mug of freshly poured coffee away and opted for juice instead. He picked at a *syrniki*. Though he usually loved the cottage cheese pancakes cook made, his exhaustion had finally caught up to him.

"We need news from Heaven. Naphtali, if not Amelia. We need to know what's going on," Dina said, sipping her coffee.

Bale looked out at the table and wondered if he had forgotten to tell cook that half their inhabitants had left. "Has Veronica made an appearance yet? What time is it?"

"It's early. She's probably still asleep," Dina said checking her watch. "It's only six-thirty."

Bale nodded, "Why don't you try calling Naphtali, or texting him, and I'll go take a nap and see if Amelia comes to me."

"What about Veronica?" Dina asked.

"Tell her we are going to need weapons for an army. The end is nigh." Bale stood, but felt heavy, each step toward his room

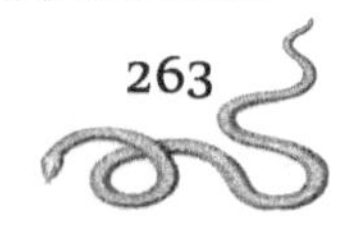

a labor of endurance. He'd never felt so human, so tired, and weak, so utterly exhausted.

"Finally!" Amelia said, as Bale's face came into form. "Where are we?" Amelia asked looking around. She was lying next to Bale in a large bed, covered in thick downs and linen sheets.

"Bed," Bale said looking around, amused.

Amelia cocked an eyebrow at him. "Really?"

"It's not like that," Bale said smirking, too tired to even smile. "I've never been this tired in my existence."

"So dramatic," Amelia smiled, propping her head up on her elbow, looking at him.

"Maybe not," Bale pondered. "I'm wondering if my strength is waning. The closer we get to the end, the weaker I feel. People don't trust so easily anymore, especially not the number of people I've needed to trust me. I am worn thin."

Amelia stopped smiling, taking a closer look at Bale. There were dark circles under his eyes, and he did look drained. She'd always thought of him as being limitless, always wise, always capable, always strong, always sure. It was only now dawning on her, that he, too, needed rest, and had moments of weakness and uncertainty- he who wasn't fallen.

As if realizing time was short, Bale rolled over to face her, sitting up. "What news from Heaven?"

Amelia sat up too, sitting cross legged in front of Bale.

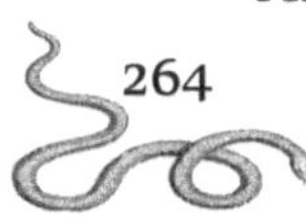

"Iesou put me to sleep, to be ready, I think to communicate to anyone who actually sleeps, but none of you have."

"Iesou did?" Bale nodded, knowing the importance.

"He told Lailah to go and get some scrolls to read and sent Naphtali to get some horses ready."

Bale's gaze snapped up to her. "Scrolls? Steeds?" His eyebrows twitched upward with urgency.

"Yeah," Amelia shrugged. "What does that mean?"

"It means I have to go," Bale leaned forward grabbing her cheeks, and kissing her hastily.

"But you just fell asleep!" Amelia was really worried about how worn out he looked. He was pushing himself too hard.

"There's going to be plenty of time for that when this is all over." Bale reached a hand up to caress her cheek, and then he was gone, and she was alone again, waiting for someone else to fall asleep.

Olivier watched as the first hues of sunlight filtered into the cabin. "Yellaina, you awake?" he asked.

"Yeah, I couldn't sleep." She stirred next to him.

"I think it's time we relieve the others." Olivier sat up and stretched his back and cracked his neck.

Yellaina followed suit. "I thought something would have happened by now. How long does a dragon take to fly?"

"It's quite a bit heavier than we are. Maybe he had to stop for breaks?"

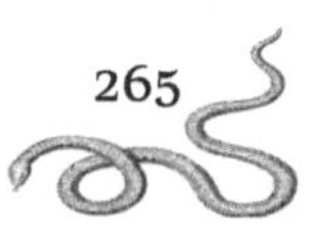

"I hope he hasn't made landfall." Yellaina's forehead crinkled in the way it always did when she was worried.

"Hey," Olivier reached out, and took her by the arms, rubbing them soothingly up and down. "One way or another, this will all be over soon. Dina, Bale and the others have the land covered. Veronica made other weapons, just in case; and she'll make more. It'll be okay."

Yellaina huffed, and looked up in his eyes, "Define 'okay.'"

Olivier looked up, thinking, and nodding, unable to come up with a suitable response. "It's subjective?" he shrugged.

Yellaina smiled pathetically at him and followed him out of the cabin, grabbing their toothbrushes, toothpaste and a bottle of water to spit over the side of the ship.

It was much brighter outside; Olivier squinted, adjusting to the light. The sun was coming up over the ocean and painting the sky pink and orange. It looked more like a sunset than a sunrise. "Red sky in the morning, sailor's warning," Noland said, following Olivier's gaze.

"Great, just what we need, a storm." Olivier rolled his eyes and shrugged. If he was being honest with himself, he really wasn't that surprised. That seemed to be their luck as of late. "You ready for a break?"

"You guys, go ahead," Noland said, turning to Emile and Achaia. "I'm good for now. I'll hang out with you guys for a bit," he said turning back to Olivier and Yellaina.

Olivier was relieved, though he was trying not to show it. If the dragon did show up on their watch, Yellaina could rouse the others, but it would basically only be Olivier left to hold the ship in the meantime. He was relieved to have Noland stay with him.

"Did you get any sleep?" Noland asked them, more quietly. Olivier and Yellaina both shook their heads.

"Before I go," Achaia dismounted from the ladder to the crow's nest and walked over to them holding out her left hand. On her finger, was a ring.

"Dude, did you propose?" Olivier asked excitedly, as Yellaina squeezed Achaia in a hug, squealing.

Noland smiled, widely. Emile stood at his side, with a hand clapped on his shoulder. Olivier wondered how his brother was holding up and was glad he was going in to take a break.

"Yeah, she's officially taken now, so hands off during nap time." Noland eyed Emile mockingly.

Emile held up both hands, as if Noland were pointing a gun at him.

Achaia rolled her eyes and laughed. "Don't know if we'll ever actually get to have a wedding, but would you be my maid of honor?"

Olivier was amused to find that Achaia wasn't looking at Yellaina, but at him. He smiled widely. "Only if I get to wear a dress."

"I have so many ideas for what to do with your hair!" Yellaina was giddy with excitement. Olivier didn't have the heart to tell her, she probably wasn't going to get the opportunity, but it was a nice daydream to hold them all over.

Achaia smiled at her, squeezed her hand, and she and Emile left to go take a turn at attempting to sleep.

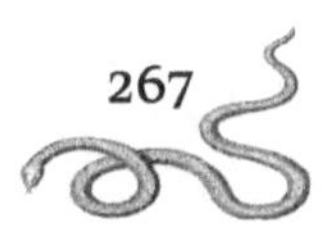

Olivier looked around the ship, taking in the sight of it for the first time in the daylight. It was ornately carved, with, ironically, a dragon at the helm. Its wings spread wide, covered the sides of the ship. The craftsmanship was par none, exquisite. "It is a Viking ship," he smiled to himself.

Yellaina looked around and smiled.

"You should check out the view from the crow's nest," Noland suggested. "It's pretty cool actually."

"Yeah, you go ahead. I will not be joining you," Yellaina said shaking her head adamantly.

Olivier laughed and raced up the ladder to the nest.

Emile and Achaia headed for the captain's quarters, where the only real bed on the ship was. Achaia climbed in first, and took the window side of the bed, leaving Emile the edge. They sat leaning up against the side of the ship, head to toe, facing each other.

"I've never been on a ship before. I was thinking it would rock me to sleep, but it isn't quite as syncopated as I thought it would be," Achaia said, sliding her legs under the covers, but still sitting up against the pillow.

Emile grabbed the other pillow from the head of the bed, and put it behind him at the foot, staying on top of the covers. "Yeah, sleep won't come easy, but I'm exhausted enough that I hope I get some anyway."

"How are you holding up?" Achaia asked, her eyes full of

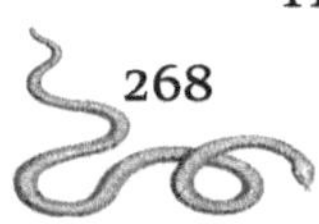

concern. He could feel how worried she was about him.

"It's actually kind of nice out here. I only have to worry about what you guys feel, instead of *everyone*." Emile smiled reassuringly at her. "I know you've been determined to hold it all together for me, Noland has too, but don't worry about it. Feel what you need to feel. I'm fine."

"You've been strong for me enough times. Let me be strong for you." Achaia leaned forward and took Emile's hand, squeezing it. "You've comforted me more times than I can count. What comforts you?" she asked.

Emile smiled and chuckled to himself. He couldn't remember the last time anyone had asked him such a question, if they ever had. "When I was young, my mother used to sing me jazz, and rub my back until I fell asleep."

Achaia nodded resolutely. "Well, I'm not much of a singer, but I can rub your back until you fall asleep."

Emile laughed. "You don't have to do that."

"We all need to take what rest we can. If it will help you fall asleep, I'm happy to try it." Achaia had a stubborn determination Emile knew better than to try and argue against. So, he nodded, and rolled onto his side.

Achaia scooted down the bed, and rubbed slow circles between his shoulder blades, alternating between lightly scratching his back with her nails, and rubbing up and down his spine with her palm. Emile closed his eyes and felt like a child again being put to bed by his mom- safe, and warm. Achaia started humming lowly in her throat, Melody Gardot's *Goodnight*, one of Emile's favorites. He'd probably listened to it enough for Achaia to know the tune if not the words. She actually had a very nice voice. The rocking of the ship, together with Achaia's voice, and comforting presence saw Emile asleep in less time than he had expected.

"Thank God!" Amelia was before him, wrapping her arms around him.

"Hey!" Emile squeezed her back. "How are you?" He held her at arm's length, and he felt tears building up in his eyes, as he held her tight, felt her in his hands, drank in the sight of her, the scent of her. She still smelled like Amelia, lavender and jasmine and maybe something like peaches.

"Me? How are you?" She leveled him with a look that warned him to be honest.

"I'm hanging in there." He shrugged.

"Things are crazy here; I think the end is coming soon," Amelia said, reaching up, and grabbing hold of his arms, too.

"I hope it does. I'm on a ship right now waiting for dragon Joash to come and attack us. I hope we can take him down with us. But I'll likely be joining you soon." Emile said this lightly, but he felt the weight of it in his chest. Amelia nodded understandingly.

"As much as I don't want you to die, I would love to have you here with me. Lailah wants to bless you all, too. But she needs you here to be able to do that. So, I think you might all have to die."

Emile nodded. "What kind of blessing?"

"I don't know, mine was to visit you all in your dreams, but that's what is necessary for now. I'm not sure what your blessings will look like." Amelia chuckled to herself. "I always knew Joash would be a huge pain in the butt, but I never imagined he'd be literally huge."

Emile laughed, "He has seven heads."

Amelia's smiled dropped, "seven?" Her voice was filled with wonder and disbelief. "He would-"

Emile smirked and nodded. "He would-"

"Can you stay for a while?" Amelia asked, looking unsure, and somehow smaller, younger.

"Yeah, I can stay." Emile pulled her back in for a hug and held her. "Does it hurt?" He asked into her hair.

Amelia nodded against his shoulder, "but only for a second. Here, there is no pain."

"In that case, I'm glad you got to go first." Emile held her tighter, not sure what was coming, but knowing that he didn't have long before he found out.

Luc slammed a fist into the cavern wall behind him, splintering the ice with fractures like a spiderweb. He screamed in rage and frustration, shaking out his fist, sending blood splattering across the floor. Jude looked up at him. "Dude, what?"

Luc stomped over to the bar, and poured himself a large brandy, and threw it back. He felt a hint of warmth in his chest, before that and the effect of the drink was already dissipating. He poured another. "KUMBHAKARNA!" Luc called. The messenger demon appeared before him, looking wary.

"Yes, sire?" Kumbhakarna asked dutifully.

"Deliver word to all the forces oppressing or possessing world leaders: They have permission to kill at will. I want the world to devour itself and bathe in blood."

Kumbhakarna nodded and disappeared before Luc's eyes. Jude stood, staring at him with a mixture of disbelief and dread. "What the Hell dad?"

"No," Luc held up a hand shutting Jude up. He looked at his half-human spawn with disgust. "If the Kingdom is coming, I'm taking as many of his pathetic beloved souls with me as I can." Through clenched teeth he warned him, *"Don't get in my way."*

Bale woke up, sucking in breath. He sat up, and kicked off the covers, not caring that he had gone to bed in briefs. He rushed back into the dining room, looking almost crazed. Dina straightened at the sight of him. "What is it? Did you even fall asleep yet?" Her eyes snapped back up to lock on his face. "What is it?" She asked again, standing at his urgency. Bale knew he probably looked half-mad. His heart was hammering inside of his chest.

"Dina, the horsemen," he said, eyes bright, the hazel of them burning blue with truth, "they're coming."

Kylie looked out of her bedroom window at the sea. A storm was brewing out over the open waters. She prayed for Achaia, Yellaina and the others. She had taken to obsessively watching the skies for any sign of dragon or fire, but nothing. How far out to sea had they gone? If the dragon did attack, would she know? Would she be able to see? She was gifted with sight. She could see miles further in every direction than the typical Nephilim, and they could already see further than humans. She should have insisted. She should have stowed away on the ship. Was it too late? She could fly after them- maybe just watch from the skies, to aid them if necessary. If they didn't need her, they'd never have to know she was there.

Resolution filling her, she started throwing clothes and weapons into a bag. She wasn't one to sit back when friends were in danger; new though they were, Achaia and Yellaina had become her friends. Besides, how was her unit to know if the dragon was slain, if Noland's unit all fell in the process? That was all she needed to justify it to herself. She would keep tabs on them and be able to come in and aid as reinforcement, or report back if she was already too late. She half ran to the kitchen, her adrenaline pumping with her resolve, to grab what food was ready and available. She threw what was in reach in her bag and took the stairs two at a time up to the roof of the safe house.

She was securing the straps of her bag around her wing joints when there was a shift in the air. For a moment all wind seemed to disappear. All was quiet and still, like the moment between the intake of a breath and its release. Then, the wind picked up like a hurricane, and the clouds were torn with the downward gust of wind. Kylie was forced into a crouch. She brought up her arms to cover her head as she looked skyward.

She saw through the fractured clouds the shadow of a beast, absolutely massive, flying toward the ocean. The dragon had tracked them, was still tracking them. Kylie was too late. There was no way she could catch up to the beast, as fast as it was flying, let alone beat it to Achaia and the others. She pulled out her phone and dialed Bale's number. He answered after the second ring. "Kylie?"

"Bale, it's here. The dragon just flew over Tjøtta toward the sea. He's tracking them."

She heard Bale's sigh of resignation.

"I'm going to follow it. I can help them. I can report back whatever happens."

"No," Bale said shortly. "Kylie, the horsemen are coming." Kylie sucked in a breath of surprise. "We need to ready the troops for the final battle. Whatever Noland's unit… It's as good as done. You and your parents ready the northern troops. That is an order." Bale waited for her reply. Kylie squeezed her phone angrily in her hand, taking a deep breath to calm herself. "My parents can ready the troops without me. I'll pass them the order before I leave," She said resolutely.

"Kylie no. Abort. Do you understand me?" Bale sounded adamant.

"With all due respect, if nothing else, we need to know what happens. Don't you agree?" Kylie argued.

Bale sighed. After a moment, he conceded. "Follow, but do not engage, you hear me? Report back to me." Bale didn't

sound pleased with the compromise, but Kylie would take it.

"Yes. I will inform my parents and leave immediately." She went to hang up the phone but heard Bale call her name again.

"Kylie,"

"Yes?"

"Do not engage under any circumstances," Bale commanded. "That is an order. The Lord's will is in motion. We do not yet know what must come to pass. You will not get in the way. You will not interfere. Promise me." He sounded serious, but also sad.

Kylie took in a breath, considering for the first time that the Lord's will did not always include their earthly idea of rescue. She breathed out slowly. "I promise."

After hanging up, she looked once again to the sky, eager to launch herself into it. Instead, she dropped her bag onto the roof for later, and ran back toward the stairs to brief her parents on the new developments and orders.

17

From the Deep

Two days had passed since they set sail from Tjøtta, and nothing. Noland checked his phone again out of habit, but of course none of them had any service this far out to sea.

Olivier was especially restless. He had taken to flying laps around the ship, to get an even wider view, but there had been no sign of a dragon, yet. Noland was beginning to dread that Joash was making war on humanity, and they were just sitting out at sea in a boat…

"Why didn't we think to pack a deck of cards or

something?" Olivier complained, shuffling his feet across the deck boards, setting Yellaina's teeth on edge. She kept quiet, but Noland knew they all had cabin fever, and desperately needed time away from each other. The tiniest things were beginning to seriously annoy.

"Let's mix up the rotation today," Noland suggested. "Yellaina, why don't you and Achaia go rest, while Olivier, Emile and I keep watch." Yellaina nodded at him appreciatively.

"I can practice some hair style ideas I have!" Yellaina looked at Achaia excitedly.

Achaia nodded, and Noland saw the resolve. Achaia was willing to give Yellaina the outlet, even though it wasn't her idea of fun. Noland smiled. The small ways Achaia showed she loved people, even though she wasn't the type to come out and say it usually, made him love her even more. Only time and paying attention helped you get to know things like that about someone. Noland was thankful for all the time they'd been able to spend together. Unlike some couples, it seemed that Noland and Achaia actually thrived when they were locked up on trains, or in cabins, or on ships with each other.

Noland wondered what Heaven was like and if they would be able to get married and share a home, or if such things were no longer important or a priority, there. Would he look at Achaia the same on the other side of life? He hoped so. He had fantasies of what forever would look like, but the truth was, he wasn't sure. Angels had been mated before the fall. Surely there was some form of family life- Noland shook his head. He had way too much time on his hands; his fingers itched for a weapon.

"Emile!" He called to Emile who was up in the crow's nest. "Training session?"

"Please!" Emile called down. He unfurled his wings and flew to the deck. "I need to do *something*. Olly, do a lap?"

Olivier nodded, and launched himself into the air, to circle the ship and keep watch.

"How long do we wait, before we try to head back to shore, or at least in range to get news?" Emile asked.

"I've been thinking about that. I just thought he would come straight after us. I never considered he'd take his time. Do you think he's just toying with us?" Noland asked.

Emile drew out his bow and pulled it in two, unsheathing two short swords. "I've been wondering that, too. Joash *is* the sadistic type to play those games."

Noland's muscles were restless and ready for action. He drew his sword, and sparred with Emile, until they were both sweating, and hungry. Olivier rejoined them, reporting all was 'quiet on the skyward front'. They took out provisions and ate a picnic lunch on the deck.

The ship rocked on the open water, the wood creaking. Emile sat on the steps up to the helm polishing his sword. Noland paced the deck, occasionally stopping to stare out over the horizon. Waves lapped against the side, sending sprays of salty mist to splash their faces, and dampen their hair.

Yellaina and Olivier stood huddled together against the

railing in quiet conversation. Achaia was desperate for a minute to herself, alone. She couldn't help feeling that they were sailing in the wrong direction. Shouldn't something, anything, have happened by now? If this was the calm before the storm, she was ready for the thunder.

Achaia looked up the mast to the crow's nest. Instead of using the ladder, she grabbed hold of a rope and started to shimmy up the swaying pole. A space away from everyone, a second alone was just in reach. She climbed to the perch and sat. It struck her that she wasn't out of breath. Before all of this, she wasn't even sure she would have thought to climb the ropes to perch herself so high on a swaying vessel. She never would have considered not needing to climb because she could fly. And yet, now she climbed for the physical strain her muscles craved locked on a ship. She craved the burn, because it made her feel human. Yet, she hadn't even broken a sweat. What used to seem impossible had become simple. She thought to herself that it was funny, how life changes you. Her skin was hot from sunburn. A light pink spread across her face and arms, over her freckles. The neckline of her t-shirt, higher than the one she'd worn the day before, irritated the sensitive flesh around her chest and neck.

She looked down at her companions. Emile was now putting his sword away and walking the deck toward Noland, who stood looking out at the sea. She followed his gaze and looked out over the water- the deep dark blue of the ocean, the depth of the water marked by the darkness of the hue. She looked out, looking for currents, or sandbars… making a study of the shifts in depth. There was a deep section off the starboard side where Noland was gazing that seemed to shift and move with the waves and to grow. Achaia stared, trying to look beneath the surface. The depth took shape. It was no longer just a blob of darker blue, but it rose. Something was coming to the surface. A whale?

Achaia thought of *Twenty-Thousand Leagues Under the Sea*, and of a gigantic octopus, and of *Moby Dick*; but the shape didn't look to have tentacles or fins… It looked like—

"NOLAND!" Achaia shrieked pulling her dagger from its sheath.

Noland looked up at her, as did the others. He looked back where he had been studying, following Achaia's gaze.

"WHAT IS IT?" He called. "CAN YOU SEE?"

Achaia looked back at the growing mass. She could make out a tail, and the shape from before—wings. They stroked the surface of the water. "DRAGON!" Achaia screamed. "GET READY!" They'd been studying the skies. Achaia had never thought it would attack from the depths.

Below, everyone scrambled to draw their weapons. They couldn't see as clearly as she could. "ACHAIA, WHAT DO YOU SEE?" Noland yelled, taking up *Olethros*, standing with his weight distributed, his feet, ready to move. But he couldn't tell where to look.

The dragon looked like it was flying beneath the surface. Its wings, she could see clearly now, were covered in scales, and were propelling it forward. It circled the ship, with every lap, drawing closer and closer.

"IT'S GOING AROUND THE BOW!"

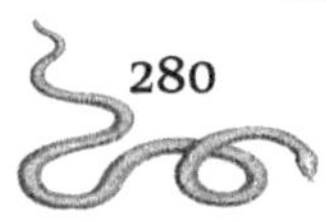

Noland stared out over the water. A dark mass moving just off the side of the ship skimmed the surface. It was massive and scaled. Its back was lined with blade-like talons as were the spines of its wings.

"Joash," Noland breathed. Emile, who stood next to him, gasped; his face had gone deathly white. "Take courage!" Noland yelled to everyone, sensing Emile's weakness. "Brace yourselves!"

As Noland gave the order, a wave crashed down on the ship, drenching them, and the dragon burst forth out of the water, its wings raining down spray on their heads. The beast was so large, it blocked out the sun and enveloped the ship in darkness with its shadow. Noland scoured the beast searching for any point of weakness. Its mass was covered in thick, though lace-like, scales: a glittering coat of silver, with scattered black scales, giving it the look of a scaly leopard. Looking higher, Noland took in the thickness of its seven necks, leading to seven heads, each one with lion-like jaws which snapped and growled. The guttural echo reverberated through the ship. Each head had a crown of thorny horns, beneath which great eyes, with catlike slits, blinked, staring down at them. Sneering at them and snapping their fangs, a few of the mouths licked their lips in anticipation. The wings beat down gusts of wind that made it difficult for Noland to brace himself even against the rail. He locked eyes with the center head, which was larger than the rest.

"Noland Amsel, you have not searched for me in vain," it said in an amused booming voice. "What shall you do, now that you've found us?" The other six heads hissed and laughed.

Noland held eye contact with the beast. "Joash, no longer shall you lurk in the shadows of deceit. No longer shall you whisper curses into the earth. Your reign is coming to an end. You are no Hydra! How many of your heads can stand against the Lord? How many can survive His wrath?" At the mention of the Lord, the beast growled and snapped its teeth.

"You are so small to boast so much," Joash said through gritted jaws. "Will you still defy me in this form?"

"And what is that in the gusts of your wings?" Noland continued, refusing to be intimidated. "It is the stench of fear!" Noland looked up at Achaia, who had managed to go unnoticed by the dragon. She looked prepared to pounce. She nodded her readiness to Noland, and he raised his sword. Emile and Olivier followed suit.

Yellaina had hidden behind the mast; Olivier stood guard near her. She held in her hand the dragon's blood jasper dagger, but Noland knew she hardly knew what to do with it, especially against such a large adversary. He regretted his decision to let her come. He wished more than anything she wasn't there. Her face was streaked with tears of fear. Her knuckles were white, clasped around a weapon, Noland was convinced, wouldn't do her any good.

She looked at him, her eyes sad, knowing. Noland looked down at the timbers of the ship. He had failed her in letting her come.

"Come then, little warrior. Show me your idea of power," Joash sneered. The dragon lunged forward and struck its mace-

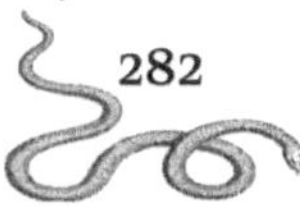

like tail at the ship's helm, smashing it into splinters. Debris flew through the air. Noland shielded his eyes and ran for the dragon's gut. He drove into it with all his momentum and body weight, but the scales didn't give way, even with the weight and sharpened point of *Olethros*. He slashed, aiming between the scales and drew black blood. The heads roared and lashed out.

Emile was airborne, engaged with one head. He was slashing at its eyes, as it endeavored to devour him. Olivier was dashing around with the other five heads, all of them befuddled, trying to keep an eye on him as he ran and flew, slashing between scales as he went.

Noland looked up. Achaia was set in a squat. As he watched, she dove. Her dagger braced in both fists, she aimed at the wing before her. Driving her dagger in at the top and dragging it down by gravity and her body weight, she ripped it from top to bottom. The beast let out a roar which seemed to shake the earth. He beat his wing, as if to swat her away. Achaia was flung to the deck. Noland lunged with every ounce of strength he possessed, while Joash was distracted, his long-handled dragon sword piercing hilt deep in the dragon's gut. Achaia landed in a roll, but had lost her dagger in the bone lining the wing.

The harder the dragon beat the injured wing, the more the meat tore away from its bony frame. Joash began to fall, failing to keep flight with only one wing. He fell forward, landing on the deck, and pushing *Olethros* even deeper into his belly, but nowhere near his heart. His mass took over most of the ship. Olivier took the opportunity to run forward, hacking, and beheading the second of the seven necks. The beast roared again, looking down at him with all of his remaining heads.

Olivier had looked over to lay eyes on Yellaina and make sure she was okay. Unfortunately, Noland realized, this had given her location away. "OLIVIER!" Noland yelled, wrenching Olethros out of Joash's mass, twisting as he did to tear away whatever muscle he could to weaken the beast.

Joash roared, lashing out with his tail, taking out the mast, Olivier and Yellaina with it.

Olivier was knocked flat to the deck, hard, his nose busted and bloodied. The mast was in the water, bobbing in the waves, but Yellaina was nowhere to be seen. "YELLAINA!" Noland screamed. He fought his way over to Olivier, slashing and stabbing at anything that came near him as he ran.

Olivier sat up and shook his head, stunned. He was a quick healer. Noland looked all over the surrounding area. Yellaiana wasn't there. Olivier jumped to his feet and joined in the search. Achaia was clinging to the sixth neck. Noland realized how small she was in comparison, being smaller than one of the smallest head's eyes. She had *Akakios*, her whip, wrapped around the beast's neck like a garrote, each end of it in her hands, and was sawing it back and forth, slicing the neck from the opposite side. The beast roared and tried to snap at her, but she clung close to its neck out of the reach of its teeth. As Noland watched, the seventh head snapped its attention toward her and lunged forward.

Noland flew before thinking. He landed behind Achaia, between her and the seventh head. As she sawed, he advanced and sliced at the beast's face. It tried in vain to snap at Noland who was agile and quick, if not as fast as Olivier. With all the strength he possessed he jabbed *Olethros* into the beast's eye, all the way through the top of its head so that the dragon's blood jasper tip of his sword protruded like a blood speckled horn in the beast's crown. And with that, the seventh head hung limp on its neck.

Noland turned around and grabbed one end of Achaia's whip. With a look she grasped his plan. She nodded, signaling she understood, and was ready, and the two of them jumped back and away, pulling the whip the rest of the way through the severed neck. The sixth head fell with a splash into the ocean. As it hit, and its blood mingled with the water, Noland watched the black oil-like substance spread over the surface for as far as his eye could see. The ocean turned to blood. But Joash's blood was no longer that of angels. It had turned to demon ichor.

Dina was quick with a spreadsheet, and together she and Bale had made a list of all the unit leaders. They each called a list of countries and gave them orders to notify all the units in their region, to spread the word as quickly as possible for all Nephilim to make for the Valley of Martyrs; the horsemen were coming.

Some received the news with anxiety, others with relief that the end was finally coming. The war to end all wars was upon them.

Dina tallied how many they would have in their Remnant. "We won't have enough. Unless heaven empties-"

"We will not be alone," Bale assured her.

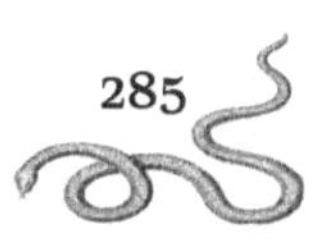

"Who will help us? Humans? They are no match for demons." Dina scoffed.

"They are not without their strengths; it is they who are made in the image of God," Bale reminded her. Dina tried to understand exactly how that was. She didn't have the benefit of having seen God or having been in heaven with the Lord. When she looked at humanity it was all too easy to focus on their weakness.

"In the Valley of Martyrs, we will stand a better chance. Let us hope they bring the fight to us." Bale looked resolute. "And may God go before us."

"May God go before us," Dina echoed.

Jude left his tomb of a room, feeling like an entirely different person, harder, sharper. Now that he wasn't fighting off the transition of Hell he was taking on some of the traits of demons. Slowly but surely, he felt the taint creeping in. He found his father screaming at a band of demons outside of the arena. His tantrum hadn't stopped for days. But his level of rage seemed to have risen to still new heights. Jude fought the urge to shrink back from him.

"GO NOW!" The veins in Luc's neck were protruding, as he shouted at the enormous gangly demons that resembled inky black eight-foot-tall praying mantis with the musculature of gorillas.

The demons were a terrifying sight to behold, especially

in such a great number. Jude wondered where he was sending them. But his father, in his fury, and could it be, fear- was even more menacing. "What's going on?" Jude asked.

Luc did a double take. "You don't look like a pot head anymore." He finally noticed, though Jude had cut his hair days before. "Good, I can take this," he gesticulated at Jude's entire person, "much more seriously."

"Dad, the demons?" Jude asked again nodding toward the mass that had just left.

"Joash is a damned moron," Luc said, sounding legitimately fearful.

"What has he done?" Jude asked, feeling his own anxiety rise in his chest.

Luc looked at him in the eye for a second. "The bastard shifted, ruining everything; and now he's gone after Achaia."

Jude's stomach dropped. "How many more demons do you have?" he asked, coldly. "Send them all."

Luc studied his face seriously. "No. *You* go."

Jude nodded curtly, unfurling his wings, disconcerted to find that they were now black as oil.

"But you come straight back with her," Luc ordered. "Or I will empty Hell in pursuit of you."

Jude nodded and took off at a run toward the surface and the opening of the icy catacombs, the reflection of his black wings chasing him like a shadow.

Sacrifce

"Many that live deserve death.
And some that die deserve life."

-J.R.R. Tolkien, The Fellowship of the Ring

Emile could feel the surge of confidence and hope as the sixth head fell, and Noland and Achaia landed back on the deck. But, it soon turned to disgust and horror. He turned his attention to Noland. He was staring over the side of the battered ship into the waves, which had grown rough. They were thick black, no longer translucent, but a solid mass of boiling demonic blood.

Emile choked on the sickeningly sweet scent, like rotting garbage, and a stopped-up toilet combined. He turned back to his fight, and had just finished dispatching the first head, when he felt a grief that knocked him back. He looked around again, dodging fanged lunges from the third head. Noland and Achaia were fighting the fourth, the largest of the heads, and the fifth. Olivier and Yellaina were nowhere to be seen. Emile, thinking they may have gone overboard in the fight, ran to the rail.

He heard a heart shuddering sob, and felt it echo in his chest. Below, in the blackish sea, Olivier was floating. He was holding on to a shattered bit of the mast riding over every passing wave. In his arms he held a body. Yellaina's hair was dyed black with the filth that they now floated in, her face washed white. She lay lifeless, stretched across the splintered raft. Bright red blood poured down her face from a gash in her forehead. The small river running from it floated across the black, like oil and water, refusing to mix. The fourth head roared in laugher as it saw Emile and Olivier, momentarily distracted.

"You think you stand a chance against me?" Joash laughed. Emile watched paralyzed by fear as the dragon raised, again, its mace-like tail, with all of its horns.

"OLIVIER!" Emile shouted. Olivier looked up, just as Joash's tail slammed down on him. Splinters of the bit of mast he had floated on flew through the air like shrapnel. Emile ducked instinctively. He prayed that Olivier had just moved too quickly for him to see. He looked around everywhere for where he may have gone. But as the chunks of wood began to float again to the surface, so did Olivier's body, punctured through with multiple softball sized holes from the beast's barbed tail. "OLI-" Emile tried to scream, but his voice broke off halfway through, refusing to finish the name. Nausea hit Emile like a punch to the stomach.

Noland screamed at him, "EMILE?" He was looking for back up, for information. Trying to block everything but the battle from his mind, Emile swallowed hard and ran back over to rejoin the fight; the last DuBois left. He kept seeing Olivier's last look of surprise on his face as Joash's tail came down. Yellaina's blood refusing to mix with the beast's, her hair stained black… Emile's fighting was sub-par, he knew.

He struggled to regain focus, but instead of seeing the third head of the beast, he kept seeing Olivier's face, as a child. Instead of his sword, he felt Olivier's tiny little hand in his, as he had walked him to his first council meeting when he was five. Instead of cries and roars, Emile heard Olivier's laugh as he had run in circles around the room with Amelia's favorite book, throwing it across the room then running and catching it again, playing monkey in the middle, with no one else on his team. He was so fast, the lightest of them all, always reading his comic books and laughing, always talking about how they were like mutants…

The dragon struck out with its good wing, knocking Emile to the deck.

"Get your head in the game!" Noland yelled, angrily. Emile felt Noland's surge of desperate frustration. Noland and Achaia were outnumbered without him. Emile stood up and lunged forward once again, slashing with all his might. He had failed Amelia, Olivier, Yellaina… He wouldn't fail Noland and Achaia, the only two he had left.

Jude reached the warm air, outside of the tunnel, and remembered it was summer. Hell was colder than eternal winter. It ran deeper than the bone. It was soul chilling in its lack of anything good or holy. Jude shook the thought from his head, ignoring the warmth of the sun on his skin, and launched himself into the sky, following the demons. If he had felt the right to pray, it would have been that he wasn't too late.

He never thought he'd be grateful to have demons for back up, but if they helped take out the dragon trying to kill Achaia, he'd take the help from anywhere. Jude acknowledged a darkness in himself, as he realized he wasn't actually concerned about the others. It would be great if they were all okay, but the only one he really cared about was Achaia. Maybe he was like his father after all.

With Joash breaking the veil between the spiritual and the mundane, Jude wasn't concerned if humans saw him and the demons or not. The secret was out. There was more going on in the world than met the human eye. Good and evil. As Jude flew, and the desperation to reach Achaia ebbed and mounted, he realized that though the line was maybe a little gray at times from the ground, from up here, good and evil really was rather black and white. The problem was there was a little of all of it on both sides. He may be flying with demons, but it was with the intention to save his friend. And Joash was the leader of the Nephilim council, and he was the one trying to kill her. Jude wondered how clear the picture would be if he could get an even higher perspective, God's perspective. Then he did it, whether he deserved to or not. He dared to pray. He prayed that though he had pledged allegiance to his father, that God saw that he had only done it because he loved.

***

Kylie could see the fire rising from the ship. She was still miles away, pushing harder than she'd ever pushed in her life. When she did arrive, she would be worthless to help, unless by some miracle God renewed her strength and gave her another burst of adrenaline. Kylie was already purely sustained by adrenaline at this point. She had been flying for hours without rest. Struggling to take full deep breaths, her breathing was shallow. She was lightheaded and hadn't eaten in at least a day.

Her wing beats were out of sync, and she was fighting gravity, hard. Flying was made more difficult by her wings not working in tandum, and beating at different times. Her vision began to blur. She prayed for renewed strength. The water beneath her was tainted, black blood coating the surface of the waves. Hopefully that was a good sign. The dragon was significantly wounded. Then, Kylie's left wing snapped with exhaustion, no longer able to bear her weight. She tumbled, summersaulting through the air, struggling to regain her balance. Her wings twisted and she landed in a tumble with a splash onto a low hanging cloud.

Picking herself up on her hands and knees, she struggled to catch her breath. She looked around trying to get her bearings. She found the fight; she was at least a couple miles off. It was not going well, and yet, it was. Kylie debated pushing through, despite her utter exhaustion. But she remembered her promise to Bale: to observe, but not interfere, and to report back. Kylie collapsed onto the cloud and tried to focus her vision. She could see Achaia's hair, and Noland. She couldn't see the others, but maybe they were obscured by Joash? Blackness crept into the edges of her vision, and she felt herself beginning to lose consciousness. "God, no. Please, let me help," she moaned as the darkness took her.

Achaia found her chances of success better the closer she was to the beast's mouth. If she stayed on the deck, it could lunge and snap at her, but if she could get back up onto the beast's neck, she could hack away without it being able to bite her, as long as Noland and Emile kept the other heads occupied. She couldn't climb as she had done before. Her hands were too slick with blood. She wasn't sure if she should hazard to fly, lest it snatch her out of the air. She tried to wipe her hands off on her jeans, but it didn't help much, as they were also soaked.

Noland was fighting the largest of the heads, and as she looked over to call for him to cover her or provide a diversion, the head lunged for him. He slipped on the slick deck and had lost his balance and wasn't in the right stance to block the blow.

Achaia lasso-whipped her arm around, sending her diemerilium snake whip, *Akakios*, sailing through the air. It wrapped around one of the beast's fangs, just as it was about to reach Noland's arm, and she yanked it as hard as she could. The beast's face whipped around to face her, and she looked it dead in its grown-man-sized eye. "No!" she said, almost involuntarily, as if she were rebuking a rowdy dog. She had even pointed her finger in the beast's face for good measure. If the dragon had an eyebrow (it was more of a scaled series of mountains on its forehead) it was cocked in surprise and confusion.

Noland was looking at her with a smirk of amusement, huffing a laugh as he got back on his feet.

"You reprimand me," the enormous jaws bellowed, "as if I were a mutt!" Achaia's whole body reverberated through with Joash's voice.

She yanked hard on her whip, pulling out the fang it had been wrapped so tightly around. "Dogs are smarter," she yelled, slinging her whip, still holding the fang, and plunging it into the beast's eye.

Joash roared in agony, struggling to blink but trying not to irritate the fang which was now two thirds embedded in his eye. Black blood rained down on the deck. The dragon flailed in rage and pain. His tail, and other two heads lashing out in every direction. Achaia and Emile were both knocked off their feet.

All of a sudden there was a flash. Noland's sword was on fire, and hilt deep in the dragon's chest. Blood flowed, and where it did, fire swelled up. Achaia got back to her feet as quickly as she could and drew back her whip again.

"His blood is flammable!" she yelled.

"I can see that!" Noland laughed. It was a mad sounding laugh, lacking any humor. Achaia knew they were all exhausted, and probably on the verge of losing their minds. She looked

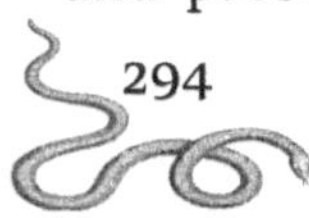

294

around.

"Where's Olivier? Where's Yallaina?" she yelled out. The look on Emile's face told her everything she needed to know. She glanced over the deck. The sun was setting on the horizon, and she realized the water had turned thick with Joash's blood, and there in it, floating side by side were the bodies of Olivier and Yellaina. Achaia also realized that the ship was damaged beyond repair. If they got out of this, they would have to fly to land, and who knew how long that would take. They were all spent. She sighed, and gulped hard, as if swallowing the realization that none of them were making it out of this. But they were so close to ending it.

Joash was screaming in pain. But it wasn't until now, Achaia realized, *what* he was screaming. "Come!" he bellowed. "Come, legion!" He sounded like he had lost his mind. Was he summoning demons? Could he do that?

She felt the boat rock as if something had hit it. Looking overboard she saw hands with fingers tipped in talons rising up out of the tar-like water. They sunk their claws into the sides of the ship and pulled themselves from the abyss with strands of ichor hanging from their mangled bodies. Black lids peeled back like alligators' to reveal blood shot eyes with black irises. Paper-thin, wide-set lips recoiled to show rows of needle-sharp teeth. Achaia had never seen the likes of these demons even in her worst nightmares in Hell. There were hordes of them, climbing the ship.

Hopelessness was fleeting, and quickly replaced by anger. *I'm not dying without taking that bastard with me*, Achaia thought

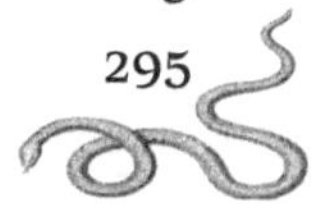

lividly as she looked back to the dragon. Achaia knew there was a flash of something in her eye, because Noland yelled after her, "ACHAIA!"

Achaia ran full speed, her wings cracking out from her back with a snapping sound of breaking bones. She lassoed again one of the fourth head's fangs, and while its mouth was open wide, she flew headfirst, full force down the beast's throat.

"NO!" Noland screamed as the beast began to choke. Achaia was without any weapon that could serve her inside the beast. She had no sword. She had lost her dagger when she had torn the wing. Noland had no clue what she had been thinking. "ACHAIA!" he screamed, lashing out at the beast. In his anger and fear he burned red hot. The blood that Noland ran across on the deck burst into flames. Emile had turned and was fighting the demons that were now crawling over the railings, shooting them with arrows before unsheathing his bow into swords for close range combat. The beast roared, and Noland saw that Achaia's hold had ripped the fang out of the beast's mouth which meant she wouldn't be able to pull herself out.

All Noland could think was "No." Over and over again he heard the word repeated in his own voice. He slashed and lunged, burning through scales. He beheaded the third neck, and he gouged out the eyes of the fifth before dispatching it. The fourth head's bellows were cut off by an awful, deep, gurgling choke. Achaia was lodged somewhere in its throat, doing what, Noland

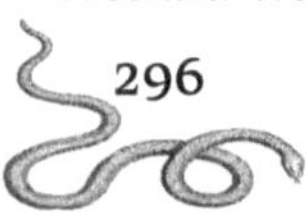

296

hardly knew. He would cut her out if he had to. He couldn't lose her now.

He slashed at the dragon's throat, being careful not to stab too deep, lest he catch Achaia, stuck inside. The dragon swung its tail knocking Noland off balance. He was dangerously close to the edge. He looked at Emile, whose back was to him. He was fighting off fifty or more demons at once. They had him surrounded. It was over. They couldn't win.

"No," Noland heard again in his mind. They could win. They just couldn't survive.

Noland squeezed his eyes shut, resolving himself to the conclusion that Achaia had already accepted. He looked to the ground. The deck was covered in demon blood. The ship was sinking… Noland gathered what strength he had left and ran full force at Joash. He left a trail of massive flames in his wake. He collided with the dragon, and the both of them fell overboard. He felt the heat overflow out of him. It burst from his eyes, his fingers, and chest. He was only slightly surprised to see his flesh turn to flames. As he hit the surface of the water, it burst into a sea of fire.

The dragon sank fast, unable to beat its wings to swim or float. Noland hacked away; his brain began to scream with the lack of oxygen. He saw stars bursting in front of his eyes. He thought he saw the dragon's own fang burst from its neck. It was Achaia, still trapped inside. He tried again to cut her free, slitting the beast's throat. He pulled her from its descending body.

The two of them tried with strained effort to swim for the surface. As Noland looked from Achaia's pale face to the sky he saw that the surface was all fire. He could survive it, but Achaia could not. He saw beyond the surface, the ship burning, and the silhouette of Emile standing in a ring of flames fighting off a horde of demons. He watched him fall. Achaia looked at him, her eyes full of fear, and realization, then gradually, acceptance. She grabbed his face with both of her hands and kissed him. Noland kissed her back and held her tight until they lost consciousness.

Jude beat the demons to the ship, or what had been a ship. The ocean was on fire, and there was a mound of something large, quickly turning to ash in the middle of it all. He didn't see a dragon anywhere, but the demons were dancing around the flames, in wonder and terror, unable to approach.

"Achaia!" he yelled. He flew around and around, feeling like a vulture. He could see the burning remains of three bodies. But none of them looked like Achaia. How many of her friends had been there? The dead were beyond recognition. Then, near the border of the ring of spreading fire, he saw her pale form float to the surface. "NO!" Jude plunged toward the water, pulling her from its grasp. She was hot to the touch, as if she'd been boiling in the sea. Her hand was clasped loosely in Noland's, but pulled free as Jude lifted her from the flaming waves. Noland's body wasn't burning, but it was blue at the lips, as if he'd suffocated. They must have drowned.

Jude clung Achaia to his chest and landed on what was left of the stern of the ship. He pounded on her chest and gave her

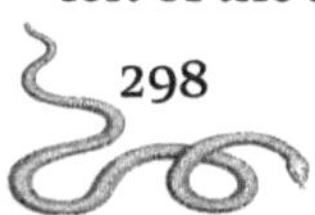

CPR until he was sure he had broken her ribs, but she was gone. There was no reviving her. "No, Achaia please," Jude pleaded. The flames were closing in tightly around them. "Damn it! Achaia, please!" Jude wailed, his hands red and scorched from the heat of her body. "I cannot follow where you are bound." Jude wept. "You were made for Heaven. I was bred for Hell." Jude pushed her wet curls out of her face. She looked so peaceful. He sniffed back his tears harshly, wiping the sweat and tears from his own face, trying to clear his head. He took hold of her body and launched himself back into the sky. He wouldn't leave her here.

19

Epilogue

> "The loneliest moment in someone's life
> is when they are watching their whole world fall apart,
> and all they can do is stare blankly."
>
> -F. Scott Fitzgerald, The Great Gatsby

Kylie came to in a cloud. No. She was on a cloud. She was in smoke. She struggled to see through the thick darkness of it. She coughed and tried her wings to see if they were broken, or if she could fly. Her wings stretched out well enough, so the tried them. She flew to the side, out of where the smoke was being blown by the wind. The sea was on fire, and it was spreading. Kylie flew in a circle around the wreckage. There wasn't much ship left. Kylie counted the remains. There were three badly burned bodies she couldn't identify. *May their sacrifice smell pleasing to the Lord,* she prayed.

She flew around again. On her second lap she spotted Noland, on the edge of the flames. "Noland!" she called, swooping low, reaching for him. She grabbed hold of his hand and let go with a yelp. He was searing hot. Kylie hovered low above the surface of the water and studied his face closely. "Noland?" He was lifeless. Tears stung the backs of Kylie's eyes. For over an hour she flew around and around, calling for anyone, listening for a response.

She was a body short, and there was no dragon in sight. It couldn't have flown far; it was too badly wounded. That was apparent from the amount of blood crawling over the surface of the deep. Could someone have been eaten by the beast? Kylie shuddered as she perched on a cloud, surveying the damage one last time. Could the beast have burned? Or sunk? She scanned the skies, for miles around. There was no dragon in sight, and no friends.

With a lump in her throat, Kylie flew back toward land, wondering if it really was better to know. Regardless, now they did. Noland's unit had fallen. Kylie had dived into the sea and seen the body of the beast. She had scanned the skies for miles in every direction, but never found the last body, or survivor. She assumed they were eaten or burned to ashes. Periodically she stopped to rest and sobbed. Her progress was slow, but when she made it close enough to have service, she called Bale.

"Kylie?" His voice was full of dread.

Kylie couldn't speak. Her breath caught in her throat, and

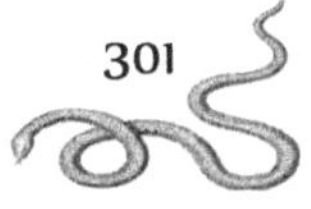

she couldn't form the words.

"They are fallen?" Bale deduced.

Kylie nodded and let out a sob.

"And the dragon? What of Joash?" Bale asked urgently.

"Dead," Kylie muttered.

"Come to the valley, Kylie," Bale ordered gently.

Kylie nodded, and hung up the phone.

Luc sat on the floor between the ice sculpted sofas of his cavernous drawing room, Achaia's body lying across his lap. Her arms and face were burned. Jude had gone to his room, utterly devastated. This was Luc's fault, he'd said. But no, this was Joash's doing. Luc had never intended Achaia to die. She'd chosen a side. Killing her would only separate her from him forever. Now she was lost to him, like her father.

Luc wiped the hair out of Achaia's face. She was so small. In life she had been so fierce. He'd never noticed how small she was. She'd been larger than life, to him. She'd gotten that from her father. Luc lifted Achaia in his arms, unsurprised by how light she was to carry, when she wasn't fighting back. He carried her princess style down the hall to the room where her father lay at rest. Well, Luc hoped he was at rest.

"I failed you brother. This is not how I meant her to return," Luc said apologetically, laying Achaia beside her father on the altar-like bed. "I continue to fall short."

Behind the closed door, in this room he forbade anyone

else to enter, and which Jude knew nothing about, Luc wept-wept to be alone, wept to always fall short of what he wanted, wept to be so hopeless, wept in anger and frustration, and self-pity.

Hours passed, or maybe days; Luc didn't care. Eventually, he felt a presence behind him, and turned. Iesou stood in the doorway, looking down on him with sympathy.

"Hello Lucifer," he said in greeting.

"What are you doing here?" Luc asked, annoyed to be found looking vulnerable. He wasn't vulnerable, just inconvenienced. He did his best to sound annoyed.

"I have come to collect what is mine. You cannot keep them, Lucifer."

Rage flooded Luc's chest. "No, if they were yours, they'd already be in Heaven with you," Luc argued. "They weren't yours."

"Yes," Iesou said, calmly, "they are." Iesou walked into the room, a slow and patient pace, which annoyed Luc further. Everything He did was right. He never did anything that didn't make sense, or that wasn't thought through. He was never rash, always so patient. It almost triggered Luc's gag reflex.

"Don't touch them!" Luc stood to his feet, standing between the Cohens' bodies, and Iesou.

"I don't need to," Iesou smiled. "Awake oh sleeper," he said soothingly.

Luc turned.

Shael's eyes opened.

Brace Yourselves!
The story concludes in

Redemption

Keep Reading With:

Awake O' Sleeper

A bonus Kingdom Come Series short story!

Book Discussion Questions

1. In the beginning of the book, Achaia hears a voice calling to her. In Abolition we never really find out where it's coming from. Who or what do you think it is?

2. Noland wonders if maybe "protecting Achaia" means allowing her to fulfill her purpose even if it means getting hurt or worse. What, if anything, would you consider to be more important than physical safety?

3. Jude doesn't seem to care if he wasn't meant to be with Achaia, since she already had a soul mate. Have you ever clung to a relationship that might not have been good or right for you? What made it so hard to let go or move on?

4. Yellaina has always struggled with not wanting to fight, and feeling like she was letting her father down by not training. However, Tobias looks on in awe as she leads the entire Remnant of Nephilim to unity. Have you ever known someone who might have seen you better than you saw yourself? How so?

5. Olivier doesn't like sitting in his negative feelings, even if it is to mourn his sister. How do you handle negative emotions? Would you rather avoid them, or face them head on?

6. Amelia finds herself clinging to her human form even though she is now in Heaven. Have you ever found it hard to leave behind the familiar even if it is for something better? Why was it so hard?

7. Joash leaves himself wide open to be possessed by Luc when he refuses to show true loyalty to either side. Why do you think it is so important to have convictions? What are you most convicted about? Why?

8. Tobias accidentally pushes his brother to make a huge mistake that will shape the rest of his life. How do you think this situation could have played out differently had Tobias tried harder to see things from Jude's perspective?

9. Veronica is struggling with a lot of feelings surrounding the death of her father. What do you make of her situation? Would you be open to forgiving her like Vito? Or would you condemn her like Vidal?

10. Emile secludes himself when he is overwhelmed by everyone else's grief on top of his own. What do you do when you're overwhelmed? Is the practice actually helpful, or is there something else you could do that might be better?

About the Author

Brandy Ange is the YA author of The Kingdom Come Series. With a BA in Bible, her fiction explores age old mysteries of the spiritual world, and mortal world alike. She currently resides on the barrier islands of North Carolina where she mentors at risk youth. For more information or to contact the author you can visit her website brandyange.me

Instagram: @vagabee

Twitter: @vagabee

Facebook:https://www.facebook.com/TheKingdomComeSeries/

YouTube: Brandy Ange

Goodreads: Author Brandy Ange

 For Bonus Content

To interact with the series in a unique way and get access to all the bonus content available become a patron.

Patreon: https://www.patreon.com/brandyange

If you Liked the Book:

Please consider leaving a review on Amazon and Goodreads!

Thank you!

Notes from the Author

RAPHA
INTERNATIONAL

Rapha House is an organization that I have admired and supported for years. They serve an important purpose in our world today, helping those who often cannot help themselves. For more details, and to see where a portion of the proceeds of this book have gone, visit their website.

https://rapha.org/

9 781947 992061